CAGED

CAGED

Book One: A Mike McMaskell Novel

Marshall Black

McHaskell Enterprises

To my beloved wife,

Words cannot express how grateful I am for your unwavering support and encouragement throughout this journey of writing my book. You have been my rock, my source of strength, and my biggest cheerleader. You have been my sounding board, my source of inspiration, and my source of motivation.

I am profoundly thankful for your consistent trust in me, which has given me immense comfort and reassurance. You have always been there to lend an ear, offer guidance, and help me stay concentrated and on the right path. You have been a genuine ally in this mission, and I immensely appreciate all you have done.

Your love and support have been the foundation for my success. Without you, I would not have been able to make my stories come to paper. Thank you for being my partner in this amazing journey.

With all my love,

-Marshall

The Beginning:

Mike McHaskell is walking down 5th Avenue, headed for the small farmers market downtown. He is lost in thought, thinking about his life here. *San Diego, California - what a beautiful city! The weather is almost always perfect, and the people are nice; not Minnesota nice, but nice. There is so much to do here: the beach, the mountains, the zoo, Sea World, Legoland, the delicious food in different neighborhoods, not to mention the great Mexican food everywhere. If you can't find some way to make a happy life here, you must be...* He is interrupted mid-thought. It's 2:15 pm. He is north of 5th & G when he notices the white cargo van. It is empty, has no windows, and the side door is open. He sees several men aggressing toward him from different directions just as the hood is thrown over his head. His world goes black. The men grab him. The trap is sprung. Mike's instinct is to fight, but his training takes over. He mentally tells himself, *You're outnumbered - let this play out.*

The moment the van begins to pull away, the *"Bastards"* start pounding and kicking him. He desperately tries to curl up into a tight ball to protect himself. It isn't an easy task for Mike; he is a big guy. 6 foot 5, solid, built like a brick shit house, an ex-frogman who could still join Team Echo with one call and be team leader today. He can barely make out the figures through the hood and quickly notes in his head: *Three guys trying to beat the shit out of me, one driver, three blocks north, and then a right turn; that means we are headed south on Broadway.* Then, nothing. Mike is unconscious. One of the men gives him a solid hit to the head, and his body goes limp.

Hours later, he starts to come to. Before anyone knows he is awake, he needs to find out as much as possible. He keeps his eyes shut, does his best to remain still, and listens for a few seconds. He hears the sounds of an airport, large engines starting up, and planes taking off and landing. He can smell fuel, oil, and harsh chemicals. Mike hears men speaking in what might be Arabic, but he's too groggy to make it out clearly. Before he can discern any more details, four men pick him up by his shoulders and feet. He does his best to remain as limp and lifeless as possible. He slowly opens one eye to see them carrying him inside a hangar, where an awaiting plane is powered up and ready to go.

Mike is far from 100%. He has sustained a concussion from that bat to his head in the van. He is dizzy, his vision blurred, and he feels like he might throw up at any second. He knows it's *"go time,"* so he attempts to catch the men off guard by quickly and forcefully rolling to his right. They almost drop him, and the men at his feet lose their grip. Immediately, he is jumped on by one of the men. A nearby armed guard hits him in the back of his head with the butt of his rifle, and Mike is, once again, knocked out cold. This time to make sure he understands that he is a prisoner, they all take turns kicking him in his body and head before putting him on the plane. By the time they load him into the aircraft, he is bleeding and almost entirely lifeless.

Welcome to Your New Home:

Mike lies on the concrete floor, shackled and chained at his wrists and ankles, wearing only his boxers. Pain radiates through his body, his head pounding, and he suspects he has a few broken ribs. His entire body aches, and there is blood on his face; his left eye is almost swollen shut. Mike has no idea how much time has passed and needs to figure that out. He tries to open his good eye and look around without moving. It is dark, but he can see he is in a Cage and thinks he is alone. Just in case he is not alone, he needs to find out what he can without anyone knowing he is awake. Mike listens for a minute, moves slowly and gently, and rubs his hands over his face. His left eye is swollen, huge, and too painful to touch. He can feel the stubble on his face, telling him it has been at least one, if not two, days since his last shave. He looks down to see the shackles and chains around his wrists and ankles, tracing them to the back wall of the Cage, where they disappear. Mike tries to take in as much of his new surroundings as quickly as possible, not knowing how much time he has. As far as he can see, it looks like an old underground parking garage filled with metal Cages. He needs more information but can only hear hushed conversations from the closest Cages. He slowly sits up, grabbing his head with one hand and his ribs with the other. He angrily mutters under his breath, *Those guys who grabbed me are on my list for later!* and looks around.

While sitting on the floor, Mike can see Cages filled with attractive young women wearing almost nothing. Each Cage appears to have a man inside as well. The women aren't chained or tied up inside the Cage; they move around freely. The men, however, are not moving around. There are pathways throughout this place, between the Cages.

He stands up to get a better look and thinks, *My God, there must be at least 100 cages here.* All the Cages Mike can see are set up in the same way: three to four women with numbers on their chests, one man chained up, one mattress, one blanket, and two buckets. He slowly walks through his Cage, taking mental notes. *This is about an 8-foot square Cage with cold concrete floors. There is one very old, very thin, and very used single-size mattress, and one small blanket, if you can call it that; it is so worn thin that it barely covers the mattress without anyone under it. The Cage has two wooden buckets; one is empty, and the other has a nasty-smelling liquid inside. That's it - nothing else. Why are there no women in this Cage? Every other Cage has women. It's the only difference I can see with my one good eye.* Mike tries to figure out what this place is being used for. *This place is not a prison; men and women wouldn't be together. It must have something to do with sex. What else could it be?*

From the looks of the construction and the few broken wheel stops he sees in a Cage a couple of rows away, he decides this must be an old parking garage that has been converted into a dungeon. It is very dark, smells terrible, is cold and damp, and only missing a dragon or a mad scientist.

There are light fixtures, but not all of them work, and the ones that do have flickering lights, which is worse than having no light at all. The entire place smells like the back seat of a New York City taxi on a hot August afternoon in 1978. It is obvious that no one is allowed to bathe regularly, and there are a lot of people here. He thinks, *If what I can see is most of the Cages, that means there are around 300-400 people here, and it certainly smells like it.* Ammonia is definitely part of the wafting aroma. He is pretty sure the second bucket is his toilet, meaning everyone else has the same wonderful bathroom facilities contributing to the smell. The only sounds are quiet murmurs, moans, and cries - mainly from the other Cage dwellers talking about the new guy. He can feel and smell the fear in this hellhole and quickly realizes he is fucked. This is beyond bad.

Mike is trying to count the Cages and people inside more accurately; he needs to know precisely how many people are in this place. He has counted three rows away from his Cage when through the bars, he sees two men walking between the Cages carrying metal rods. He immediately knows they are electric cattle prods, and they are walking straight toward him. They stop in front of Mike's Cage, laughing. The taller man says, "Hello there, big man. I see you are awake." At the same time, the shorter man quickly pulls a lever next to Mike's Cage. The lever is attached to a large wheel that connects the chains shackled to his arms. In an instant, Mike's arms are pulled apart, and his body slams into the concrete wall behind him. He is already in pain from the beating he has taken and sleeping on the cold concrete floor. His head hits the wall again, and he sees stars for a second. Mike also loses his breath when he first impacts the wall. He will be more prepared if these '*assholes*' do this to him again.

The taller man enters Mike's Cage and says, "This is how this is going to work: when we enter your new home, you will obey our commands. I hope you understand."

Mike looks at the man with death in his eyes and asks, "Or what?"

"Well my new friend, or this," The tall man has no mercy when he drives the cattle prod into Mike's chest. Ten thousand volts of electricity surge through Mike's body, causing him to convulse and tremble uncontrollably. It feels like an eternity has passed before his body eventually gives out, and he is left suspended by the chains on his wrists, utterly devoid of any motor control. His bladder has also involuntarily released, a testament to the immense pain he has just endured.

"It is understandable that you asked such a foolish question," the man says, "but now you know the consequences. Hopefully, you will not make the same mistake again. Although, I am sure you probably will. You Americans are stupid, like Dirty Harry or Chuck Norris. If you do not follow instructions, this is only a tiny fraction of the consequences that you will face. Have a nice day, stupid American." He turns to the small man in charge of Mike's chains and, in Arabic, orders him to "release the Big Man." Immediately, the lever is reversed, and the chains that have been tightly secured to the wall are suddenly loose. Mike collapses to the ground, and his captors proceed to give him a series of kicks, culminating in a final blow to the head that renders him unconscious.

This time when Mike awakes, he immediately jumps to his feet, ready for a fight. He is alone in his Cage. They have left him to his injuries, and he is still chained up like an animal. He still has no idea where he is, who these people are, and what they want from him.

In the Cage closest to him are three women and one man. One of the women looks directly at Mike; she seems out of place from the others in her Cage. She is somehow a bit cleaner than the others. Also, she is not as young as the other women, but she is beautiful, 5'7", with long, very dark, very straight hair, and the way she carries herself suggests that she comes from money or held a high-powered executive position before this place. She seems different from the others, and he needs more information. Mike thinks, *Maybe she could help. Even if she doesn't think she knows anything, she might be able to fill in some blanks.* Mike is hoping she speaks English. He hears some of the people here whispering in English. He also speaks a few other languages but doesn't want to give away any information about himself. So, he speaks to her in English and says, "Hello."

The woman that is looking at him walks toward him inside her Cage. The other occupants of her Cage turn away from him, huddling together in fear, and appear too terrified to speak with him.

"Hello," says the woman, with a thick Indian accent, as she places her arms through the bars.

Mike is relieved that she speaks English. Although there are at least eight feet between them, the comfort of communicating with a friendly face in this strange place is welcome. He asks her, "Do you have any idea where we are?"

As she answers, she looks around at all the Cages. "No, I'm afraid not," she says apologetically. "None of us have any idea where we are. We all just wake up here, just like you." she turns her attention back to him, "My name is Marisa. I'm from Calcutta."

"I'm Mike. How long have you been here, Marisa?"

"I have been here for almost three months, I believe. You might have noticed that women are not chained like men are. That is because this is a..."

Mike cuts her off, asking, "It's a Baby Mill, right?"

"Yes, but it is more than just that," says Marisa.

Baby Mills are a type of human trafficking that sees many women end up there in two ways, stolen off the street or tricked into believing they will have a better life in a different country, only to be sold into the sex trade. In particular, younger and more attractive women are sent to these Baby Mills, where they are treated like livestock and bred for the black market.

This is because babies, especially those with attractive parents, are worth a great deal of money. Thousands of couples fuel the baby trade every year by illegally purchasing black-market babies.

Mike finds himself in the middle of the world's largest Baby Mill, run by the notorious terrorist Shariek Blon Mosomid. He is driven by greed and his religious beliefs, but his passion for money far surpasses his faith. Shariek is sought after by all Allied Countries for his crimes of Human Trafficking, Terrorism, and other nefarious activities.

Mike asks with a kind and caring tone, "Marisa, you said you had been here about three months. I'm sorry to ask, but you don't look pregnant. Are you?"

Marisa tries not to show how worried she is. "No, I am not," she says sadly, "If I don't get pregnant soon, I'll be sold off to the Body Traders," Marisa adds, "They gave us three months to get pregnant. If we do, we will stay here until we have the baby. They move the pregnant women to a different area, but it is still here. If we do not get pregnant, they will either sell us off or, if they decide we are not worth enough to sell, they may even kill us. I have seen this happen."

Mike is in shock. He has heard of these places, but to be here in person is something else entirely. During his time in the Navy, especially as a Seal, he had seen some of the worst evils imaginable. But what he is witnessing now is even more devastating. He is standing in the middle of it, and, all of the horror and pain of the situation is all too real. The terror in the eyes of the women in the room is almost too much for him to bear. He can hear their muffled screams, cries of anguish, and moans of pain. Mike McHaskell has always been the one to come in and save the day, but today, he is powerless to help any of these people. It is a painful experience that he will never forget.

He is pulled from his thoughts by a woman pushing a cart entering the area, closely followed by his two new friends, the rod-carrying bastards. The woman is wearing scrubs, and her cart is full of medical supplies. They walk straight to Marisa's Cage.

"Okay, you bitches, move to the side of the Cage. Put your hands through the bars, and do not move," The taller guard barks orders at the women.

As instructed, the women move to the far side and place their arms through the bars.

Then, the shorter man pulls the lever connected to the man's chains inside Marisa's Cage. He flies towards the wall, slamming his malnourished body against it with a thud. He is pinned to the wall, just like Mike had been earlier. This gives Mike a new perspective on what happens when the lever is engaged; he doesn't like it from this angle either.

The women in the Cage move to the furthest side. One at a time, the guards pull each woman from the bars, turning them around and yanking their shirt down without caring if it tears. A number is tattooed above each woman's right breast. The guard reads it aloud to someone; we will call her the Nurse for now.

"80936!" yells the taller man.

"936," repeats the Nurse as she checks her notepad. "No, not her — next."

The guard pushes the woman back into the bars and yells, "Put your filthy arms back through the bars!"

Then he grabs the next woman and repeats the same process until he yells, "80933."

"80933. Yes, that one," says the Nurse. "Bring her."

The taller man grabs the woman by the arm and drags her to where the Nurse is standing. He then pushes her into the cart and yells, "Do what you are told!"

The Nurse says, "Put your arm on this," pointing to the cart. She then ties a cord around 80933's arm and takes a blood sample from the captive woman, "I am done with her. Next."

The guard grabs the next woman, repeats his routine, and yells, "80931". Mike jumps to his feet and grabs the Cage, having seen Marisa's number while they were talking. He realizes this is not good for her, but he knows he can't do anything about it.

"Oh, big man, I guess you found a friend?" the taller guard turns to Mike and laughs, "Well, do not get too attached, ha!" Without taking his eye off Mike, he pushes Marisa hard to the ground and kicks her in the side. Then he yells at her, "Get up and go outside to the Nurse!" Marisa moans in pain as she crawls out of the Cage.

"Arm here," says the Nurse, and Marisa complies. The Nurse is rough with Marisa; she hears the guard talking to Mike and knows it will upset the big man. The Nurse uses a double tourniquet and repeatedly pokes her arm with the needle, not even attempting to draw blood, just to cause pain and bruising afterward. After finally taking her blood sample, Marisa is thrown back into the Cage as hard as the two men can throw her. Then they lock the Cage and release the wheel with the chains that are restraining the man against the wall.

The Nurse pushes her cart out of sight, and the two guards take a few steps toward Mike. "Big man, we will be back for you. You have some tests to take as well. See you soon," the guards laugh as they walk away, banging their prods against the Cages.

"Marisa, what was that all about? Why were they taking your blood?" Mike is very concerned about what he has just witnessed.

Marisa gets up off the floor, her knees scraped and her hands bloodied from the fall. She then walks to the side of the Cage closest to Mike. With tears in her eyes, she explains, "That lady is our Nurse. Today, she was taking our blood for testing to see if we are pregnant," As she speaks, she brushes herself off, "Mike, if mine does not return positive this time, I think they will kill me. They have told me many times that I would be an excellent example to make. So the other women do as they are told. They think I am not the 'right kind' of woman. I am highly educated, the CEO of a unicorn company, and fiercely independent, or at least I was before I ended up here," she begins to cry a little, "I am 27, Mike. Older than all the other women here. Some of them are not even women yet; they are just girls. I do not think I am what they want."

Mike is gripping the bars so hard that his left-hand bleeds from a jagged piece of metal. He sees the blood and loosens his grip. Inside, his anger and anxiety are growing. He is captive and cannot help any of them. All he can do for now is talk to Marisa. "I don't know what to say. I'm so sorry this is happening to you. When will you get the blood test results? Do you know how much time you have if the results aren't what you need?" He is trying to figure out how to fix the problem and needs information. He has forgotten he is talking to a woman who needs to become pregnant in order to survive.

Marisa buries her face in her arm and starts to cry. She wants to tell Mike everything; for some reason, she feels that if she tells him, maybe he can help. But he is just another Caged prisoner. *What can he do*? Still, she tells him through her tears, "The results will be back tomorrow. I am not sure how long I will be here if they are not good. It could be a day or two if I have already been sold, or it could be less if no one has bought me yet and they have decided that I am not worth selling." Marisa can't go on. The other women in her Cage sit her down on their only bed and hug her. They all know this is her last chance.

Night Night, you Filthy Pig:

It is challenging to keep track of time here, as there are no windows, only concrete walls and steel doors. Mike cannot see outside, and there are no clocks. He needs to figure out some way of telling time.

After what feels like an eternity, a large, chubby man appears, pushing a cart from one Cage to the next. He has several large containers filled with food, from which he takes something out at each Cage and then throws it onto the floor. "This is for the men only!" he bellows as he proceeds to strike two young women with an empty bucket for attempting to take some of the food that has fallen on the ground outside of the Cage.

Inside the Cage, the fat man leaves two carrots, an ear of corn, a small potato, and a small piece of meat, approximately 4-5 ounces.

Mike watches as the man follows the same routine at every Cage, eventually arriving at his. "Whoa! You are a big man!" he exclaims upon seeing Mike for the first time, "You might need an extra helping of corn or potato." After that, the fat man proceeds with his duties and walks away.

Mike looks at the food and thinks, *This is American food: meat, potatoes, and corn. I didn't expect this. Maybe hummus and rice or vegetable soup. But what does this mean? Am I still in the United States? No! Could it be? Or am I close to an American settlement somewhere?* He tries to make the crazy pieces fit together, but there are still too many empty spaces in this puzzle.

Mike's Cage door slams open, and his new friends walk in. "Hey, big man, it is your turn. Are you going to behave?" says his taller nemesis. Before he can answer, he feels a sharp pain in his right hip; the short guy has shot him with a tranq dart from outside the Cage.

Mike looks down to see a dart sticking out. He thinks, *Where in the hell am I? A tranquilizer dart? So, the little man is too afraid to enter my Cage. Noted.* Then he looks at the guard and says with as much force and anger as possible, "What the fuck!? A tranq dart? What's wrong, little man? Do I scare you?" His body succumbs to the dart, and he falls to the hard concrete floor.

"Night night, you filthy pig," his Jailer says. Then he spits on him.

You Are My Guest:

Mike wakes up, this time in what appears to be a dog Cage, barely big enough to fit his massive body. He is in a room that looks more like an office than a garage. He looks around; there are windows, but he can't see much, and a large desk is in front of him. Whomever this office belongs to is an Arabic man with money. It is decorated with gold-framed paintings on the walls, gold telephones, and a minibar. Mike thinks, *A mini bar? That's a little strange. Why have a mini bar? Most Muslims don't drink.* If this is Shariek, then it makes sense. He needs to see what is outside the windows. The sky is blue without a cloud. He pushes his face into the corner of the little Cage and can only see the tops of buildings and a little bit of the skyline, but nothing he recognizes from the U.S. He can barely make out some writing on the building tops; it is Arabic and reads "Allah." He catches a glimpse of a very large blue building and thinks to himself, *Where have I seen this building before? Come on, Mike, think!* He is trying to remember where he has seen the building when he suddenly has company.

"Hello my friend," says a tall, clean-cut Arab man as he enters the room. It is positively, Shariek. "Let me introduce myself. I am Shariek Blon Moso-mid; you may call me Shariek."

Shariek is a tall man, standing at 6' 3" - not as tall as Mike - with dark black hair, dark brown eyes so dark they are almost black, and a dark, short, close-kept beard and mustache. He wears a custom-tailored white long-sleeve Kaftan with cuffs and matching pants, a white Ghutra, and a black Igal. This man dresses to impress; he wants Mike to know he is a man of means and a very powerful one.

Shariek walks past the windows and remarks, "What a beautiful day outside." This is to show Mike that he is in control and that he has the freedom Mike wants but does not have. After his stroll around his office, he sits at his desk, which blocks Mike's view. The desk is large, carved from wood, and inlaid with gold. Everything on top of it is also made of gold. The gold paper trays, a gold stapler, a gold phone, and gold pens are all overly ornate. Mike thinks, *If I can just get my hands on one of your ridiculous gold trinkets, I'll be out of here and free all the people you have in the Cages.*

Shariek interrupts Mike's thoughts, "I'm sure you have some questions for me, my friend, do you not?"

"Is it permitted for me to speak?" Mike asks.

"Of course it is. You are my guest."

"Oh? I am your guest. Well, if I am your guest, how about you open this Cage and let me out so I can shake your hand?" Mike would love to shake his hand and kill him with the gold paperclip Shariek has in his teeth.

"I think not. But you are most welcome to kiss my foot," Shariek stands up from his chair and walks to Mike's Cage. He bends over him, sniffs, and makes a face as though Mike stinks. He turns his back on Mike and looks out the window, again displaying his power before speaking, "You must understand, you have only one job here. You may think of yourself as a Stallion. Yes, a Stallion; I like that. You will make me big white American babies. And you will do this, or you will die."

"I know you are confused. I will give you some sense of what is happening here. I sell babies, you see. It is very simple. You will be given a harem of women and will fuck them until they are with child. If you do not like that, you can think of yourself as the Stallion and receive a stable of women. Yes, that is what we will call you, my Stallion with a stable of women." Shariek pauses to let it sink in. Now Mike knows what exactly is expected of him.

Shariek continues, "Later tonight, we will begin to fill your stable with nice American women from Ohio and Minnesota. I hear women are nice in Minnesota; they are all very attractive. You will like them, and I am assured they are all virgins," He turns around and looks directly into Mike's eyes, "You will obey me and make me big American babies. If not, my friend, you and the women I give you will die." He walks away from Mike and says, "Now you must leave. I have a very important meeting, and you are taking up too much space on my floor."

Shariek opens his office door, and four Arabic men walk in. They start banging on Mike's Cage so he won't be able to see the small man with a syringe. He feels a sharp pain in his back and thinks, *Shit! They drugged me again*. He looks at Shariek, memorizing his face so he can come back and kill him for what he is doing later.

Whatever it is they keep injecting him with is something that works quickly. He is out again within a few seconds.

Everyone Has A Boss:

Everyone has a boss; even Shariek has a boss. Sheik Zubair Majeed funds the entire Network. Shariek will let Majeed use Mike for a bit and get a few babies out of him, but he has other plans for Mike. Not just the women Majeed has in mind for Mike to make babies with; Shariek also has access to Mike's little soldiers. He can create as many little Mike McHaskell babies as he desires. The offspring are not just meant for programming, sleepers, or sales; they will be used as propaganda. Shariek has plans to double-cross Majeed and sell Mike's genetic material across his Network. After the Sheik is finished, he will make his money off Mike.

Today, Sheik Zubair Majeed will be in Shariek's office to tell him what he wants done.

As soon as the filthy American is cleared out, everything is cleaned and prepared for Majeed's arrival. Shariek is sitting at his desk when Majeed is shown into his office. "Hello, Zubair."

Sheik Zubair Majeed is wearing a gold-embroidered white long-sleeve Kaftan and matching pants, with a black sheer Bisht Thobe Cloak Eid with a gold tip, and a white Ghutra with a black and gold Igal. It takes a Sheik to out-dress Shariek.

"Shariek, it is good to see you again, my friend. I hear you have acquired a fine specimen."

Majeed sits in an elaborate, gold-and-white-embellished, overstuffed chair, looking out the windows in the office. Shariek joins him in a matching chair. There is fresh tea in an ornately engraved, highly polished brass teapot and two matching etched glass cups sitting on the table between them.

"Yes, I have," says Shariek, "He is perfect for our plan."

"That is good, Shariek. When will he receive his women?"

"Today. I have his mates in the house now. They are being prepared and will be given to the Stallion tonight," Shariek explains.

"When can we expect results? I know it may take some time, but we must keep to our schedule."

"His women are ready; I have made all the necessary preparations. The Doctor will help to expedite the process. They will all be ready for the plan in a few months; it is a guarantee," replies Shariek.

"Good. Make sure I am not disappointed, Shariek. I have other business to discuss, also. I was contacted by a man in China who has a business we might be interested in. I need more information from him before I can make a decision."

"What kind of business?" Shariek asks, "As you know, I am always looking for new sources of income."

Majeed explains to Shariek the essence of the new business: "He is in the business of human body parts. Quality organs on the black market. I think it could be a good fit for our database."

"Interesting," replies Shariek.

Mike has extensive training to know how to handle being drugged and beaten. He has learned many things about managing the drugging he just received. He is able to pull away just slightly from the needle as soon as it goes in. The guy giving the shot was so scared of him that he probably didn't notice he had pulled away.

Because he didn't get the entire dose of drugs, and he knows how to fight the effects. Mike is coming in and out of consciousness as he is dragged back to his Cage. The men think he is unconscious and are not looking at him, which is lucky for him. He can pick his head up slightly, so it won't bounce off the floor, and he can get a good look around.

As he is dragged past one of the rooms, he spots four unconscious white women having their clothes removed. They are on metal tables, surrounded by what looks like medical technicians taking photos. He doesn't see the man just inside the room door, but the man sees him and notices that he is awake. Mike sees him just as he is struck along the side of his head with something hard and flat, knocking him out once again.

He wakes up back in his Cage, again chained up and lying on the concrete floor. His head is pounding. He thinks, *How much more can my head take, fuuuuuuk!* He gently starts rubbing his head and eyes. He wishes he could snap his fingers and go home, but he is stuck in this hellhole and can't leave without saving all the women.

Mike looks into Marisa's Cage, but he can't see her. The other women in her Cage are huddled around something and crying. "Hey! Where is Marisa? Where is she?" he yells. The women move aside and reveal Marisa's badly beaten, lifeless body. Her head is smashed, and she lies in a pool of her own blood. Mike starts to shake with rage, an emotion he cannot control, especially regarding the mistreatment of women.

What The Hell! Who Are You?:

Mike hears a door opening, and shortly after, he sees a wheelbarrow piled with two naked white girls heading towards his Cage, with another wheelbarrow with two more right behind. The two men, whom he hasn't seen before, stop at Mike's Cage door and speak in Arabic, "Pull the lever and get the big son of a bitch back." One of the men pulls the lever, and he is again pinned to the back wall. The other man then opens his Cage door. Then the two men pick up the naked women one by one and drop them on the Cage floor. Before they leave, one of the men throws a thin, worn tunic in the Cage for each woman. After they lock Mike's Cage, the men release him, take their wheelbarrows, and leave without saying a word.

He looks at the women, trying to figure out what to say and do next. He thinks, *They can't be more than 18. Where did they come from? What happened to them?* So many thoughts run through his mind.

The first to wake is a curly-haired, slender blond, standing at 5'6" with green eyes. She lies naked on the floor and looks up at Mike. He sees terror in her eyes and gently says, "No, no, wait, I won't hurt you. It's okay." She crawls across the cold, hard concrete and backs up against the Cage bars. She curls up, trying to cover herself as much as possible. It is cold, dark, and smells horrific. A stranger, a very large man, is staring at her, and she is completely naked. This is the most scared and uncomfortable she has ever been. She looks around and sees the other women unconscious and naked on the floor, with Cages all around them.

Still trying to stay away from the massive man standing over her and curling up to cover herself, the Mama Bear instinct kicks in; she has to save her sister. Her sister is one of the other women still lying on the floor, and she tries to wake her up. "Christina," the woman says, "wake up. Are you okay?" Christina slowly nods her head up and down to indicate yes. She sits up and rubs her eyes.

Christina has long brown hair and stands at 5' 3", looking like a little athlete. She opens her big blue eyes and rubs her neck as she says, "Where are we?" Looking down, she realizes she has no clothes. "Wait... why am I naked?" She looks at her sister, "Why are you naked? Claire, what's going on?"

Claire grabs for Christina and pulls her closer, saying, "I don't know, I don't know, come here." Then Christina catches her first glimpse of Mike.

She is terrified. A mountain of a man is standing over them, and he is practically naked himself. "What the hell! Who are you? Why are you chained up? What's going on? Why are we here? Where is here?" Christina starts to become hysterical. She is so confused and overwhelmed that she begins to tear up and tightly grabs Claire.

Mike has no idea where to start. Instead of answering her questions, he says, "We should check on these other women. Do you know them?"

Claire wants to protect her little sister, so she is the one to answer. Her voice is a little shaky as she says, "No, I have never seen them before today." Christina nods in agreement. The two women are trying desperately to cover themselves in a hopeless attempt at modesty.

Mike leans over the other two women, still unconscious on the cold concrete floor.

Christina asks tearfully and fearfully, "Are they dead?"

Mike places his hands on their necks, feeling for a pulse. "I can feel a pulse; they're alive." He tries to wake the woman closest to him, shaking her lightly. "Miss, hey, Miss. Wake up, come on, wake up." The woman is a redhead with very light, freckled skin and an average build, 5'6" tall. She eventually wakes up as he shakes her arm.

She puts her hands on her head, rubs her temples, then looks around, asking, "Where am I?" Mike backs away from her, not wanting to scare her more than she already is.

"We don't know," Mike says, asking, "Are you hurt?"

"I don't think so," she answers, "but I am naked. Why am I naked? Where are my clothes?" She is shocked to wake up in an unfamiliar place with strangers and without any clothes. She curls up on the floor. Claire hands her one of the tunics to put on. While Mike was checking on the other women Claire and Christina had put on the tunics that were left for them.

"Do you know this woman beside you?" Mike points to the last unconscious woman lying on the floor.

"No, I have never seen her before," the woman says.

Claire reaches out and pulls her closer to where she and Christina are sitting, introduces herself and Christina, and then asks, "What is your name, sweetie?"

She answers, "Terri, my name is Terri."

Mike decides to explain what he knows so far to the women, hoping it might help them to be calm and talk to him about how they got here.

"My name is Mike. I've been here for approximately two days, I believe. There isn't a good way to keep track of time here. I still have no idea what is happening. The best I can come up with is that it seems we were all abducted, kidnapped, and then brought here for some reason I haven't figured out yet. Wherever 'here' is, I haven't figured that out, either. What is the last thing you remember before waking up here?"

Claire decides to answer first, "The last thing I remember is that my sister and I were in the Great Mall of Arabia with our parents on vacation. We were in a really nice clothing store, and I was helping my sister try on an outfit that she couldn't zip by herself, so we were in the dressing room together. Then, we woke up here."

"Exactly," Christina adds, "I was trying on that cute blue sequin body suit and couldn't reach the zipper. Claire came into the dressing room to help me zip it. That's the last thing I remember before waking up naked with you staring at us. How did we get here?"

This is great, Mike thinks, *we must be in Saudi Arabia*. He has been to Jeddah before and is familiar with that mall. It starts making sense: The food and the skyline of Jeddah Tower in the window of Shariek's office. Suddenly he realizes, *We are in Jeddah*!

Mike hopes the women will have more information than they realize, so he says, "Okay, ladies, you're doing great. Maybe, together, we can figure out where we are."

The remaining woman on the Cage floor begins moaning and clutching her left side. She opens her eyes to see Mike and the three women standing over her. Her eyes fill with terror, and she screams as she scurries into the corner of the Cage.

Terri slowly walks over to her with the last tunic in her outstretched hand. "Hi, I know you're scared; we all are. My name is Terri. We're not going to hurt you. We are all kind of prisoners here. Are you okay? Have you been hurt?"

The woman tries to take a deep breath and winces. She then takes a few short, quick breaths and says, "My name is Sammy, and my left side really hurts. I've never felt anything so painful in my life. Why am I naked?"

"Can I take a look at your side?" Mike asks.

Sammy balls up in a defensive move, turning her head away from Mike's eyes, "No! Don't get any closer!" she shouts.

Claire reassures her, "It's okay. Don't be afraid, Sammy. Can I look at it?"

Sammy slowly nods her head in affirmation. Claire lifts her arm and examines Sammy's ribs; they are deeply bruised, displaying various colors, including black, red, purple, and yellow. Whoever has done this to her has repeatedly hit or kicked the same spot for several days. Claire then looks back at the others. "I'm pretty sure she has at least a couple broken ribs. She'll need medical attention." Claire takes the tunic from Terri. "Sammy, we all arrived here naked. Please, let me help you put this on," she helps Sammy put on the last tunic.

Mike knows the kind of medical attention these women will receive won't help fix what is wrong with Sammy. Therefore, he decides not to tell them about the Nurse and her purpose, at least not for now.

"You asked what the last thing we remember was? I remember eating at the food court in the Mega Mall in Minnesota. My food tasted funny, so after a few bites, I ran to the restroom. I was sure I was going to puke! The restrooms weren't close to where I was sitting, and I wasn't sure I would make it. I remember throwing the door open and falling into the stall over the toilet before I woke up here," Terri says, "I don't know where the Great Mall is, but I wasn't there. I was in Minnesota."

"The Great Mall is in Saudi Arabia," Mike says, "and I wasn't there either. I was walking along 5th Avenue in downtown San Diego. Next thing I knew, some guy was pulling a bag over my head, and a couple of other guys started beating me senseless. I don't remember anything else until I woke up here." He isn't going to tell them everything; he only tells them what they need to know to make them more comfortable with him. He needs them to help fill in some of the blanks and paint the picture. It seems to be working; even Sammy starts talking about what has happened to her.

"I am doing a year of college abroad in Germany," Sammy recalls, "I remember going to a nightclub in Tier with my friends and getting dressed up. We went out to a totally German Techno Disco. We ordered drinks and started dancing before they arrived at the table. After a few songs, I went back to our table and had a few sips of my drink, and then nothing. I experienced a total blackout until I woke up here, naked and beaten up, five minutes ago."

"Okay, so none of us were anywhere near each other, we don't know each other, except my sister and me, and we don't look alike; we're not celebrities, we're not like Bill Gates' kids or anything, so what do these people want with us? Why are we here?" Claire is trying to wrap her head around what is going on.

They all look toward Mike. He knows he has to tell them something, but what? How does he explain to these four women that they have just been put in his stable? He is the Stallion they will have to breed with or die. He decides he won't say anything, not yet, anyway.

The little fat man strolls into the garage with a fully-loaded cart and causes quite a stir. He is short, plump, and a perfect square - 5 feet tall, 5 feet wide. Oddly, he seems to be a nice man just doing his job, even though his job is feeding innocent people just enough to keep them from starving, being held against their will, and almost naked in Cages. He is strangely jolly as he walks along the corridor filled with broken captives.

As the man walks directly to their Cage, the four women move closer to each other and away from the door. "It's all right," Mike says, motioning for the women to step back. "This little Asshole is our meal wagon. He won't hurt anyone." Claire, Christina, and Terri get behind him and try to hide. However, Sammy is too scared to be near Mike and stays as far away from him and as far back in the Cage as she can.

The little fat man stops his cart right in front of Mike's Cage. "So, big man, I see you have received your harem. They are attractive for American women. You should like them, I think," he turns to the women, "This food is for you; soup to make you feel better. You all get one bucket; whether you share it or not is up to you, but you only get one." He fills a small wooden bucket with what looks like split pea soup and then pushes it through the Cage bars.

"Thank you," says Mike.

"You are welcome, big man," says the little fat man.

The little man continues with his job of feeding the Caged. At each Cage, he leaves one bucket of soup for each group of women. He chats with some of the Cage dwellers but not all. Mike notices that the little fat man seems to like some prisoners more than others. He makes a mental note of it; this may help him out later.

Mike has the bucket in his hand; he turns to take it to the women. After seeing their faces, he realizes they are looking at him with total disdain and disbelief, unable to process what has just come out of the fat little man's mouth. The women all take a step closer to him.

Terri is the first to speak up, "Okay, what did that man mean by 'harem'?"

"Mike, what is going on here?" Claire asks.

He knows that his time is up, and he has to tell them what this place is. He isn't sure exactly what to say, so he weighs all his options in a split second. *Should I tell them the whole truth? No way; that would definitely freak them out. I should tell them part of what I know. What part? Shit! These women might try to kill me. I'd better just tell them a little now and see how they react before I tell them everything.*

Mike takes a deep breath and starts to answer, "What I know so far is that we are here because..." Suddenly, the door to the garage swings open and slams into the wall, interrupting him.

Shariek walks through the door as if he is marching in a parade, followed by some of his men. He marches directly to Mike's Cage and says, "Ahhh, I see the women I selected for you have arrived" He stops at the Cage door and peers inside. He examines the women as if he were inspecting cattle he has just purchased. "You see, my Stallion, they are all beautiful, just as I promised." Claire gives Mike a look that would kill a lesser man.

Mike quickly answers, "Yes, Shariek, they are just as beautiful as you promised, but we need some time to work out a few details first."

"Yes, yes. Let me help you with that." Shariek turns to one of his men standing at the door and says in Arabic, "Bring him in." Two large men, dressed in all black with only their eyes visible, large scimitars strapped to their backs, and guns holstered at their waists, come through the door. The men are dragging a man with a black bag on his head and his hands tied behind his back toward Shariek. They stop in front of Mike's Cage.

They are holding the man under his arms, his legs dragging behind him, his head hanging down.

"I believe you are familiar with this man, ladies," Shariek says, looking directly at Claire and Christina and smiling as he quickly yanks the bag off the man's head.

"Oh, my God! Daddy! Daddy!" both women scream. They rush to the front of the Cage and try to reach their father through the bars. Claire and Christina are desperate to get to him. Shariek has instructed his men to be close enough for the women to think they could touch him but not close enough for them to actually do so. They both try with all their might to get through the bars, but he is just beyond their reach. Tears stream down their faces.

"Ladies, let me tell you how this is going to work. You are here to provide me with big American babies. Each of you will breed with the big man and provide me with at least one child. I will give you three months to become pregnant. If you do not become pregnant within three months, I will sell you to the highest bidder," He explains to the women, "I want you all to understand that this will be happening, and you will be doing as I have told you."

Shariek removes one of the large scimitars from its sheath, and the two men holding their father step back slightly behind his shoulders. Still holding him up by his arms, they put him on his knees, and he looks up at his daughters. His face is bloodied and bruised, and there are tears in his eyes. Mike immediately understands the situation and grabs Claire and Christina, pulling them back to him and turning their heads away from their father, so they won't see what is about to happen. Shariek's men release their father just before Shariek raises the scimitar and swings forward, striking the man in his neck. With one swift motion, his head is removed, falling to the floor and rolling forward to rest on the bars of his daughter's Cage. His body hits the ground with an unmistakable thud. As blood begins to pour out of the headless body, Sammy screams and collapses lifeless to the ground. Terri rushes to Sammy and cradles her head in her lap. Sammy is breathing but passes out again. The screams made Claire and Christina panic; they try to pull away from Mike to see what has just happened to their father.

He pulls them tighter to his chest. "Don't look, just don't look," he says, doing his best to keep them from seeing their father's beheaded and bleeding body.

Shariek, proud of what he has done and satisfied with the message he has just bestowed upon these filthy Americans, wipes his scimitar on their father's shirt and spits on his body. He smiles, knowing he hasn't finished making his point to the women.

"Now, ladies, I have another surprise for you." He motions to a guard standing at the doorway. They can hear a woman screaming from the other side of the door; it is muffled, but Claire and Christina immediately recognize the woman's cries. Two more men, identical to the two with their father, throw a heavy-set woman, arms bound behind her and gagged with duct tape, through the doors. She falls to the floor, slamming her face into the concrete. They grab her legs and begin to drag her closer to Shariek. "It would not be a family reunion without your mother," says Shariek.

Their mother is on the ground behind Shariek. She looks like she has been beaten worse than their father; her clothes are ripped, her face is bloody, her right eye is swollen shut, and her feet are covered in cuts. The two girls begin to scream, and their bodies start to shake, but this time they do not leave Mike's embrace. "You two have a choice. You can choose to do as I say, and your mother will live. Or if you do not do as I say, she will be cut from her privates to her throat. It is your choice to make. I will leave you to think about it," Shariek says, then turns and leaves the garage. Making sure to leave their father's head resting along the bottom rung outside of their Cage.

Two of the men drag their mother out of the garage by her hair. She begins kicking and cries out in pain as they begin to pull her. The two men stop and one of the men turns and punches her in the face. Her head slams backward hitting the ground, and she falls limp and silent.

Christina collapses to the floor, staring into the decapitated face of her father, and begins to shake uncontrollably. She is going into shock. Claire pulls Christina away from the front of the Cage, turns Christina's head towards the back wall, and sits her on the floor. Claire then sits behind her, wrapping her arms and legs around Christina as tightly as possible. She does her best to comfort and console her sister, but it is useless. Christina is overwhelmed by what she has just seen, which is more than anyone should ever endure. Her body gives in, and she faints. Claire strokes her hair and speaks in a soft, motherly voice, "Everything will be alright. I will take care of you. Rest now. I've got you." Now Claire is lying beside her little sister, with her arms and legs around her. She has no idea how they are ever going to be able to escape this horrible place. Something tells Claire that Mike will save them; she doesn't understand why, but she believes in him.

All the lights in the garage go out. *Thank God,* Mike whispers.

During the night, Christina takes up position behind Mike on the mattress, with Claire behind her and Terri behind Claire. They need each other to stay warm, and Christina wants to hide behind Mike to feel as safe as possible in this place. Claire has given Sammy the blanket because she is still too scared of Mike and the whole situation to lie with them. Sammy is sleeping on the ground, her back against the wall and facing away from the others.

Mike only sleeps in short spurts throughout the night. He watches and listens while he is awake. In the depths of the night, just like every night, two men dressed in all black remove their father and the dead or dying victims from all the Cages around the garage. He listens closely while they are in the garage that night, as neither man has ever spoken, not to anyone in the Cages and not to each other. Tonight is no different; not a single word is uttered. This is the only activity throughout the night.

This is Truly a Place of Horror:

Mike slowly and quietly leaves the women on the mattress; he is sitting on the floor facing the doors used to enter the garage. The overhead lights begin to turn on, and the low murmur of the Cage dwellers starts. All four women are still sleeping, and that is good. He has been waiting for the lights to come on for a better look around this morning. After Shariek's "Power Moves" yesterday, he knows he must figure things out quickly. Mike thinks, *This guy is a psychopath and an egomaniac. Not a good combination.* He will have to use all his training and experience to get out of this place in one piece. He has to start working out a plan today; the only problem is that he doesn't have enough information to create a plan that will work. On top of that, he now has four women with him, so he will also have to get them out.

Softly, Claire asks, "Is it still there?"

Mike knows exactly what she is asking, and he quietly answers, "No."

She gets up and sits next to him so they can talk without waking the others.

He is still looking around, trying to figure out what to do, when Claire whispers, "Mike, what are we going to do?"

He doesn't look at her when he answers, "Right now, I'm not sure, but I'm working on a plan."

Claire can see how intense he is, but she has to tell him what she is thinking. "I need to protect my sister. I think you and I both know that if they haven't already killed my mother, they're going to. That man is a psychopath. I don't know if we will make it out of here alive."

Mike stops his surveillance and looks Claire in the eyes. "We will get out of here. I promise you, we will," he says adamantly. Claire doesn't understand why but deep inside, she believes him.

The door to the garage swings open, and the two guards, who like to beat on Mike, walk in. "Hey, big man, guess what?" says the taller bastard. "I think I want one of your women. Well, you have four, so you can give one to me. Not that you have any choice, of course."

Looking straight ahead at the guard, Mike tells Claire, "Wake them up. Get to the back of the Cage... Claire, move them now."

Claire wakes up Christina and Terri. She grabs their arms and pulls them to the back of the Cage saying, "Come on, let's move." They then wake up Sammy and huddle together in the back corner of their Cage.

The two men walk to the Cage's door; one throws the lever, Mike's arms fly up, and he bounces off the wall. The tall man enters the Cage, walks past Mike with a smile, and tries to grab Christina by the arm. Christina screams, then kicks the man in the shins and pulls away. Claire stands up, gets between Christina and the dirtbag guard, and punches the man with all her might. This angers and embarrasses the guard, so he grabs Claire by the shoulders and shakes her. "Filthy American woman, you must learn your place. Women do as men wish. You will not do that again!" He backhands her across the face, knocking her off her feet and back into the other women. Claire looks at him with utter disdain as she lands on the ground, and blood begins to flow from her nose and mouth.

The guard steps back and says to the women, "I will take what I want. You cannot stop me." Just as he begins to step toward Christina, Mike pulls himself up by his chains to the top of the Cage and, in one swift move, wraps the chain connecting his legs around the man's neck. He kicks so hard that the man's neck is instantly broken. The chain cuts so deep that it almost decapitates the guard. Blood sprays from his neck onto the women as they scream. This is truly a place of horror.

As this is happening, the other guard yells for help. In a matter of seconds, five guards rush into Mike's Cage. They release his lever just long enough to get the big man off balance and then pull him back to the wall. The guards start beating Mike, and he fights for his life. Claire jumps to Mike's defense, punching and kicking in vain, trying to protect him. One of the guards hit Claire in the head with a bat, dropping her to the floor, he then jabs her with his cattle prod, holding it in place and shocking her unconscious. Then he kicks her body out of the way and returns to beating Mike.

At this point, the five guards are torturing him with thousands of volts, making his body convulse uncontrollably. Mike's head is repeatedly hit against the cement wall, and soon enough, blood starts streaming from his nose, and his eyes roll back into his head. As he is losing consciousness, the last thing Mike sees is Claire lying below him, her face covered in blood and her eyes closed. He can hear the screams of the other women in his Cage, and the last thought to cross his mind is, *I think they might have killed me this time. I don't think I will wake up from this. I hope those women get out; maybe my brothers will find them when they find my body.*

As quickly as it begins, the ordeal comes to an end. The men rush out of the garage, leaving the dead guard's body outside the Cage.

"Claire, are you alright? Claire, wake up, come on, please wake up," Christina wipes the blood from Claire's face with her hands, desperately trying to wake her sister. She is crying and covered in blood. "Please wake up; please wake up."

Claire slowly opens her eyes and tries to speak, she can see Christina is frantic, but she can't get any words out. She looks at Christina and mouthes, "I'm okay," then nods and gives a slight smile.

"Oh, thank God you are okay! I think they killed Mike," Christina tells Claire, "He looks dead, and I don't think he is breathing."

Terri leaned over Mike, her voice filled with disbelief as she exclaimed, "He's still alive! He's barely breathing, and they almost pushed him to the brink of death. I can't believe he's still alive, but look at him - how is he going to make it through this, here in this place?"

Claire slowly turns to look at Mike. She can't believe her eyes; Christina is right; he does look dead. She stepped closer to him and placed her ear on his chest, carefully monitoring the rise and fall. "He's breathing very shallowly," she said, "and his heartbeat is so slow and weak. We have to do something to help him."

Mike is pinned to the wall, the guards leave him in this state for their safety, they claim, as they leave. But he is unconscious and poses no risk to anyone. The real reason the guards leave him hanging there is they are hoping Mike will die before anyone discovers what has occurred. The women tug at the chains, but they won't budge.

Claire is trying to figure out what to do next and needs to know how long she and Mike have been unconscious. "How long was I out?" she asks. Christina looks at Claire and shrugs her shoulders.

Terri says, "I'm not sure. It wasn't very long. The guards finished with Mike shortly after they knocked you out. They grabbed the guy Mike killed, dropped him outside the Cage, and locked us up again. As soon as they left the garage, Christina began trying to wake you up. So, maybe somewhere between five and ten minutes."

Claire is silent for a minute, taking a little extra time to process everything. She has a head injury, as well as Mike. "If I was out for five or ten minutes and they finished with Mike soon after me, that means he's been out for at least ten minutes now. Are you all okay? Did they hurt you?"

Terri explains that the men only aimed to inflict pain on Mike after he killed the guard, so they left the three of them alone. She and Christina are fine; the guards didn't even glance at Sammy.

The women are trying to figure out how to help Mike when the door to the garage swings open once again. They jump and grab ahold of each other, sure that whoever has come back is there to finish them off.

It is Shariek, followed by a dozen of his guards.

Shariek looks angry and shocked. "What the fuck happened here? Why is the big man beaten and bleeding?"

"Mr. Shariek," pleads Claire, "Mike was only trying to protect us. This man," she points to the dead guard on the floor, "came in and tried to take my sister. He told Mike he could take one of his women for himself since you had given him four. Mike was only trying to protect his "Harem," as you called us, when they did this to him and hit me. Please don't be angry with him; I promise we will do what you want us to do. Please don't punish us for this."

Shariek is very angry; he turns to the guards and begins yelling, "I told you all! No one is to touch the white women until they are pregnant. Do you have any idea how much I have invested in these Breeders? Millions! My orders are clear and must be obeyed. No exceptions. They will not be touched by anyone but the big man, or as we now know his name, Mike.

Now release his chains!" He walks away from the Cage and says, "And remove the chain you so foolishly put on his legs before he can use the weapon you idiots gave him again."

Mike is the only man with chains around his ankles due to the guards' fear of his massive size. They had no idea that he could kill one of them using these chains. Shariek commands the leg chains be removed, as he does not want to see another guard lose their "head" to his Stallion.

Two guards enter the Cage and remove Mike's leg chain while his arm chains are still pulled tight, pinning him to the wall. Even when he is unconscious and motionless, they are still afraid of him. After securely locking the Cage door, one of the guards releases the lever for his arm chains. His limp and beaten body falls to the ground with a solid thud. The guards then turn and leave.

Claire kneels beside Mike, her heart aching at seeing him in such bad condition. She carefully places her left hand over his heart, feeling for a pulse. It is faint and weak, but it is still there. She gently wipes the blood from his eyes, nose, and mouth with her right hand. She keeps a close eye on his chest, watching for any sign of movement, but unfortunately, it is very shallow and slow.

Claire desperately attempts to wake Mike, calling out to him, "Mike, can you hear me? Can you open your eyes?" But there is no response; not a single sound, not a moan or a grunt, not even a twitch of an eye or muscle or an extra breath. Nothing. She knows she has to keep trying.

This time, Mike is in terrible shape. He suffered a significant concussion, and his heart stopped beating. The guards had no idea that the cattle prodding had actually restarted it at some point. He is as close to death as he has ever been. The women are scared about what will happen if he dies; they never say anything aloud, but they all think about it.

They have nothing in the Cage to try to clean his wounds. The only water they can find is a pipe above their Cage, dripping a little, but they have no way to collect it. The only cloth they have is the clothing they are wearing. Claire motions to Terri, "Help me get his underwear off. We can tear it into strips and use them as bandages." The two women start removing his boxers and then begin tearing them apart. Claire hands Christina a large piece of fabric. "Tear this into two strips as long as you can. Then try to soak up the water from the wall and floor with the strips." Christina gets to work, tearing the boxers and wetting them.

At that moment, Claire's only focus is on creating the bandages, but she can't help but notice Mike's impressive manhood. She and Terri exchange embarrassed glances, both blushing and quickly looking away, neither saying a word. Christina is able to make four bandages and soak them with the only water she can find, handing them to Claire and Terri. When she sees Mike in all his glory for the first time, she can't help but exclaim, "Oh, my God! That thing is....wow!" Christina has a habit of saying whatever is on her mind without any filter, often getting herself into trouble because of it. She is young and hasn't yet learned the art of discretion, never considering the consequences of her words.

"Thanks for the bandages," Claire says, trying to ignore Christina's outburst and gesturing for her to come and help, "Help me lift his head." Claire is well aware that Christina has no control over her words and that responding to her will only make the situation worse.

Claire does her best to clean and bandage Mike's wounds, but there are too many cuts and gashes for the number of bandages they have. She decides to start by cleaning as many wounds as possible and then focus on bandaging the worst ones. She begins with the gashes on his face and neck, and as she wipes away the blood, he moves and groans a little, a good sign that he is starting to wake up. Suddenly, his eyes open, and he speaks, "I'm still alive? I didn't think I would be."

"You surprised us too. We thought the guards did you in for sure. They beat the hell out of you," Terri says.

Claire asks Mike, "How do you feel? I mean, it's a dumb question, but are you okay?"

Mike answers slowly, "I'm not sure." He runs his hands through his hair. "My head feels like an elephant stepped on it, or maybe even sat on it, and I think it might still be there. My whole body hurts. My ribs ache, and it's hard to take a breath. Can I ask why I'm naked?"

Claire answers, "We needed to clean your wounds and try to bandage the worst ones. Your wounds, your clothes. Besides, now you know how we felt when we were thrown in here completely naked."

He looks at Claire and gives a half-smile, wincing in pain before asking, "Really, how am I alive? The last thing I remember after killing that guard is being rushed by a group of his friends. If they told Shariek what I did, there's no way he would have let me live."

"It was all Claire," says Christina. "The guards told that monster, and he came here to kill you, but she was able to talk him out of it; for now, anyway. Claire is really good with people; she can talk anyone into anything. You know, she can even sell ice cubes to a polar bear! She's done this our whole life and has kept me out of a lot of trouble. I'm not sure how she does it, but she always does."

"I don't think I talked anyone out of anything," Claire insists, "At best, I bought us some time. At least they removed your leg chains."

"So I have to ask, what's with your penis?" Christina blurts out.

"For fuck sake, Christina! What the hell is wrong with you? The dude is practically dying on the floor over here; give him a break," says Terri.

Terri stands out from the other three women; she is not particularly feminine and has no inclination to become close to Mike. She doesn't bother to shave her legs or under her arms, and her behavior is more masculine than it is feminine. Claire has a suspicion that Terri might be more interested in other women than men, but she keeps her thoughts to herself. Claire doesn't have any strong opinions either way, but if she can help anyone to feel less awkward in this environment, she is willing to do so.

"Geez! I was just asking. I didn't mean anything by it, Mike. It's out there for us all to see, but still, I'm sorry," Christina apologizes.

"It's okay," Mike says, "This whole situation is pretty strange, and Claire is right. Now I know how you ladies felt when you woke up here. It's not too comfortable waking up naked in front of strangers."

"You're right; we are all complete strangers here, but we need to focus on what we must do next," Claire starts, "We have to come up with a plan. To protect you from that man, I had to make certain promises. Promises that we will do as he wishes. From what I understand, that means, in his own words, we need to breed with you. You are our Stallion, and we are expected to produce pure-bred big American babies for him. That monster is expecting results. I believe he will let those guards take our lives if we do not do as he says."

Mike looks at all four women, then turns to Claire, "Thank you for saving my life. But please don't do it again; Shariek could have just as easily killed you for speaking up. These people don't think women are worth much here. They are to be silent and do as they are told. You are right; we do need a plan. Since he has allowed me to live, we have some time. Shariek wants what he wants, but he is smart and knows I will need time to heal. We will use this time to make a plan to get us the hell out of here."

"I knew it was risky, but I had to try, not just for you, but for our mother. I understand he will kill any of us without a second thought. I'll be more careful from now on. We can talk about all of this later. You need to rest for now. I'm certain you have a concussion, so we'll have to keep waking you up and checking on you," Claire says, acting like a Den Mother.

Mike closes his eyes and tries to get comfortable, attempting to get some much-needed rest. His mind is racing, trying to devise a solution, but his battered and exhausted body eventually wins out, and he drifts off to sleep.

As Mike lies resting, Claire and Terri talk about the promises they have made to Shariek to ensure Mike's and their mother's survival. Terri is convinced that their mother is already dead, and it seems that Claire has the same opinion. However, Christina is a different story; she still holds onto the hope that her mother is alive. Christina appears to be quite naive and innocent. They know that Shariek expects progress, which means someone has to become pregnant.

Terri looks around at the Cages and says, "All the women here seem pretty young. Like, no one over 25. Have you noticed that?"

Claire is also scanning through the other Cages, "I did; I guess they think the chances of getting pregnant are better when you're younger. I'm 19, and Christina had just turned 18 the day before when whoever it was grabbed us. That's why we were out shopping; it was a shopping spree birthday gift from dad. I can't believe we'll never see him again; he was such a great dad."

Terri knows she has to keep the conversation moving, as she doesn't want Claire to dwell on what had happened to her father. "I'm 20, and I'll be 21 in a few months. I'm sure you noticed, but I'm not really into guys. I don't have anything against them; I'm just not interested. I hope that doesn't make you girls uncomfortable. To be honest, I'm not into girls, either. I just don't have any interest in any of that."

Sammy has been motionless and silent for hours, with the other three women leaving her be. The trauma has left her almost entirely unresponsive, so when she suddenly speaks, it shocks them all. "I'm 19 years old, and I am attracted to men, but I have no desire to breed with anyone. Just tell me how we're going to get out of here. This place is worse than any horror movie I have ever seen; I can't take it anymore."

"We will all get out of here eventually, although it will take some time. Mike is too injured to do anything at the moment, but he is trying to come up with a plan. I'm not sure what it is, but deep inside, something makes me believe he can do it. We need to figure out what we can do to help him," Claire is adamant that she will do whatever she can to aid Mike in getting them out of this situation.

Christina blurts out her solution, "I will do it! I will get knocked up by the big guy. He is a big guy, but I will do it."

Claire firmly grasps Christina's hands and looks her in the eyes seriously, "No, Christina, I won't allow you to do that. I'm the one who made a deal with the devil, so it's my responsibility to keep the promise. It's strange, I know, but I feel like Mike trusts me, and I think I can get him on board. I'll talk to him and explain that we've decided I should be the one to try."

"Oh, thank God!" Terri exclaims in relief, "Christina is absolutely right; he is a big man, and I know there is no way I could handle that. If I'm being honest, it won't be a good time; that thing is gonna hurt. We all saw it."

Sammy is visibly distressed, her voice trembling as she speaks, "I can't do it, I never have before, and I just can't. There's no way," she says, her eyes filling with tears. She curls up into a ball in the corner of the Cage, wrapping the blanket around her tightly, and begins rocking back and forth in a desperate attempt to soothe her fear.

Christina chimes in, "Well, you know Sis, you have never either, so....."

Claire cut her off firmly, "And neither have you! Let me decide what's best for us. Things can change here in an instant, so you need to be careful about what you say, not just about me. You cannot say anything to the men here. They will take your life in a second, so think before you speak. I'm not trying to be mean, but we all must be careful. This place is like the pit of hell, and we have made a deal with the devil to stay alive. I think it's best if we all get some rest. We will take turns watching Mike. I will sit with him now, and you two can sleep. But before you do, please try to rinse the bandages and get more water on them."

Without another word, Christina and Terri pick up the homemade bandages and wring them out. They take them to the dripping water and soak them as much as possible before returning them to Claire.

Christina feels terrible about how she acted. She never wants to hurt her sister, so she sincerely apologizes to Claire for her actions and vows to try to do better from now on. With their tasks complete, Christina and Terri try to get some much-needed rest.

Claire keeps a close eye on Mike, and after a few hours, she notices he is trembling. She puts her hand on his forehead and feels he has a fever. She is concerned that he might have internal bleeding or infection from his wounds since this place is not particularly sanitary. Not knowing what else she could do to help him, she holds him in her arms.

A few hours later, Mike's temperature has risen. Claire attempts to wake him, begging him to open his eyes. When she receives no response, she quickly alerts Christina and Terri, instructing them to bring bandages and additional water. She knows that Mike's fever can be dangerous and that they must take steps to reduce his temperature.

Christina quickly soaks the homemade bandages in the dripping water and hands them back to Claire. "That's all I can get. The water is slowing down," she says. Claire then takes the bandages and squeezes the excess water, letting it drip into Mike's mouth.

Terri passes the last of the bandages to Claire, drenched in water. Shee begins to apply them to Mike's head, saying, "We need to lay them on his head and do our best to break his fever. We have to make it happen."

Taking turns, soaking up whatever water they can find, they pass the damp bandages to Claire. She waves the bandages in the air trying to help cool them down before carefully placing them on Mike's forehead and around his neck. This process goes on for hours, leaving all three women completely drained and exhausted.

Mike utters in a hushed tone, but he speaks, "Oh my, I must be the luckiest man alive. Three gorgeous women, barely clothed, fussing over me - wow!" He begins to chuckle, but the laughter quickly turns into a coughing fit that causes a sharp pain in his fractured ribs. Fortunately, his fever has broken, and he seems to be on the path to recovery. Claire is in awe of him. He is an incredible man with unparalleled strength, both in body and spirit.

"Maybe, you should just be that lucky guy and let us help you for now. You need to rest as much as you can," Claire squeezes another bandage over his head.

Mike gives a single nod, seeming to be too exhausted to give any more of a response. Claire is relieved that he is only taking a nap this time rather than being knocked out as he has been earlier. She cannot bear the thought of it happening again.

The next day Mike wakes up with Claire facing towards him, Terri behind him, and Christina with her back against the wall and legs outstretched so that Mike's head rests in her lap. Sammy has finally gotten up the courage to sleep next to them and is lying with her back to Claire's back.

"You're awake," Claire whispers.

"I am, and I'm feeling a little better," Mike says in a low, rough voice, "Thank you for helping me. I owe you ladies my life. As God as my witness, I will repay you. That is a promise."

"I'm glad you feel that way because we need to talk," Claire says, precise with her words, "My main focus is protecting my sister. We need to keep her safe."

"Okay, we will," Mike agrees with Claire.

She looks him in the eyes and says, "Mike, you need to tell me. What is this place really? What is going on here?"

Mike says uncomfortably and quietly, "It's a Baby Mill."

She looks at him with a questioning face, almost mouthing the words before asking, "What is a 'Baby Mill' Mike?"

"This is just one part of a much bigger operation," he says, "I'm not sure if you really want to know all about what this place is; it's very disturbing. It's dark and pure evil. Are you sure you want me to tell you all about it?"

"How can it get any more disturbing than what we have already experienced? Please just tell me what we are dealing with here. I can't protect my sister unless I know what I'm protecting her from," says Claire.

Mike takes a breath and begins to explain it all to Claire, "Okay, here goes; it's not just a Baby Mill, but an entire Network. The leading players are 'Buyers', 'Sellers', and 'Hunters'. The 'Buyers' are sick people looking to purchase Men, Women, Children, and even Babies. Some of these people may come as a shock to you, while others you may have already expected to be involved. Regardless, they all have the money and power to do whatever they please. We are talking about Kings, Presidents, Russian Oligarchs, American billionaires, Saudi Royalty, and anyone with enough money to be considered a 'Buyer'. It all begins here. These people have the financial means to get this terrible cycle of horror into motion.

"As disturbing as it may sound, demand is the first thing needed. Unfortunately, there is no shortage of that. The 'Buyers' log onto the dark web. Some sick fuck set up an entire database to ensure these people can find exactly what they want. It is like an 'App' on your phone. That is where Shariek comes in; he is responsible for the 'Acquired' on the App. We, Claire, are the 'Acquired'. All of us here are the 'Acquired'. It is a scary thought, but it is the truth.

"When a 'Buyer' logs into the App, they can search 'Acquired' inventory, as precisely as they want. They choose hair color, eye color, height, weight, body type, measurements, shoe size, skin color, or anything you can think of. All of this determines the value of the 'Acquired'. Unique attributes - something unusual or distinctive - can drive up that price."

The other three women see Mike and Claire talking and overhear a little. They stare at them in disbelief, hoping what they have heard was out of context or not what they thought they had heard. Finally, Christina can't sit there any longer and asks, "What are you two talking about?"

Mike looks at Christina, Terri, and Sammy, "I think you all should know what we're up against here; it's worse than you probably think." They all move closer to him so they can hear his story. He fills the other women in and then continues with his explanation.

"If the 'Acquired' inventory doesn't meet a 'Buyers' needs, they can place a Custom Order. This allows the 'Buyer' to choose exactly what they are looking for. For example, if I wanted to order someone like you," Mike motions to Claire, "I would go through the App and use checkboxes to select the following characteristics: American woman, white, 18-22 years old, blond hair, green eyes, between 5'5" and 5'6", slim build, and any other features I can think of. Then, there is a section to add special requests for anything not on the list. Maybe someone wants you, but they want you to have a prosthetic leg or be a trained French Chef. They add that to their list. After they have listed everything they desire, the 'Buyers' place a deposit into an escrow account. Once the money has been verified, the request list is sent to the 'Hunters'."

"'Hunters'? What the hell is a 'Hunter'?" Terri can't believe what she is hearing.

Mike continues, "I am getting to that now. Shariek's Network spans the globe, and he employs 'Hunters' who, seek out and 'Acquire' people who meet the 'Buyers' requirements. Each morning, the 'Hunters' get notifications through the App of new requests. They have their own Network of 'Finders' who look for prospective 'Acquired.' When a match is found, the 'Finders' send photos to the 'Hunters', who forward them to the App for prospective 'Buyers' to view and approve. If the 'Buyer' likes what they see and clicks approve, the 'Hunters' go to work."

"They go to work? What do the 'Hunters' do, Mike?" Christina's eyes are wider than ever.

"They hunt," he explains to the women, "They go out and 'Acquire' the people the 'Finders' sent photos of. That's why they are called 'Hunters'."

Claire touches Mike's arm to stop him and says, "So, let me get this straight. We were 'Ordered'? Like a pizza or something?" She holds her hand out and motions to the other three women.

"Yes, as disturbing as that may sound. Shariek ordered all four of you and me."

All of what Mike explains is beginning to sink in for the women. They are all starting to realize they have just been purchased, and it is overwhelming. Tears stream down Christina's face. Sammy bursts into tears and turns away, pulling her knees to her chest, and Terri has a look of utter shock and terror on her face.

Claire is the only one still maintaining her composure, "Please go on, Mike. We need to hear it all, even if we don't like what you tell us."

He places his hand on Claire's and says, "This gets worse from here. Are you sure you want me to keep going?"

Claire looks at the other women and softly says, "Yes. Please, go on."

Mike continues, "Okay. After a person is 'Acquired', they are sent to one of the intake facilities around the globe. At these facilities, they are evaluated to make sure they meet the 'Buyer's' requirements."

"I don't remember going to any intake facility," Terri says, looking at the other women with a questioning expression.

Claire realizes why they can't remember being there, "That's because we were drugged."

Sammy turns back around and says, "I saw that place. I woke up there for just a few minutes. I remember being touched all over my body, but it's fuzzy. People were moving my arms and legs, and someone was taking pictures. A woman was using a measuring tape on my chest, and I tried to fight her off. That's when I was hit in my side by something that really hurt. The next thing I remember is seeing Mike looking over me here in the Cage."

Claire asks for more information, saying, "Mike, you said that attributes determine the value of the 'Acquired'. What attributes?"

He carefully chooses his words, "These can be anything from a specific age to sizes of things...I think you know. But the highest value attribute for a woman is being wholesome. The intake facility confirms and sends proof to the 'Buyers'."

"What the hell does 'wholesome' mean?" Christina thinks she knows what Mike means, but she has to ask.

"It means you're still a virgin; that makes you worth more," Terri is irritated by this piece of information, saying, "That makes all of us worth more to these sick bastards."

"You get the gist of it?" Mike hopes that is all he has to say.

"They send proof? What proof, Mike?" Claire demands.

"I don't see why we need to go into this any further," Mike says firmly, "They have proof; that's enough. Once the 'Buyer' approves the purchase of the 'Acquired' and the intake staff clears them, they are shipped all around the world in Shariek's private airplanes. Before Shariek's men leave the 'Acquired' with the 'Buyer', the funds are transferred to all involved. Shariek takes his fee, the 'Buyer' gets their new 'Acquired', and everyone else gets paid simultaneously."

"Okay, but what is this place? Why are we here?" Christina feels dirty after hearing she has been bought and paid for.

"Do you see those marks on your arm? They're on all of our arms. They're needle marks. During intake, they take blood, and we were probably tested for genetic defects and traits," Mike explains.

"Is that why we are here?" asks Claire.

Mike answers, "There is another darker side to that App. People can also order babies; Shariek's App calculates the probability of what children should look like based on those same blood tests. The approximate height, body type, hair, eye color, etc. It's like this: you and I both have light-colored eyes. My hair is light brown, and yours is blonde. I am tall, and your body type is more slender. So, odds are, we will have tall kids with light hair and light eyes. If a 'Buyer' wants a child like that, they can pre-order a baby from you and me."

"This just keeps getting worse, Mike," Claire's eyes fill with tears. All four women are sickened by the thought of someone "pre-ordering" a baby.

"I know, it's horribly cruel. This is pure evil in the flesh," Mike looks around the garage and says, "Pure evil."

Christina wipes the tears from her eyes, "So all these people are part of this disgusting Network. They have all been ordered and are now being bred like cattle. We are going to be bred like cattle…This gets more and more terrible every second."

"I am so sorry, ladies. I wish none of this were true. But yes, that is the purpose of this place; it's a Baby Mill," Mike says.

Claire realizes the women aren't the only ones who were 'Acquired'; she apologetically says, "I'm sorry. I was just thinking about us women, but you're also in this system. Sorry, Mike."

Mike knew all about this place and Shariek's Evil Empire. He has had more time to come to grips with all of this and he says, "It's okay, Claire. You guys just found out a horrible truth. I understand how that feels. You're upset; anyone would be upset."

Claire reluctantly asks, "What happens if we don't get pregnant? If we don't have a baby? We can't let him take…"

Mike cuts Claire off, saying, "We won't. I promise we will get out of here before it comes to that."

Claire presses Mike for answers, "What will he do to us if we don't 'produce' for him?"

Mike hates to tell the women the truth, but he knows he has to "Unfortunately, we have all seen Shariek. We know who he is and what he looks like. That makes us all a threat to him and his Empire. When I first arrived, I met a young woman named Marisa. She had been here for about three months and was unable to get pregnant. Shariek had her beaten to death inside her Cage while the other women with her watched. Shariek is a true monster. I couldn't do anything to save her, but I will get us all out of here."

Claire is clear about what needs to happen, "Then, we will have to try to produce for the monster. We need to do everything we can to keep ourselves alive so we can escape. Mike, you will have to help us survive."

Mike respects women too much to ever force any one of them to do anything. "First, we need a plan. I can get us out of here before we hit the three-month mark. We just need some time. If we run out of time, then we can talk about Plan B."

"If one of us can get pregnant, it might give us more time to devise an escape plan," Claire says.

"Claire, I'm not just going to save us; I'm going to save everyone here. I won't leave anyone behind," Mike declares, determined to save everyone, "This place is pure terror. These women and men will die if we don't get them out. We have to save everyone, not just ourselves."

Just then, the door to the garage opens, and the Nurse, pushing her cart, enters the room, followed by a couple of guards. She makes her way to the Cage closest to the door and, in a loud voice, commands the women to move back to the corner. Claire and the other women haven't seen any of this yet. The guards remove the shirts of every woman in the Cage, then instruct them to put their arms through the bars. One by one, they yell out the numbers tattooed on their chest to the Nurse, who takes blood samples from those whose numbers are on her list.

Claire and the other three women look down at their chests, wondering why they do not have numbers. "Why don't we have numbers, Mike?" Claire asks.

"I don't know. I've been thinking about that since you got here. Why are we being treated differently? Why is our Cage separated from the rest? What does Shariek want from us? I just don't know... yet," answers Mike.

They all watch as the Nurse takes blood samples from the women in the other Cages, and then she heads for their Cage.

"Okay, you filthy American Whores, each of you needs to be given this shot. Put your arms outside of the Cage now. Do not fight me. If you do, I will send in the guards to make you comply," demands the Nurse.

"Why do we need that shot? What is it?" asks Claire.

"You are new here, so let me tell you: It is chorionic gonadotropin. It is a hormone that will cause you to "come into heat," thus speeding up the process of becoming pregnant. I do not usually give this to the whores for at least two months. However, Shariek has demanded that I give it to all four of you now. You will receive one of these shots every few weeks until you are pregnant," explains the Nurse.

"I don't want to take it," says Sammy.

"Then I will have the guards pick you up and bring you to me. Either way, you will be getting this shot. How you get the shot is up to you. Do you understand?" asks the Nurse.

The women do not want the guards to enter the Cage again, so they yield and put their arms through the bars. The Nurse gives each of them a shot of the hormone.

Christina pulls her arm back, rubbing it and complaining, "Damn! That hurt."

Mike can only observe helplessly; he is still too weak to stand and is lying on the floor at the back of the Cage.

"Do not worry, big man; you will not be left out. You are getting one of these shots too. But I think I will send in the guards to give it to you," says the Nurse.

The women are frightened and thought they had prevented this by allowing the Nurse to give them the shots. They were wrong. The guards are coming into the Cage again. What if they start beating Mike again? They fear that this time, they might kill him.

Two guards unlock the door and enter the Cage. "Big man, do we need to knock you out again? Or are you going to behave?"

"He's going to behave," Claire assures them as she looks at Mike. Her expression tells him not to fight these men; Claire needs him alive.

Mike nods and says, "Just do the damn thing," one guard jabs him in the arm and quickly pushes in the thick liquid. He pulls the needle out and the two men rush out of the Cage.

As they lock the Cage door, the Nurse says, "Okay, all done. You might not feel well for a few days, but it will pass. Then you will be ready for the big man's seed. Good luck, big man. It is all up to you now. Do your job with these women; it will please Shariek."

They move on to the next Cage, giving tests and shots. The Nurse instructs the guards to remove one of the women from the adjacent Cage and take her with them when they leave the garage.

Almost immediately, the women in Mike's Cage begin to feel off. A few minutes later, Christina is the first to be affected. She feels awful as if she has the flu, and it hits her fast and hard. First, she starts to sweat, and then she begins to shake. Mike watches as the sweat soaks through her tunic.

He is concerned by Christina's reaction. "Hey, are you okay?"

Claire has started feeling the effects too, but she is like the mother in a house full of sick people. She feels awful, but she will take care of Christina before she succumbs to anything she feels. Terri is lying on her back, trying to stay cool against the wet concrete. Sammy has passed out in a pool of sweat against the back of the Cage. Christina is shaking and holding onto the Cage bars, moaning in discomfort, while Claire is holding and trying to comfort her. A woman from the next Cage looks over at Mike and the girls.

"It's the shot," she says.

Mike hasn't talked to anyone other than Marisa in the other Cages. He doesn't know if talking to her is the reason she was killed, so he doesn't want to take that risk with anyone else.

"Do you know what is happening to them?" he is nervous as he speaks to her.

"Yes. That shot is for veterinary use; it's too strong for humans, but they use it anyway. Some people have a bad reaction to it; I think she is having one now," the woman tells him.

"What can I do to help them?" he asks.

"You can't do anything; it just has to run its course, but they should start to feel better soon. Everyone should try to get some rest; they will be much better tomorrow. It's painful, but it won't kill them."

"My name is Sarah. Marisa and I were roommates before we were captured and brought here," Sarah says, looking at Christina as she rests her head on the cool bars of the Cage. "You need to drink plenty of water. I know how you feel, but believe me, you'll feel better tomorrow."

Christina nods in thanks and sits there in misery. Mike attempts to help Claire by wetting the back of her neck with a rag, but he is still weak and can't stand for long. Claire smiles at him, assuring him she will be alright and that he should lie back down.

"Sarah, why did they take that woman?" Mike doesn't want to put the woman at any risk, but she has the information he needs.

"I think the doctor is checking her out. She's been here for a few months, and still nothing. I know why; she hasn't been with Shahid yet," Sarah says, pointing to the man in her Cage.

"So, the doctor will figure that out, and then what happens?" Mike asks.

"I don't know, but I am afraid for her and him too. They expect results here, and you can't get results if you don't try."

Mike looks at his Cage mates; they are preoccupied with their misery and not listening to what Sarah is saying, which gives him a tiny bit of happiness that they haven't heard any of it.

"Thank you, Sarah. We're still trying to figure out how everything works here; what you just told me helps."

A few hours later, Shariek enters the garage with the woman they had taken from the Cage earlier in tow. Two guards remove Shahid from his chains and take him out into the middle of the garage, accompanied by the woman.

"Attention, everyone! This man has not fulfilled his duty. This woman has not yet been bred; she has been with this man for months, yet he has failed to do his sole job: breed with his women. As a result, he is sentenced to death." In one swift move, Shariek points a handgun at Shahid's head and pulls the trigger. Screams echo throughout the garage, jolting Sammy, Claire, Christina, and Terri awake. They all scream in misery, crying while lying on the ground.

"Now, as for this woman, she has only one job and has chosen to test my patience. She will be made an example of." Shariek strips the woman naked, and one of his guards gives him a Scourge Whip with small metal hooks on the ends. He whips the woman until she falls to the floor, screaming in pain. He then commands the guards to come and seize her, binding her securely to the Cage. Shariek continues whipping until her skin peels from her back.

Mike's girls look on in terror, their bodies now covered in sweat, vomit, and writhing in pain. Terri is on her knees, covering her face. Mike holds Claire and pulls her head into his chest. Christina is still clinging to the Cage bars on the floor, weeping. When Sammy sees the whipping, she faints again.

"We need to get the fuck out of here," Mike says to Claire, looking at the carnage unfolding in front of them.

Hours pass before the effects of the shots begin to wear off enough for the women to get some rest. Terri has a relatively mild reaction, consisting of sweating and discomfort. Although she is still hot and sweating, it has eased enough for her to fall asleep. Claire has a fairly mild response as well. She is sleeping next to Christina, who is starting to feel a little better. Christina's splitting headache is beginning to subside to a dull ache, and she is still sweating profusely. She has the worst reaction out of the four women. Mike crawls over with some water-soaked rags for her to suck on, as dehydration from the sweating will worsen her headache.

"Hey, how are you feeling?" he asks.

"I can't believe how horrible I feel; even my hair hurts," she says.

"Wha

"Nothing; I just need to sit here and not move," Christina presses her head against the bars. "You shouldn't be moving around Mike. Your injuries are starting to bleed again." The cool bars feel good on her head.

"I will be okay. I'm worried about you and the others. I'm so sorry this is happening to you," Mike wants to make things better for the women, but he is unable to do anything.

"Thank you for trying to make me feel better. The wet rags feel good on my face. Now, please, go back to sleep. I know we will all feel better tomorrow; we just need to let this shit run its course," Christina closes her eyes and tries to fall asleep.

Formation of A Plan:

Mike knows from his time spent in the Military's SERE (Survival, Evasion, Resistance, and Escape) training that he needs to follow specific steps. First, you need to know your enemy. *Check,* he thinks. *Then observe their routines. Watch and scrutinize who comes, goes, when, how, where, and why.*

For example, he tries to remember, *When does the fat man with the food come in to feed the men? When does he come to feed the women? How many buckets of food does he have? Are there any tools or items I can use to our advantage?*

Then he has an idea, *What about the Nurse? I know she has things I can use. The only problem is time; we don't have enough of it. Every day brings Shariek closer to losing his patience and making an example out of one or all of us. I need the women to help me with all of this. I will get them involved tomorrow when they feel better, Mike says to himself.*

He is awake most of the night, watching over his women as they sleep. He goes over everything he has learned up to that point, trying to devise a plan. He is making progress, and things are getting better for the ladies after a few hours. They stop shivering, and, except for Christina, they stop sweating. Mike, completely worn out, finally gets some much-needed sleep.

Claire was the first to wake up in the morning, and she began the day by taking some rags and soaking them in water. Unknowingly, she roused Mike from his slumber when she brushed the wet rag across his lips.

He opens his eyes and asks, "How do you feel today, Claire?"

Claire continues to wipe his mouth and face with rags. "I think I'm over the worst of it. I feel much better. How do you feel? You still look weak, Mike."

"I will be fine. I just need a bit more rest. But I will need your help. I need all of your help." Mike knows time is short, so they have to plan their escape.

"Of course, we will do whatever you think we should. Let me get everyone else over here so we can talk," she stops wiping Mike's face.

Claire slowly wakes the other women and gives them as much water as possible. Once everyone is alert enough, they all gather around Mike.

He addresses all three women with a heavy sigh, "It's been a difficult few days, and I'm afraid it won't get any better. We need to come up with a plan to get out of here, and it starts with paying attention to the details. Who's coming and going, when, why, where, and how long they're here - all of it. We can't write anything down, so Claire and Terri, you'll have to figure out a way to remember it all. Let's make it a game if we can, that way it'll be easier to recall. And, of course, we must be careful not to let them realize what we're doing." Everyone agrees and they start to discuss what they already know and how they will remember it all.

"What can we do?" asks Christina. "Sammy and I are just sitting here."

Mike says, "I need you to keep a lookout."

"Look out? What the Hell..." Christina feels left out and doesn't like it.

"No, wait," Mike interjected, "This is really important. Claire, Terri, and I need to be certain that the guards don't realize that we are observing them. They can't catch wind of what we are doing. Your job is to let us know if they seem to be watching us. If you notice them paying too much attention, you need to distract them. Keep their focus away from us and onto you or something else happening in another Cage. Do you both understand? This is essential. I need to hear you both say that you understand."

Christina and Sammy both agree, "Okay, yes."

Mike and the women turn their attention to the short, fat man pushing the food cart who has just walked through the doors to the garage with an irritating smile on his face. Mike smiles back at the man, then turns to the women and says, "Okay then, you all know what we need to do, and we need to start right now with this little fat man."

"Hello big man," says the fat meal delivery guy as he gets closer to their Cage. "I see you are awake. I heard that you might have passed on to meet Allah."

"No such luck; I am still here and alive," Mike replies.

"From the way you look, I would say just barely," says the fat man.

Mike is very dehydrated; his lips are cracked and swollen. They have all been licking the wall behind the Cage to get water. Mike is still unable to stand for long, so Claire and Christina take turns squeezing wet bandages into his mouth. This, however, isn't giving any of them enough water.

Mike asks the fat man, "Is there any way we can get some water?"

"It's right there, in that bucket," says the fat man.

In the corner of the Cage are two small wooden buckets: one for waste and the other filled with a stinky liquid. None of them think it is water.

"Yes big man," the fat man tells them, "when the Chamber Maids come and clean out your waste bucket, they refill your water bucket."

"Wait, that is a water bucket?" Christina cringes. "Oh! I'm so sorry guys. I didn't know; I peed in it."

"For fuck sake, Christina!" says Terri. "What the hell is wrong with you?"

"Okay, okay, she didn't know," Claire says, "Mike, I will take care of it. When they come tonight, I will get fresh water. Thank you Sir," Claire turns to the fat man and bows her head.

The fat man's face contorted in a look of indignation as he hurled the bucket of Mike's food towards the Cage, and then continued to march away, mumbling something incomprehensible in Arabic.

As the fat man walks away, Mike notices his Kufi, a Muslim prayer hat usually worn by devout Muslims. He remembers seeing him wearing it every time he has seen him. The little fat man never touches the food with his right hand, and his disdain for Claire and all the other women, point to a devoutly religious man. He isn't sure how yet, but he is determined to use this little fat guy to his advantage.

Mike, Claire, and Terri keep track as the fat man delivers food to all the Cages. He leaves the garage to refill his cart every time it is empty, making four trips in order to have enough food for all the Caged people. After his final trip, they compare notes.

Terri gives her report, "I counted 24 buckets on the cart, and he refilled it three times."

"Are you sure? I counted 22 buckets on the cart when he was at our Cage and counted again while he was at the one next to us. You're right that it took four trips in total. That's a lot of people," Claire says.

Mike nods in agreement, "Yes, there are a lot of people here. I counted 22 buckets as well. It's okay, this is our first time, and we are all nervous. So, when we get conflicting answers, we need to decide how to proceed. If more than one of us comes up with the same answer, we should go with that. But if we all come up with different numbers, we should choose somewhere in the middle. So, in this case, I think it's safe to say 88 buckets in total."

They all agree that this is the best option. With no time to argue, this is the best chance of getting it right.

Claire began to count silently in her head, and when she finished, she spoke in a hushed tone, filled with surprise and disbelief, "Wow! That means there must be 350 people here... all in Cages like us."

Mike agrees, "Wow is right. We are all living in Hell, which is why we need to find a way to get everyone out of here — every last person."

Three days later, two men carrying a fire hose enter the garage. Behind them, two women with a cart full of buckets come in, yelling in Arabic, "Wash the lice! Wash the fleas! You dirty infidels." They repeat this to each Cage throughout the room and pass out one bucket to each Cage.

The people in all the other Cages begin to remove their clothing and take something out of the bucket they were just given.

Oh shit, what kind of fresh new hell is this? Mike says to himself.

One woman comes to Mike's Cage and, in Arabic, says, "Wash the lice, wash the fleas; you must be clean for your meeting with Allah." she throws

Mike a raggedy Jabba Thobe; it is filthy and full of holes, "Cover yourself, you dirty American. You are unclean and indecent."

Christina asks, "What did she say?"

Mike makes sure to translate only part of the message for the girls as he puts on the Thobe.

The old woman throws the bucket at Terri as she mumbles, "Dirty whores."

"Thanks bitch," Terri replies, handing the bucket to Claire.

Inside the bucket are three bars of soap, three washcloths, and a scrub brush.

"I think this is lye soap," Claire knows she needs to warn the ladies, "so be careful not to get it in your eyes; it will burn, and it could even blind you."

Christina doesn't care if the soap burns her skin off. "At this point, I don't care if I go blind as long as it gets me clean. I still have blood from that scumbag on me, and it's coming off now!"

Lye soap, perfect, Mike thinks, and then he says to Claire, "Can you figure out a way to keep one of the bars of soap? It might just be our ticket out of here."

"Okay, I think I know how to keep a bar and maybe one of the rags too. But first, I agree with my sister; I am going to take advantage of this and get myself cleaned up," answers Claire.

"Great, Claire. If you can keep it, I will explain what it's for after our gracious hosts leave," he says to her, impressed that she is so quick to have a plan.

Then, the two men turn the fire hose on to full power, blasting everything and everyone in all the Cages, just like they would hose down an animal's Cage, but these Cages are filled with people. Claire watches the people in the other Cages to see what they should do. They all quickly rub the soap on their clothes as soon as the water starts, then drop their clothes, wash their bodies with soap, and rinse everything as best they can. After observing this, Claire thinks she has a better idea. She instructs everyone to keep their clothes on and wash their bodies and clothes at the same time. She explains, "Get the rags wet and rub the soap onto them. Then clean your skin with the rag and use the soap on your clothes. When they rinse you off with the hose, everything will be clean, or at least cleaner anyway."

When the men arrive at their Cage, Mike says, "Okay, hold onto the bars if you can. This will be cold and might hurt, but at least we'll be clean."

The two men blast Mike and the four women as they laugh, "It is like washing pigs; it is a waste of time. They will still be unclean even if they wash off the lice and fleas," the men say as the girls scream and yell.

Sammy screams in pain as the cold water blast smashes into her ribs. The men enjoy her screams and point the water directly at her. Mike steps in front of her at the Cage bars and shields Sammy with his body. He notices that she is getting weaker and she is coughing from the hard blast of water hitting her side. Mike thinks he hears gurgling as she breathes, and he hopes he is wrong. He wonders if one of her broken ribs has pierced her lung.

Claire's plan works; they are relatively clean and almost smell good. Except for Sammy, everyone feels a little better. This washing has not been good for her.

After about an hour, the men finish washing the entire garage and its occupants. They roll up the fire hose and yell at the two women, collecting buckets and soap from each Cage, to hurry up.

"Return the bucket with the soap and rags to me now!" says one of the old women, "You are still filthy, but at least you do not smell as bad as before."

Claire, with a shove, pushes the bucket past the woman, stretching her arm as far as she can outside the Cage, knocking a few other buckets off the cart and spilling their contents all over the floor. She steps back as the woman swings one of the buckets at her, narrowly missing her arm.

Her face contorted in anger, the old woman begins to call Claire names and says in Arabic, "Cursed am I to deal with these infidels. Allah, give me strength, and strike these devils from the earth." She begins to pick up what Claire has spilled, her irritation so great that she fails to notice anything is missing.

"Thank you," Claire says with a smirk, "We do smell better. Here is the bucket."

Christina leans against the wall in the back of the Cage while all the commotion is happening. Behind her, against the wall, is a bar of soap and one of the rags.

After all the buckets are collected, and the old woman has made her last trip through the door, the two men follow close behind.

They've done it. They have lye soap and a rag, which may not be much, but it is a start. Knowing that they are able to trick their captors if they work together gives them a huge confidence boost. This makes them think that maybe, just maybe, they could get out of there alive.

Mike is beaming like a proud parent after his or her child's first day of school as he says, "Claire, you did it. You are amazing."

Claire smiles at him and says, "Thanks, but I couldn't have pulled it off without Christina. She had the soap and rag pinned between her back and the wall the entire time. So now that we have the soap, why did you want it?"

"Lye soap is corrosive when combined with water and urine," Mike explains, "See these chains on my arms are connected by rings on my wrists. All held together by a simple square steel bolt. If we combine lye with water and urine and keep applying it to the bolt, it will take time, but the bolt will eventually weaken, hopefully, enough that I can break them. If my hands are free, we have a real chance, a good chance of..."

"Weaken? Corrosive? What the fuck are you talking about?" Terri interrupts, "That will take time. We don't have time. Remember? That madman wants results. That doesn't sound like a good plan to me at all."

Mike needs to sound confident, and he says, "I won't lie to you; it might take weeks. But, for now, it's a start, and we need to move forward in any way we can. Everything will come together; you'll see."

"Mike is right. We need to keep moving forward. Our goal is to get out of here, and if this soap might help us even a little bit, we need to try it. So let's do it," Claire says.

Mike is thankful that Claire is on board. "Let's take small steps forward, ladies. That will help us reach our goal. I need the soap, the rag, and 'Christina's Bucket' for our first step." He mixes equal parts of water from the "pee bucket" with the lye soap. He then tares a small end of one of the rags and mixes them together to create a putty-like material, smashing the mixture into the rings binding his wrists.

"We will need to change this every day for it to work," Mike explains.

Claire asks, "How will we know it's working?"

"You'll start to see something in a few days. I need you to take turns putting it on for me. Lye will irritate my skin and make it very raw over time. If you ladies can take turns making new wads and putting them in the same place, it will keep me from getting it on my skin," Mike tells them.

So, Sisters?:

Mike, Claire, Christina, and Terri start talking about their lives. He asks them where they are from, how old they are, and all the usual things. They ask him the same types of questions.

Like every man out there, Mike has one question on his mind. After all the usual questions have been exhausted, he finally asks, "So, sisters?"

"Sisters, yes, but not biological sisters," explains Claire, "My father married her mother when Christina was two years old. Her father was killed in Iraq; he was a Navy hero and a SEAL Team member. My father adopted Christina," Claire starts to tear up, "Oh, my dad..." She remembers what happened just a few days ago.

Christina explains, "Claire's mom died in childbirth. Her dad had to raise her alone for three years before my mom came along."

Claire hates not being in complete control of everything; the only thing here she can control is herself, so she collects herself. She takes a breath, puts her thoughts about her father into a neat little box, and stores it away. Then she rejoins the "getting to know you" conversation as if they were at a Sunday Brunch.

After they talk about their lives before this awful "Sex Dungeon", the conversation turns to, "*What do you miss the most?*" They have only been here a few days, but it seems much longer. The question catches Terri by surprise.

"What do I miss the most? For fuck sake! I miss my freedom!" Terri doesn't mince words, "I want to get out of this hellhole! That's what I miss."

"I know you all might think this is silly," Claire says, embarrassed, "I mean, Terri is right. I could say I miss the same things, which I do, of course, like food. I mean, that soup is terrible. But what I really miss is a razor and shaving gel."

"What?! You miss... what?" Terri can't believe what Claire is saying.

"I mean, don't get me wrong, but I take care of myself. I shave my legs and underarms—the whole thing. I have a daily ritual to stay presentable," Claire says with a smile, pointing to Terri's legs, "Look at me; I almost look like you now, Terri."

"Yeah, you're right; it hasn't been long, and I already feel like a 70's porn star down there," Christina reveals.

Claire's face turns bright red, and Terri bursts out laughing. Mike joins in, and then Sammy and Christina. Claire snorts as she laughs, which makes them all laugh even harder. It is a tiny bit of levity during their torturous ordeal, and they desperately need it.

You Will Have Your Peace:

They are all still engaging in small talk when the little fat man returns with the green soup the girls hate so much. Mike wants to take advantage of this opportunity, so he quickly devises a conversation in his head. "Sir," he says to the little fat man, "As-salamu Alaikum," which means "peace be with you," a standard greeting between Muslims. The fat man is pleasantly surprised to hear Mike speaking Arabic.

"Wa-alaikum as-salam," replies the little fat man.

Mike instantly knows he is on the right track. If the man was not religious, his response would have been "Ahlan beek."

In Arabic, he says, "Sir, my name is Mike, and I have a request. I am not married, but I'm growing a beard. It's not something I want to do; I know it angers Allah. But I do not have any way to shave."

Mike has noticed that some of the other men in the Cages are clean-shaven, and he is betting that this little fat man is how they get the things they need.

"Are you Muslim?" the little fat man asks.

Continuing in Arabic Mike says, "Yes, I am. I was in the United States Army stationed in Afghanistan for six years. I could not bear to witness the suffering of the Afghan people. Seeking peace for myself, I talked to the local Imam and told him of my struggles. He showed me the way to

Allah and brought peace to me. He gave me the structure to get my life on track to serve Allah."

"My name is Assim," says the little fat man, now known as Assim. "My brother, you will have your peace and be right with Allah. Tomorrow I will bring you a razor, and you can shave as you should."

Of course, everything Mike has told Aasim is total bullshit; it is just the next piece of the puzzle, a small step towards the goal of escape, and Mike thinks it will make Claire happy if he can get a razor into their Cage.

After Mike's conversation with him, Assim generously provides the women with a bit more soup than usual today. Although they aren't overly fond of the taste, they are grateful for the additional nourishment, as it is all they have to maintain their strength.

After the girls eat and Mike's new friend has left, he desperately needs to rest. He has been up and standing for as long as he can, trying to build his strength and endurance. His body is healing, but without medication or proper nutrition, the process is slow. As soon as Mike closes his eyes, he drifts off to sleep.

Dude! What the Hell?!:

It is not easy to sleep in this place. The floors are cold hard concrete, and the mattress is very small, thin, and worn. Because it is so small, they have to take turns sleeping on it. Also, they are all practically naked, making it hard to stay warm. Moans of pain and despair fill the air. There is also the occasional woman going into labor, but Mike can't hear any of it tonight; he sleeps like a baby. The girls do their best to make him comfortable. Christina is again leaning against the wall with Mike nestled between her legs, the back of his head resting on her stomach. She is slowly brushing his hair with her hands. Claire is snuggling against Mike's side, sleeping to the left of Christina, her arms and legs on Mike to help keep each other warm. Terri is sleeping on his other side in the same way. Sammy has moved closer to Claire's back, but she is still distant and silent.

Terri is abruptly startled out of her sleep, her eyes widening in shock as she exclaims, "Dude! What the Hell?!" She then turns away from Mike with her back to him.

Mike has awoken, as some men do. Things happen. It isn't something he is thinking about here, and until now, it hasn't happened because he was so beaten up and in constant pain. His little soldier is at full attention, pointing towards the ceiling. It is a sign that he is healing nicely and that the shots are working.

"Oh my gosh! I'm sorry; I didn't know it was happening. I was asleep. I'm so sorry," Mike says to Claire and Terri, his face burning red in embarrassment.

Claire looks at Christina, who is fixated on Mike's manhood with her big blue eyes not blinking. Claire then slowly moves her leg, pushing his little soldier between his legs and covering him.

"It's all good now. Go back to sleep," Claire says, wanting to keep everyone as comfortable as possible; they have so little space, and they need to remain a team, working together and being as comfortable as possible with each other.

Christina leans her head back against the wall and falls asleep, thinking about *Mike's little soldier and how she has felt since that damn shot*. Terri is not having any of it; she stays on her side, facing away from him. Embarrassed, Mike closes his eyes and wills himself back to sleep.

Sammy:

Everyone in the garage has finally settled, and the garage is dead quiet. However, the silence doesn't last. Claire is awoken by Sammy's coughing, which starts mild, but quickly becomes more intense. Sammy begins to choke and can't stop coughing long enough to catch her breath. Claire knows this is not good, and she has to take action.

"Mike, Mike, wake up. Something is wrong with Sammy," Claire says.

Mike and Claire get up from the mattress, leaving Christina and Terri sleeping, and move towards Sammy.

"Sammy, Sammy, can you hear me?" Mike gently shakes her shoulders.

Sammy's coughing is becoming more and more severe, and she is now expelling a crimson foam. Mike instantly understands the situation: Sammy has at least one fractured rib piercing her lung, resulting in her lungs filling with her own blood that she is now drowning in. He has to seek help for her, but in truth, it is for the other women. Help to prevent them from witnessing another cruel and agonizing death, right in front of them.

He starts yelling, "Help! We need help here! Someone, please come and help!"

His yelling wakes up everyone in the garage. The lights are off, and only a thin light can be seen coming from under the doors. Suddenly, the door flies open, and the lights come on. Two angry men enter the garage and charge straight to Mike's Cage.

"It is the middle of the night. What did you do to her?" they scream.

"She needs help! Please, help her; she needs a doctor!" demands Mike. He knows they will not do anything for her, and that she will likely die soon. However, he doesn't want this to happen in front of the others; it is already hard enough to keep everyone together. Seeing Sammy die a horrible death like this will make matters much worse. He knows all they will do is throw her body in a pile somewhere. Which, sadly, is a better alternative than seeing men dragging her dead body out of the Cage, as he has seen done so many times before.

The two men grabbed Sammy by her shoulders and feet, lifting her up and carrying her away through the doors.

"Sammy, you'll be alright," Mike tries to comfort her and the others. "They will take care of you."

Tears stream down Christina's face as she keeps asking where they are taking Sammy and if she will be okay. Claire grabs Christina and holds her tight, and Christina begins crying hysterically.

Terri and Claire think the same as Mike; deep down, they are aware that they will never again lay eyes on Sammy and that their captors will not offer her any assistance. They both try to provide Christina with comfort, but it is of little use. Christina weeps for most of the night, her mind overwhelmed with thoughts of Sammy, and she can't help but fear that something similar will happen to all of them. Despite their efforts, she is unable to drift off to sleep until it is almost morning.

Claire is always the first to wake in the morning, this time having slept very little. When she gets up, she checks on Christina and the others. Everything is still quiet when Mike wakes up and whispers, "Hey."

"Good morning," says Claire.

"Rough night. How is Christina?" Mike is worried about her.

"She finally fell asleep a little while ago; she is really freaked out by what happened with Sammy last night," Claire says, taking in a deep breath., "Mike, I think we both know what happened to Sammy, right?"

"I think we do," Mike agrees, "But for Christina's sake, let's try to keep that between us, okay?"

"Of course, it's the best we can do for now," says Claire.

I Have Brought You a Gift, My Friend:

Assim steps through the door, and they are taken aback to see him arrive without his usual food cart. Although they aren't sure what time it is, they know it is too early for food. Puzzled, they watch as he makes his way directly to their Cage, leaving them wondering why he is here.

"As-salamu alaikum, Mike," says Assim.

"Wa-alaikum as-salam, my brother," replies Mike.

"I have brought you a gift, my friend." Assim removes a small, dirty bag from his back pocket and hands it to Mike through the bars of his Cage. He tells Mike, "You will need to use this today; it is going to be an important day for you."

Mike wonders what Assim means by this, but he does not ask, knowing that Assim will not put himself at risk by telling Mike anything else.

"What do you mean by important day?" interrupts Claire, speaking directly to Assim.

Without a second passing, Mike turns and smacks Claire across the face. She falls to the ground against the bars of the Cage. "You do not speak unless spoken to," Mike shouts at Claire, "You will learn your place. Do you understand?"

The yelling awakens Terri and Christina. Claire is in shock; she is lying on the ground with Christina and Terri at her side, and a small trickle of blood is coming from the left side of her mouth. Then the look in Mike's eyes tells her everything. She is still a bit shocked, but she completely understands what is going on now, with just that one look, and she plays her part perfectly.

"Yes, I am sorry. Please forgive me," Claire says, looking away and starting to cry.

"I am sorry for that outburst, my friend," Mike tells Assim. "These women do not know their place, but with Allah's help, I will teach them."

Smiling, Assim says to Mike, "Sabah al-kheir," Good Morning.

Christina is devastated. Her big blue eyes well up with tears streaming down her face as a deep sadness settles over her. She can't believe what has just happened. Mike hitting Claire is crushing to her.

Terri is a different story; she looks at Mike with hatred and fear, her defenses up, ready to take him on if necessary. She is not going to let him hit her like he has, Claire.

The worst is Claire; Mike is filled with immense guilt and regret for what he has done; her face is bleeding, and he is aware he has hurt her. He had to hit her in order to gain Assim's respect and make him believe that Mike was devout, as this was essential for the plan to be successful. Despite the disapproving looks from Terri and Christina, Mike rushes to Claire's side, unable to ignore the pain he has caused her. He feels so insignificant after having to resort to such violence. Still, he knew that it was necessary for the plan to move ahead.

"Claire, please forgive me," he begs, his eyes filling with tears, "I had to convince Assim that I was the kind of man he was for our plan to work. I didn't want to hurt you. I swear I would never do that. I just..."

Claire puts her hand over his mouth to prevent him from saying anything else and says, "Mike, I understand. I'm okay. I understand why you had to do it. I could see in your eyes what you were trying to tell me. I forgave you as soon as I looked into your eyes. I'm really okay."

Mike bends over and kisses Claire for the first time, "Claire, you are un-believable. You can't imagine how sorry I am," he says, kissing her again, "I have something for you," He hands her the dirty bag containing razors and shaving soap. Claire looks into the bag, smiles, and then glances back at him with a massive grin before kissing him back.

Video to The World:

It doesn't take long to understand what Assim has been talking about. Shariek comes through the door with a camera crew, heading straight for Mike and the girls.

Shariek greets Mike, "Hello, my friend! I heard my favorite Stallion lost one from his stable last night. No matter! I will replace her with a suitable match for you as soon as I am able."

After hearing this, Christina bursts into tears again. Claire wraps her arms around her tightly and whispers, "Christina, please keep quiet and try to hold it together. We must remain silent anytime that man is here. He is very dangerous."

Christina takes a deep breath and holds it in, trying to regain her composure. She then wipes her face and nods in acknowledgment.

"Today, I will be producing a quick but important video. Today my Stallion, you will be making your television debut," Shariek announces.

"What do you have in mind?" Mike asks.

"I am glad you asked, my friend. For years, your country has oppressed my people. Today, I show the world that we will no longer tolerate it. We can take you from anywhere we wish and Cage or kill you if we choose to. The reign of the Great Satan is over."

Shariek's men cheer, "Praise be to Allah! Praise be to Allah!"

"I have deprived you of your freedom, your self-respect, and soon I will take away your children. Once I have completed my task with you, I may even go so far as to take your lives," Shariek declares ominously, "But first, we must make this video and show it to the world."

Claire, her arms still tightly wrapped around Christina, manages to prevent her from having another emotional meltdown. Terri is able to keep her composure because her rage is fueling her determination not to show any sign of weakness to their captor. The women are appalled that Shariek wants to tape them for the whole world to witness, but Mike appears to be completely unfazed. Claire can't help but question why he is so accepting of this.

"Okay! Everyone, take your place. Haha, let us begin, shall we?" says Shariek. He then positions himself in front of the Cage, ensuring everyone can see Mike and the three women inside. He looks into the camera and shouts, "Action!", then begins his speech.

"To all the people of the world, I am here to deliver a powerful message. For far too long, the oppressive Imperialist Pigs have taken away our land, killed our children, and stolen our wealth. But today, that ends. Behind me are four of your American children, who have been stripped of all their possessions, rights, and dignity. This time, we, have done the taking. No longer will these imperialist powers be allowed to continue their heinous acts. This is merely the start of our journey. We will not rest until we have restored what is rightfully ours. I am here to declare, that, as of today, our Campaign of Terror and Intimidation is officially underway. Striking at the core of your soul. We will take your women, kill your men, and breed you out of existence. These four are only a small sample of our accomplishments. We have thousands of women in Cages like this. We can kill them at any moment. We have total control; you are not safe. We will be coming for you. We will exterminate your children, and with the help of Allah, death to America will be complete. Remember these faces," the camera pans across Mike, who tries not to show his face for very long, and the three women in his Cage, "This is just a small sample of what will be accomplished very soon. By the grace of Allah, we shall reclaim all that is rightfully ours and has been taken from us by the abhorrent Americans."

Shariek's men shout the Takbir in unison, "Allahu Akbar! Allahu Akbar! Allahu Akbar! - God is the greatest!"

"Cut! That was good, was it not?" Shariek looks at Mike.

"That was really interesting, Shariek," Mike says sarcastically, "I especially liked the 'thousands of women' part."

"I thought it was powerful," proclaims Shariek, "Maybe a bit over the top, but that is what I was looking for."

Mike knows that Shariek doesn't care about any religious feud; it is just to keep his people behind him. It is all for show, but it helps more than Shariek realizes. While he had his back to Mike, during the filming, Mike was tapping Morse Code with his right hand on the Cage bars. He gave the information he knew so far: "*Jeddah, Saudi Arabia. Inside Underground Parking Garage, Jeddah Tower, Three American Women, less than three months to get out, Fed American Food, Potatoes, Corn.*" He is able to repeat the message three times during the filming in the hope that someone will see it.

"Well, my friend, I would love to stay and chat with you, but I have a video to upload," Shariek says as he turns and heads towards the exit, followed by his film crew and the guards.

"No one will ever see that video, Shariek," Mike shouts, "It won't be seen in America! I promise you!"

Shariek turns around, "Oh yes, my friend, it will. I assure you. Your American Pigs will see this video. Goodbye now. I must return to my work," he turns and disappears through the door.

"Ok, what the hell was that all about?" asks Terri.

"Step three," Mike says, "step three." He knows they have some time before the video goes live, so he can't risk anyone tipping off Shariek about the Morse Code message. This means keeping the girls in the dark for a while.

After Shariek leaves, Mike and the women try to go back to sleep. They are exhausted and didn't get much sleep the night before. While they are resting, the women who empty and replace the buckets come around. They don't like it when Claire asks for a new bucket, but somehow she manages to get them to give her a new one for water.

Well, Now That Was Something:

As always, Claire is the first to wake the following day, followed by Mike and the rest of his Cage mates.

"So, did you get us some clean water?" Mike asks Claire.

"Well, I wouldn't exactly call it clean," Claire says as she hands him the new small wooden bucket, "Here, you need to drink some of this."

Mike takes a quick swig, "I wouldn't call it spring fresh, but it's better than licking that damned wall."

"You know what? I think I'm going to shave," says Claire. "Thanks to you, I can. But Mike, you can't watch. So you need to turn around and look outside the Cage."

Mike settles on the floor near the door and surveys the other Cages. In an attempt to lighten the mood, he pretends to have a remote control in his hand and begins to channel surf. "Ah, here's a show called 'Caged'," he says with a smile, "I think I'll give it a watch and see if I can learn something that will help us out of this place. Does anyone want to join me? It looks quite entertaining."

Christina says, "Oh, so now you're a comedian? You're not funny, but I'll give you this one since you got us soap and a razor. Go watch your show. We have things to do over here."

Claire and Christina begin to make shaving cream with soap and a bit of water. While Terri has no interest in shaving, she still engages in small talk with the two girls. Mike, however, can't help but sneak a glance at Claire as she is shaving her legs. He has been trying to be respectful and not look at the girls in any way that would make them feel uncomfortable, but this time he can't help himself. His eyes sweep over Claire's entire body before she notices. He thinks she will be angry. Surprisingly, she just smiles at him, and Mike smiles back before quickly turning away to avoid anyone else seeing.

"Okay, Mike, you can turn off the TV. We're finished. You have no idea how much better I feel. I almost feel like a civilized person again," Claire says.

"I'm sorry, but the razor isn't very sharp anymore; it wasn't very sharp to begin with," Christina asks Mike, "Do you still want to use it?"

"Sure, thanks. I need to get this beard off. I have to keep up appearances with my new Muslim friend, the little fat food man Assim," Mike walks to the back of the Cage, where the women shaved, and Christina hands him the soap and razor. He works up some lather with the soap, but his broken ribs make it difficult to raise his right arm and apply it to his face. He has to get the beard off, so he grunts and bends over in an attempt to reach his face.

Claire observes the pain this is causing him. "Mike, sit here and let me help." He sits on the ground with his back against the wall and his legs stretched out. Claire takes the razor from his left hand and scoops the lather he has out of his right hand, straddling his legs. She kneels in front of him and lathers his face with soap. Then she sits back on her knees before beginning to shave his face.

"Okay, try not to move," Claire says as she slowly and carefully begins to shave his face. He winces, and Claire says, "Oh my gosh! I'm so sorry I cut you and the cuts on your face! My gosh, you're bleeding. I'm so sorry."

"It's okay, don't worry," Mike says, "Keep going, I can't do it, and I need you to do it for me."

Claire takes in a breath and inches closer to Mike. She is now sitting on his lap as she finishes shaving his face.

Terri and Christina observe what is happening; Mike is visibly aroused. Claire must sense it, but she shows no response. In an effort to give them some privacy, Terri and Christina shift to the furthest corner of the Cage, although it was not much privacy. Just as she finishes shaving Mike's face, he leans in and tenderly kisses Claire, who puts the razor aside and returns the kiss. They embrace, and with nothing between them, they quietly fall into each other.

"Mike, I've never..." Claire whispers.

"Shhh... I'll be gentle. Just tell me if you want me to stop," says Mike.

"No, please don't stop," Claire says. "Oh wow."

Christina can't help but look. She will later describe it as something beautiful. "It was just magic; in a terrible place, Mike and Claire showed love and beauty. I didn't want to look away; I couldn't look away."

Mike smiles as his lips press against Claire's neck and mouth. They both gasp for air; neither of them wants to let go, so they remain in an embrace, their hearts beating in unison. "Are you okay?" He whispers to Claire.

"More than okay," Claire smiles at him.

"This is crazy. Look at where we are, but I can't help it. I think I'm falling for you, Claire," Mike professes, "You are like no woman I have ever known."

Claire shares the same sentiment but refrains from expressing her opinion, wanting to take in the moment's beauty and commit it to memory, despite being in this incredibly horrible place.

Suddenly, remembering they are not alone, they turn their heads and see Christina and Terri, both wide-eyed and staring at the couple, still holding each other.

Christina smiles from ear to ear, "Well, now that was something!" she says.

Claire is embarrassed, although not as much as she had expected, "Okay, okay. You two have seen enough. Could you please turn around? I need to get myself in order. All of you. Please, turn your heads."

Mike, feeling a bit uncomfortable, attempts to turn his body and head towards the wall in order to give Claire the privacy she has requested. "Oh, of course," he apologizes, "I understand."

After a few minutes, Claire sits next to Mike. Christina plops beside her, and then Terri takes her position on the floor with her back to the front of the Cage.

Christina asks, "So when can we talk about it?"

"We can't," Claire says.

Terri and Mike smile and laugh just a little, while Christina grins, looking like a kid caught with her hand in the cookie jar.

They sit in silence. Mike holding Claire's hand and working on a plan to get them out of there. He wonders if the Lye was having any effect on the metal. Then he thinks, *Shit Mike! What the hell did you just do?*

Enter The Central Intelligence Agency:

Director Albert Walker Gray of the Central Intelligence Agency is sitting at his desk when his right-hand man, Deputy Director Markus Delphy, walks in carrying a laptop.

"Sir, you need to see this," says Delphy, "He is in Jeddah, Saudi Arabia." Delphy hits the space bar on the computer, and a video plays.

"To all the people of the world, I am here to deliver a powerful message. For far too long, the oppressive Imperialist Pigs have taken away our land, killed our children, and stolen our wealth. But today, that ends. Behind me are four of your American children, who have been stripped of all their possessions, rights, and dignity..."

"Turn off the volume," Director Gray barks, "I don't need to hear that idiot."

"Do you see? It's him - Mike. He has infiltrated Shariek Blon Mosomid's Network," says Delphy, "Now we know where he is, or at least we're close."

Director Gray studies the video, then turns back to Markus, "I want everyone on this; I mean everyone," He orders, "Markus, I want Mike back now. Do you understand? I'm sure he's working on an escape plan and will need our help."

"Yes Sir, I will have all available Field Agents press their contacts in Jeddah," says Delphy as he walks out of the Director's office. He then calls Margaret, saying, "Margaret, we got him. We know where Mike is."

"Finally! He made contact?" Margaret is relieved, "He's been gone for months!"

"Yes, and I need all Agents in the Saudi area," Delphy says, "Please get them on the phone with me as soon as possible."

"Right away, Markus," answers Margaret.

"Hang on Mike," Delphy says as he stares at the video. "We're coming for you."

Shipping a Piece of You:

Shariek enters the garage, this time accompanied by only one guard. He walks to Mike's Cage, carrying a clear plastic jar with a blue lid.

"Mike, I have something special I need you to do for me. I need you to fill this jar with your seed. My database has just found two women who are perfectly matched with you. It is much easier to ship a piece of you to them than to ship them here," says Shariek.

Shariek hands Mike the jar and says, "Normally, I would not interact with this kind of thing, but you are by far the most valuable Stallion in my herd. I feel we are more like friends. Next time I need you to do this, your Nurse will deliver the jar."

Mike stares at the jar, noticing the words, "SPECIMEN KEEP FROZEN" printed across the lid. There is a number followed by the words, "Big Man" printed next to it. *I guess this must be my number,* he thinks. Next to his name and number is a date, and after reading it, he realizes it is almost four weeks after he was taken off the street in San Diego.

"And if I don't want to fill this cup, Shariek?" Mike asks.

"Mike, why must you always resist me? Please do as you are told. I will not have you beaten if you do not comply this time. I will have the blonde one punished. I know you like her; I have seen it," Shariek threatens.

Claire watches the exchange; she is determined not to be used like this. She is not going to stand by and let Shariek use her to get Mike to do anything. Just as Claire is about to speak, Christina jumps in and says, "He will do it! I will make sure of it."

"The sign of a good woman," Shariek says, "You see Mike; your women are learning their place. You must always do as you are told. My man will stay here until you have filled the jar. I have a shipment leaving in one hour, and that bottle will be onboard. I hope you understand."

Shariek turns to his guard, speaks, and then leaves the garage.

"You will do this. I will come back in ten minutes, and the jar will be full," says the guard as he turns and walks away.

"Christina, why did you say that? Maybe Mike has a good reason for not wanting to do what that psychopath told him to do," Claire exclaims.

"It's okay, Claire. Of course, I'm going to do it," Mike continues, "Shariek would make an example of you, and he would enjoy it. I can't let that happen. I just can't agree with whatever he tells me to do. I have to put up some resistance."

"Mike, you don't have to protect me," Claire says.

"What's the big deal, anyway? Just do it, and it'll be over. It's not like you haven't been doing it your whole life or something," says Christina.

Mike stares at the jar, thinking, but not saying a word.

Claire looks on, noticing that he is struggling with something, "Mike, what is it? What is going through your mind?" she asks.

"It's just that when this leaves here, part of me could be used in this system of horror. Somewhere out there, there might be a person who is half of me, and I would have no way of knowing. That makes me very uneasy. That's all," says Mike.

Claire whispers into his ear, "Thank you for doing this. I know it's for me. I'm sorry this is happening to you."

Mike shakes his head and hugs Claire; she can feel his hurt through the hug.

"Christina and Terri, could you please give Mike and me some privacy?" asks Claire.

They nod in agreement and turn around, facing out of the Cage. Mike then turns toward the wall and sits on the ground.

"Thanks, Claire. Now, if you can also turn…" asks Mike.

Claire interrupts, "No Mike. I'm going to help you. You're doing this for me. I want to do this for you."

Claire took the bottle from him and pulled up his Thobe. "Just close your eyes. I will take care of everything," Claire says, kissing him passionately.

Mike closes his eyes and tries to relax. When he opens his eyes again his task is complete, he sees Christina and Terri staring at him, his little soldier specifically. Embarrassed, he quickly covers himself and moves to the corner of the Cage.

Claire replaces the cap on the jar and gets the guard's attention. "Here you go Sir," she says, holding the jar outside the Cage. The guard collects the sample and walks out of the garage.

"Mike, I am really sorry. I didn't mean to look. I shouldn't have. I'm so sorry," says Christina.

"It's okay," Mike tries to talk himself out of the embarrassment he is feeling, "it's hard to get privacy in this small Cage. Again, it's okay. I just want to drop it. Please. Can we drop it and just go to sleep now?" Mike pleads with the ladies.

Claire also saw the date on the bottle. She knows it has been three weeks since *"that darn shot"* and that the Nurse will return soon to administer another. She tried to stay calm last time, but that shot really affected her. Her symptoms were less severe than Christina's, but it was still no picnic.

Just as she suspected, the Nurse comes to their Cage the following day, accompanied by two guards carrying cattle prods.

"Okay, everyone, get up; it is time for blood tests and your shots," yells the Nurse.

This time, she uses rapid testing for pregnancy, pricking the women's fingers from outside the Cage. Each woman holds out her arm. Mike is sitting against the wall, so the guards don't chain him up this time. He watches their every move and takes mental notes.

"Ouch! I fucking hate this shit!" yells Terri. She is the first to have her finger pricked. Claire is next, followed by Christina. All the tests came back negative. Afterward, the Nurse gives each of the women their hormone shot. Mike is given his shot on the same day each week and today is not his day.

"Don't worry Big Man. You will not be left out. Tomorrow, I will be back for you," says the Nurse. She then moves on to the next Cage.

Within a few minutes, Christina again begins to show symptoms, this time more severe: nausea, vomiting, and shaking.

Mike yells to the Nurse, who is working on the woman in the adjacent Cage, "Hey, something is happening to her."

The Nurse looks over at Christina, and seeing that she is vomiting, approaches her and places her hand on Christina's head. She does not have a fever, but she begins sweating and looks pale.

"She will be fine," the Nurse hands a tablet to Christina, "Put this in your mouth; it will dissolve and ease your stomach. The hormones are powerful, but it is the fastest way to get this job done."

The Nurse hands Mike a second tablet, telling him, "She will feel better now. Give her this one in the morning. Big Man, you need to do your job. It has been three weeks, and nothing." Then she walks away to continue her work.

That night, Mike can't help but notice Christina's body's reaction to the shot. Her tunic is soaked and see-through, as if she has just walked out of a pool of water. He is staring; the hormone shots he is being given seem to be more in control than he is.

Claire notices, "She is beautiful, isn't she?" she says softly.

"Claire, I'm sorry. I shouldn't have been looking at her," says Mike. "That was a dick move."

"It's okay. Boys and now men have been looking at Christina our entire life; she just has that 'It' factor. And Mike, you might have to do something about it soon. Don't forget where we are."

"Claire, you know how I feel about you. You are the only thing that should be on my mind," says Mike.

Claire, in an understanding tone, says, "Hey, we get that shot once every three weeks, but you get one every week. Mike, if it makes you feel even half the way it does us, you are showing incredible self-control. Hats off to you for only looking."

"Claire, you have no idea. But I think you understand what I mean."

I Think Maybe:

Weeks go by, and Mike and the girls continue their surveillance. They assign code names to the guards: Guard one is dubbed 'Tiny', two is 'Stinky', and three is 'Dumbass' based on their respective personalities. They work out the Nurse and Assim's daily schedules, which are always the same. Everything is running like clockwork, which is great news for Mike as it means he can devise a plan knowing exactly when things will happen.

"Mike, I need to talk to you," Claire says quietly.

"Okay, what's up?"

Claire whispers, "No, over here, please. I don't want anyone else to hear."

"Sure," Mike says quietly as he and Claire walk into the corner of their Cage.

"How long have we been here?" asks Claire.

"I'm not sure; I've been trying to keep track. My best guess is six weeks," Mike answers.

"Six weeks? Okay. When do you think we can try to escape?" Claire asks.

She appears notably anxious. Mike can tell that Claire isn't telling him everything; there has to be a reason for her acting differently. "We're not ready yet," he says, "The metal isn't weak enough to break the chains, and we don't have much of a plan yet. What's going on? Is something wrong? Is there something I should know about? Claire, tell me why you are so on edge?"

The couple have been intimate for a few weeks now. Usually, after the others have gone to sleep, they hope they are asleep anyway.

"I'm not sure...I think, but I don't know for sure. I think maybe...," Claire struggles to find the right words to tell Mike what she needs to say.

"What's up, Claire? Please, just tell me what's going on?"

"Mike," Claire answered, "I'm pretty sure I'm pregnant."

A huge smile grows across his face, "Wow! Really? That's amazing. That's the best thing anyone has ever told me." At that moment, he forgets where they are and the plans Shariek has made for their offspring. Suddenly, reality jerks Mike back to the present, and panic sets in. He utters in a hushed yet determined voice to Claire, "Holy shit! Shariek! I swear on my life that I won't let him come near you or our baby," Under his breath, he says, *Fuck!*

Claire nervously looks down at her stomach, her hands placed protectively, before looking back up at Mike. "That's exactly what I'm worried about. We can't let Shariek or anyone else get their hands on this baby. For now, no one knows. I haven't had a blood test since that witch gave me the last shot, so as far as anyone knows, I'm not pregnant."

"How do you know?" Mike asks, "I mean, what makes you think you're pregnant?"

"Mike, women know. I have been feeling sick for the past few days, and my boobs are sore now," Claire says in a low voice, "We must keep this to ourselves for the time being," she glances at Christina and Terri, still asleep, "If they find out, everyone will know. I don't want Christina to be concerned about me, and she will be if she finds out."

He agrees to keep it between the two of them, for now. They need to make a solid plan and implement it quickly.

Looking for Mike:

Downtown Jeddah, Saudi Arabia. Two men, Max and Ricky, are holding a Saudi man by his ankles, dangling him off the side of a high-rise apartment building, and threatening to drop him unless he gives them the information they need.

"Where the fuck are the Americans? You piece of shit! Tell us where they are, or we are going to let go!" says Agent Maximilian Colburn II.

Maximilian, a.k.a. 'Max' as his friends call him, or 'Jr.' as his dad calls him, is Mike's best friend and brother. Max's parents, Max I and Rebecca Colburn took Mike in after his parents and sister were killed when a private jet crashed into and destroyed their family home. Max Sr. was a Navy Seal while Max Jr. and Mike were growing up, and he was the leader of Seal Team Echo years before Mike. Both of them followed in his footsteps, and it was Max Sr. who honed his sons' skills. Joining the Navy and becoming Seals, just like their dad, became their calling.

Max Jr. is a lean, muscular man, just over 6' tall. In every way, Mike is his brother. Max always does everything he can for Mike, and right now, he is doing everything he can to find him. The brothers joined the Navy and became SEALs together. After leaving Seal Team Echo, Max followed Mike into the CIA, where they remain inseparable.

Agent Enrique 'Ricky' Perez was also a member of Seal Team Echo and a brother to Mike and Max. Ricky is tall, standing at 6' 1". He comes across as hard and more intimidating than Max but less so than Mike. Ricky is more of a; you never want to find yourself alone, anywhere, with this kind of guy, guy. Ricky has one unique skill: he was born without a conscience, a perfect attribute for his current line of work.

"Last chance, you little shit! Where are the Americans?" demands Max.

"I truly do not know," the man with a heavy Arabic accent begins to beg, "Please, my friends, I do not know anything. If I did, I would tell you. Please believe me." The man hanging off the building knows he is begging for his life. He does not have the information they want and knows he is in trouble.

"I don't think this shit-bag knows anything, Max," Ricky says.

"I do not, I do not," the man pleads.

Max decides, "You're right. He doesn't know shit. We can let him go."

"Roger that," says Ricky. With that, Max and Ricky simultaneously open their hands and step away from the edge of the towering building. The man plummets, screaming and thrashing in terror. In seconds, his body is reduced to a gruesome mess on the pavement forty stories below.

Just before the men walk through the door on the roof, Max stops, looks across the city, and says, "Fuck Mike, where the hell are you?" He has no idea he is looking at the building where Mike and the girls are being held captive—the Sheik Juffali Hotel.

"Max Colburn for Director Gray," he calls using a secure line at the U.S. Embassy in Jeddah.

"Max, what's the news?" asks Director Gray.

"Nothing yet Sir," Max answers, "We have questioned six of Shariek's known associates but haven't obtained anything worthwhile from them."

"We need to be careful not to tip off Shariek; he doesn't know who Mike is yet," says Director Gray, "It's important that those men don't talk to anyone after they talk to you. No questions are the best questions."

"You don't need to worry about that Sir," says Max.

"Good to know we're on the same page," replies Director Gray, "Find him, Max. And do it quickly. That's an order."

"Yes Sir. I will Sir. You have my word. I will do everything I can to find him quickly," Max promises.

I Thought Maybe You Were Dead:

After Mike's conversation with Claire, his mind turns to his brothers, *Where the hell are the guys*? he thinks, *It can't be that hard to find me. I practically gave you my coordinates.* Mike is aware of how difficult the situation is. He knows that they are doing everything they can to find him. He also realizes that they need more help, *I have to help them find us. What else can I do? Maybe they didn't notice the Morse Code in the video?* He is trying to come up with a plan in his head.

"Claire," Christina calls, "Hey, I need to talk to you."

"What's up, Sis?" Claire replies.

Claire is trying to hide her nerves; Christina has never seen her like this. She is usually like a rock; nothing ever gets to her—absolutely nothing.

"You're making me nervous," Christina says, "You're jumpy and sick. I saw you this morning. What's going on? Are you worried about the three-month deadline? I know I am; I can't stop thinking about what will happen when the time is up."

Claire is relieved that her sister thinks she is sick because of nerves and not the real reason; this makes it easier for her to lie, "That worries me, Sis. My nerves are rattled, and my stomach is upset because I am so worried...."

In the middle of her explanation, Shariek walks through the door to the garage and heads straight for Mike's Cage. As he approaches, he raises his arms as if welcoming old friends to Fantasy Island. "Hello, my friends. Ladies, it is good to see all of you. And, of course, Mike, my best and biggest Stallion, is in his stable," Shariek says.

Mike smiles sarcastically and replies, "Hello, Shariek. It's nice to see you again. It's been a while; I thought maybe you were dead."

"No, my friend," Shariek says, "as you can see, I am alive and well. In fact, I have a surprise for you."

"I am not a big fan of surprises Shariek," Mike says.

"Ahh! But I promise you; you will love this surprise," Shariek says. "I know you're having trouble seeding your females, so I have asked the doctor to examine you. I want to make sure you do not have any troubles. It is my gift to you."

Mike glances at Claire, then at Shariek, "I am trying; you're right, I haven't been successful yet, but I am working on it."

"Yes, my friend, I know you are making a valiant effort. Will you come with me? And will you behave, or do I need more guards?" asks Shariek.

"Okay, let's do this. I will come with you and behave. You have my word, Shariek," promises Mike.

"Excellent, my Stallion. But I think we should leave your chains on. Yes, that will be best," Shariek motions to the guards and says, "take him to the doctor, and if he gives you any trouble...you should stop him. I hope it does not come to that. I do not think his women would like it if I had to get them a new Stallion."

Mike is delighted to accompany Shariek, it will allow him to study areas he hasn't seen yet, which he needs to do to create a viable plan. He knows the Doctor might examine him in full detail, but he is willing to accept this minor inconvenience in exchange for the valuable intel he might gain. As an added bonus, Shariek is utterly oblivious to who Mike is and his true intentions, which makes him smile.

Without another word, Shariek turns and walks out of the garage. Stinky and Tiny, the two guards, unhook the chains from the wheel and lever. They begin yanking on the chains pulling Mike out of the Cage door as forcefully as possible. "Guys, guys, I will come peacefully," Mike says.

Shariek pops his head back into the garage, "And bring the dark-haired girl; the doctor must inspect her as well," with that he was gone.

Oh, Shit! Mike thinks. *Christina? Okay, what's going on? The plan just changed.*

Tiny stepped into the Cage and, firmly grasping Christina's arm, said, "You, come with me."

Mike and Claire exchanged a worried glance, aware that if the doctor discovered Christina was still a virgin, they would be in deep trouble.

"Mike, just go, but what about Christina?" Claire's voice was filled with anxiety as she tried to get her point across to him.

Mike nodded, silently thinking, I'll figure something out. He then nodded again to Claire, letting her know he understood her.

As soon as the guard lets Christina out of the Cage, she runs to Mike and wraps her arms around his waist, holding on as if her life depends on it, and maybe it does.

My Name is Dr. Umar:

Tiny and Stinky lead Mike and Christina down a long hallway. Mike is taking mental notes, counting every door and window, the number of steps between, and what, if anything, is inside the rooms. After three doors and forty paces, they arrive at a Medical Office. Inside, a man in a lab coat is seated on a short, round chair with rollers on one side of the room. Tiny pushes Christina inside, and she stumbles and almost falls, catching herself on the exam table. Mike gives Tiny and Stinky a death stare as he walks past.

The man speaks, "My name is Dr. Umar. I understand you are having difficulty conceiving a child," looking at Christina and then back to Mike.

Christina is at a loss for words and stumbles on her reply, "Um, well, ahh, I mean..."

Mike jumps in to explain, "Well, Doc, it's not that we're having trouble. You see, we haven't been as active as we could be. I'm just one man, and I have three women to take care of. And, well, it's only been a few weeks."

"Let us do an examination. We can find out if there is any reason for concern. Young lady, you will be first. Climb up onto the table," orders the Doctor.

Christina looks at Mike, scared and unsure of what to do.

"Doc," Mike jumps in again, "I don't think there's anything wrong with her. Maybe give us a day or two, and we can come back? I mean, we are trying. When I arrived, I was hurt and sick. However, I'm much better now, and I think I can do better tonight, if you know what I mean," Mike is desperate to come up with anything that would keep the Doctor from examining Christina.

"You have been sick? What seems to be the problem?" asks the Doctor.

Christina slowly backs away from the exam table while Mike shows the Doctor where his imaginary stomach pain is.

"Do you see this, Doctor? It hurts when I press on it," Mike says as he walks up to the table, chains dragging behind him. Mike speaks like a Dutch Uncle, changing his story like a child trying to stay home from school to miss a test he hasn't studied for. He has the Doctor feeling all over his stomach.

Christina backs herself into the corner of the room, trying to make herself invisible and hoping the Doctor will forget about her.

The Doctor examines Mike and says, "I see you are a large man, which can cause a problem for some women. A large penis can damage a smaller woman's vagina. I have also seen larger men like yourself have a low sperm count. Perhaps, that is your issue. I think it would be best if we get a sperm count first. You will not have sex for two days. After that, my Nurse will collect a sample from you, and I will check your numbers. If they are not low, I will check the young lady for any damage you might have caused her. Yes, that is the best way forward. The guards will take you back now. Remember, no sex for two days."

It Ain't Easy Man:

Understandably, Mike and Christina are relieved when they leave the Doctor's office, having been granted a two-day reprieve. Stinky and Tiny escort them down the hall, and Mike counts his steps - *thirty to door number two.* Mike pretends to trip and throws himself into the door, which opens to reveal an empty room with telephones on a desk. Stinky quickly pulls the door closed.

Tiny yanks Mike's chains and yells at him, "No trouble from you! You do not go where we do not tell you, or we will hurt your woman!"

Mike grabs the chains and says, "These things aren't easy to walk around with. It ain't easy man."

Christina takes Mike's arm to help him up. As he stands, he says, "Thanks, honey," and pulls her closer.

Stinky and Tiny ensure they go directly to the Cage without further detours or disruptions.

As soon as the guards leave the garage, Claire asks, "Okay, so what happened?"

"I think we're in trouble," Christina says, "They want to examine me, Claire. They want to see if Mike has done any damage to my vag — whatever that means."

"They didn't do an exam today? Thank God, I was so worried!" exclaims Claire.

"It gives us two days to get the hell out of here," Mike explains.

"Do you have a plan, Mike? Can we leave within the next two days?" asks Claire.

"Not yet," Mike says, "but I am working on it. Something has to work."

"Mike, we need to talk about it, for fuck sake!" Terri, looking visibly upset at the prospect, interjects.

"I mean, that's the answer, isn't it?" Christina says, "We're running out of time. Terri and I aren't pregnant; there's no way we could be. At least Claire has a chance."

"She is right Mike," says Claire, "I think we have to resort to Plan B."

Mike seething with rage, mutters profanities under his breath as he thinks of Shariek. He desperately tries to find a solution, but nothing comes to him. He has been defeated, for now, and is forced to do something he never thought he would have to do. Plan B is their only option; they have no other choice.

Time for Plan B:

Later that night, Mike and Claire lay together on the floor, holding each other and discussing the Doctor's visit and what had happened that day. He pulls her close and says, "Claire, I can't figure out how to get us out of here in the next two days. My wristbands are still too solid. I know where the phone is, but I don't have a way to get there until I go back to the Doctor. I don't know what else to do."

Claire knows what must be done to keep them alive. She attempts to prepare him for what he needs to do with her soothing voice. Claire whispers in Mike's ear, "Mike, you have to do this for all of us. If Shariek finds out you haven't kept your promise, he will not only kill Christina but you as well. Remember what he did to that man in the Cage next to us? I have told you my first priority is Christina. She must be safe. I need you to make sure she is safe," Claire keeps repeating the same thing in Mike's ear, kissing him and assuring him everything will be alright. Until he eventually falls asleep.

"Christina," whispers Claire.

Christina can't sleep; she is worried about what might happen. She is anxious and turns to Claire.

"Come closer to me," Claire whispers.

Christina moves over closer to Claire.

"You know what you have to do, don't you?" Claire asks softly.

"Of course. I said I would, and I'm ready," Christina says.

Claire, getting emotional, says, "You know I love you, right? You're my little sister, and I don't want anything to happen to you."

The two women start to cry, "This whole situation is so fucked up," Christina says through her tears.

They fall asleep, hugging each other. At around 3:00 am, Claire wakes Christina and tells her, "It's time. Everyone is asleep. Do what you need to. I'll wake him."

"Mike, my love," whispers Claire, "wake up, my love."

Mike replies, "Yes, honey, I'm awake," he has been awake most of the night, racking his brain to no avail.

"It's time," Claire says quietly to Mike.

Christina slowly and quietly makes her way to him. He squeezes Claire's hand and nods.

Mike knows it is Christina's first time, and she is much more petite than Claire. *This could be a painful situation for Christina*, he thinks, *go slow and easy*. But he is unable to perform; his "little soldier" will not stand at attention.

Christina looks down at Mike's penis, then back at him. "What the hell, Mike? Am I not good-looking enough for you?"

The truth is, Christina is beautiful. She is petite and toned, with silky smooth caramel skin, long brown wavy hair, and mesmerizing blue eyes.

Mike is very attracted to her but loves Claire; he never wants to cause her any pain.

"Honey," Claire whispers into Mike's ear while holding his arm, "I love you, and you love me. Now, you need to love Christina."

This works, and Mike is ready; Christina does what she has to do. She is a virgin, and her face shows nothing but pain. It is not going as well as either has hoped. Christina looks like she is about to cry.

"Hey, let's stop. I don't want to hurt you," Mike says with concern.

Christina's big blue eyes look right into Mike's, piercing his soul as she smiles and kisses him. She says, "I'm okay, we have to do this."

Soon enough, Mike is spent, and Christina's pain is too much. She hopes she has done enough to pass the physical exam. She kisses him and says, "Thank you, Mike. That may have just saved both of our lives."

Mike looks down and sees blood. With concern, he asks Christina, "Are you all right?"

"Yes, I'm okay. It's my first time; it happens to some women. I guess it could be the 'damage' the doctor was talking about."

Mike can't help but wonder if he has just hurt Christina. He thinks, *Claire never bled, and I've never been with a woman who did. I hope she's okay.*

Claire is on his right, Christina on his left, and tonight Terri is asleep alone at the back of the Cage. Mike holds both women and thinks, *I need to get them out of here.* The only thing on his mind is protecting both of them; *he loves them.* For the first time in his life, he realizes that he loves someone, maybe even two women. He also fell in love with the baby the instant Claire told him she was pregnant. *Now, what do I do about Terri?* He thinks, *A problem for another day.*

Assim:

Mike wakes up in a flash; his mind has been working on the problem all night. *Assim!* he thought, *I can get Assim to alert the team to our location inadvertently. That's it! Assim is the answer!*

"Good morning," whispers Claire.

"Hello, my love. How are you today?" Mike asks.

"Mike, thank you for protecting my sister. I know it was difficult for you, and I love you for what you did for us. She will be safe now, and that's the most important thing," Claire tells him.

"I love you too," Mike says, and they both smile at each other.

Mike has been developing feelings for Christina over the past few weeks, not just because of what happened last night. She needs him, and he wants to protect her; something is there, but he doesn't know what it is yet. Last night makes him think; he still isn't sure what he feels for her, but whatever it is, it is growing.

"Good morning," Christina whispers, then kisses Mike's cheek smiling from ear to ear. Her smile lights up the room, full of pure love and joy, even in a dismal place like this.

Just then, it hits Mike — it is love; his affection for both women is genuine. He can't bear the thought of losing either one of them. "Good morning. How do you feel this morning?" he asks.

"I'm very sore and hungry," Christina replies.

"I want you girls to have my food today, Claire; you're getting too skinny anyway," Mike announces. For weeks, he has been giving his food to all three women, only eating as much as he absolutely needs to survive. Claire is secretly eating for two, and he has plenty of muscle to burn. Plus, they will be out of there soon, and he is trained for this.

Assim is the answer; Assim is the way out, his mind returns to the little fat man, and a huge smile crosses his face.

American Food:

"Okay, let's review the clues," says Agent Max Colburn, "Somewhere near the Jeddah Tower, in a parking garage."

"That's not all," Agent Ricky Perez adds, "Mike's message was also about American food, potatoes, and corn. Why would he tell us that?"

"Yeah, that's a weird clue," Max says, "Mike wouldn't pass anything that wasn't necessary; he didn't have much time. He knew that everything in his message was important, so we must figure out why he thought American food was necessary to tell us."

"Margaret," Max calls Langley on the phone, "Mike dropped a clue about American food, such as corn and potatoes. What do you think he meant by that?"

"Most sweet corn and potatoes are exported from Saudi Arabia; they are the seventeenth largest exporter of corn in the world," says Margaret, "I don't see how that helps us find Mike."

"I don't think the item was the clue. Maybe it was the way they are served, as corn and potatoes. Mike didn't say masa or potato bread or pasta; he said 'potatoes and corn,' and that keeps sticking in my mind," Ricky says.

"Then we look for a cook who makes American food," says Max, "Someone who could work for Shariek and maybe has his own place."

Margaret is still on the line with them and answers, "That would make sense. I'll research on my end for American food restaurants, caterers, and cooks. Call me later, and I'll give you what I can find."

Pork:

"I've got it," Mike is talking to himself, but it's loud enough for the girls to hear.

"You've got what, Mike?" asks Claire.

"I know what we need Assim to do," Mike explains, "I need to get him to cook something special for us, something that people here wouldn't normally eat--something he would have to look for, drawing attention to himself."

"Like what, Mike?" Christina asks.

"Pork, Christina, Pork!" Mike exclaims, "Most people here won't eat pork; they consider it unclean," he continues, "Yes of course, Pork! Perfect!"

The Clock is Ticking:

The door opens, and the Nurse walks into the garage. She heads straight for Mike's Cage, not stopping at any of the other Cages, followed by Stinky and Dumbass.

She nods to Dumbass, and he yanks on the chain wheel handle. Mike slams into the wall, and he hears the metal bolt crack on his right wrist. *Yes! Finally*! he says to himself.

"Bring the one with red hair," the Nurse barked at Stinky. Stinky opens the Cage door and grabs Terri, pushing her to the Nurse. "Put your arm here," the Nurse said.

After drawing blood from Terri's arm, the Nurse demands, "Okay, I am done with this one. Bring the dark-haired one."

Christina is next. She walks calmly to the Nurse, puts her arm out, and allows her to draw blood. "You go now," the Nurse says as she pushes Christina toward the Cage. She almost falls but manages to catch herself.

"You! blond one, come now!" The Nurse crossly says to Claire.

"Claire, don't..." Mike is interrupted by Claire, who calmly says, "It's okay. It will be okay."

Claire walks past Christina, who is holding her arm where the blood had been drawn.

"Put your arm here," orders the Nurse.

Claire does as she is told, looks at Mike, and smiles. She winces when the needle is inserted into her arm.

"Blonde whore, you are finished," says the Nurse, "Let him go." Dumbass releases the chains, and Mike is free. He grabs Christina and waits for Claire to reach him.

"Oh, and Big Man, the Doctor changed his mind. Tomorrow he will artificially inseminate the one with brown hair using your sperm. No sex tonight! Do not forget," the Nurse commands, "Unless she is already pregnant, we will know tomorrow."

"From bad to worse," Mike says, holding Claire and Christina in his arms.

"Hey guys, I am fucked here," Terri says, "I mean really fucked."

"No, you will be okay," Mike says, looking at his right wrist. "We leave tomorrow."

What do you Feed the Devil?:

Like Clockwork, Assim walks in, pushing his cart of food buckets. As usual, he begins going to each Cage in a counterclockwise pattern.

"As-salamu alaikum, Assim," says Mike.

"Wa-alaikum as-salam, my brother," replies Assim.

"My friend, I have another favor to ask of you," Mike explains, "I'm having trouble breeding with these women. They are not pure; they are devils. I need to feed the devil inside them. What do you feed the devil?"

"I am not sure," Assim says, "but I do understand your dilemma. I can pray on this and let you know."

"I am truly blessed to have you as my friend, Assim. I do this for Allah and Shariek," Mike proclaims.

Assim continues his rounds but returns to Mike after he finishes his work. He has an idea: "They are unclean devils. They need unclean food," says Assim. "The flesh of a pig will feed their unclean souls."

"You are a wise man, Assim. We will be friends in Heaven, sitting by Allah's side," Mike thanks him.

"I will find a remedy for you. It may take time, but I can do it. I know the right person to ask and will see him today. Please do not despair, my friend. We will overcome those devil women together," Assim promises.

Bowing to Assim with his right hand on his chest, Mike says, "As-salamu alaikum, Assim."

"Wa-alaikum as-salam, Mike," Assim returns the greeting.

A More Direct Approach:

"All right, you little bastard, who here cooks American food using corn and potatoes?" asks Max.

Max is talking to the third of only four food suppliers to local restaurants and caterers. This time, they are using a different, more direct approach.

"Look at your wife. Do you see my friend's gun in her mouth? Well, you have until the count of three before he pulls the trigger. Do you understand me?" Max demands.

"Sir, I am only a provisioner of food. I do not know what American food is. Is not all food just food?" the storekeeper cries.

Max counts, "One."

"Please, I do not understand the question you are asking. Yes, many people cook food for Americans. Like steak and chicken? Just today, I had a long-time customer ask for pork, but I do not have any pork. I do not have unclean food in my store."

"Pork? Who is this man that asked you about pork?" Max demands.

"Assim Negiari, he is a good man," says the storekeeper, "He asked me for pork to feed devils, but I could not help him."

"Where can we find this, Assim?" Questions Max, "Where is his kitchen?"

"At the Shatie Market near the waterfront. Please, truly, that is all I know," cries the storekeeper.

"I believe him," Ricky acknowledges.

"Okay, Ricky," Max gives Ricky 'the nod.'

Ricky pulls the trigger, killing the woman, then turns the gun on a terrified shop owner shooting him several times in the head.

"Assim Negiari," Max informed Director Gray from his cell phone, "This is the guy we need to find, Mike. He is very religious, so I don't think he'll tell us no matter what we do to him."

"Then follow him. Use any means necessary. Get Mike back today, Max, today," the Director commands.

"Yes Sir," Max says, "We will."

The Day has Arrived:

Mike is trying to break the screws holding the chains on his wrists; they are looser and cracked but are still not broken. "Hey, Terri, why don't you take out some of your aggressions on these chains?" Mike suggests.

"What do you want me to do?" asks Terri, with a confused look.

"It will hurt, but I want you to kick the metal cuffs on my wrists. Nail them hard; I can take it. Use the back of your heel, and give 'em hell. But hurry – the Nurse will be here any second to take Christina and me. And I need my hands free," Mike tells her.

Terri looks at him and agrees, "Okay, I hope I don't hurt you, but we need to get out of here." She puts all her strength into it, kicking his right hand and striking the cuff dead center. It doesn't break, but it bent.

"Good job. Now do it again," Mike says.

Claire and Christina watch, wincing at every blow Terri delivers. Claire says, "Terri, be careful; please don't hurt him," Terri smiles back at Claire and winks.

On His Trail:

"Sir," Max says to Director Gray, "I have four Apache Choppers, two ISR Drones, and a Marine Platoon on standby from Base Sieb."

"Good; use every resource you need, Max. Listen, Mike is our top priority. In the video, there are four Americans, but if you have to make a choice, it's Mike. Understood?" the Director says, "Max, that is a direct order."

Max doesn't need the Director to give this order; Mike is already his top priority. "Understood Sir," he answers, "I will keep you apprised." He hangs up the phone and turns to his staff, "SITREP, people," Max says to his command unit. They have their eyes on Assim, who is loading a Toyota pickup with plastic totes.

"Sir, we have eyes on Assim; he is at the market," says one of the Techs.

"Do we know yet what he is loading? Is it food? Corn? Potatoes?" asks Max.

"No Sir," reports another Tech, "Everything he is loading is in closed containers, so we can only speculate."

"God damn it! Ricky, we need to know what's in those containers and if this guy is even our guy," Max yells over the radio to Agent Perez.

"Max, I think I can go check. He is taking longer to return to the truck each time," Ricky replies.

"No," Max orders, "You could blow our cover. If that little asshole gets spooked, our lead is gone."

"All right, people, command decision; this is our guy. All assets on him," Max declares.

The Command Center comes to life as Techs and Operational Staff contact all Assets in the field via phones, radios, and computers.

Max mutters under his breath, *Jesus, I hope I'm right*.

Times Up:

"Holy shit! that hurt," Mike cries out after Terri kicks the cuffs again. This time, she busts the bolt on his left wrist, freeing both hands. He smiles, knowing he can begin his 'Campaign for Freedom'.

"Good job Terri," Mike says, "Claire, quickly, I need a piece of your tunic to tie the cuffs back together." She removes a small piece of twine used to close the top front of her tunic and gives it to Mike.

"This will work. Give me a hand," Mike says, "Through the hole and back." He instructs Claire to tie the cuffs back together so they don't look broken. For the past few weeks, he has been stuffing small pieces of the rags into the cuffs to keep the metal from cutting his wrists. The guards won't think twice if they notice the twine.

"Okay, good. Now, here's the plan: when they come to take Christina and me to see the Doctor, you two start counting to 500. When you reach 500, you need to create a disturbance," Mike explains to Claire and Terri.

"A disturbance?" Claire asks.

"Yes, more like a fight," Mike explains, "You and Terri need to have a loud, dramatic chick fight. It will hopefully distract the guards enough for me to do what I need to with the Doctor."

"Hells Ya!" Terri says, smiling and laughing while looking at Claire, "This bitch is going to get a beating."

"Good, so you know what to do," Mike says.

"Well hello, my big friend!" Shariek exclaims as he walks in, holding a piece of paper high in his right hand, "You did it, my Stallion! I knew you could!" he walks toward Mike's Cage.

Times up, mumbles Claire.

"I knew you could do it; I had no doubt. You have proven your worth, my Stallion," Shariek proudly says.

"I guess that is good news?" Mike asks.

"But of course it is!" says Shariek, "Now, you are aware of my love of videos, correct? I have another big surprise for you, mostly for her, but a surprise nonetheless. You see, we have many rooms here. Some like the Cage you are in now, and some are more comfortable. I just had one made up for your conquest. She will spend the next few months in luxury, in a room just like every American girl's room, with some exceptions, of course. I can show you now," Shariek removes his cell phone from his left breast pocket, "You see, this is a live feed of her new living arrangements. They are very nice, are they not?"

Playing on Shariek's phone is a video of a pink princess's bedroom, complete with everything a nine-year-old girl could want.

"I don't understand Shariek," Mike says, confused, "you want to…?"

Shariek cuts Mike off, saying, "Of course you do not. That is because you have a very small mind. I will enlighten you. Every day, at a particular time, a short video will be uploaded to the entire world. It will show a normal American girl living her life happily for months as she grows larger with the child inside until the last day. On that day, I cut the white baby from her stomach and proclaim that no American girl is safe."

Claire almost vomits, and Christina and Terri begin shaking uncontrollably. Mike feels his rage building, but he has to contain it, for now, for the sake of the girls.

"You're one sick fuck Shariek, one sick fuck," Mike says, now burning with controlled rage. He realizes why the girls aren't tattooed like the others: Shariek wants them to look like clean, All-American girls. If they have tattoos, the camera will show them, making them look like numbered prisoners.

"My Stallion, you need to make me more babies. I have two more rooms to fill," Shariek announces, "tomorrow, the blond one will go to her new room and show the world her new, happy life until I take what I need from her."

All three women hold onto each other tightly. They have just been told they will be used as incubators and afterward discarded like trash. They have never been so scared; tears stream down their faces.

"Today, I will let you say your goodbyes," Shariek says as he walks out of the garage through the doors.

"Oh my God! Oh my God!" Claire exclaims through her tears.

"Claire, don't worry; he will never touch you," Mike declares, "Ladies, today we get the hell out of here.

The Team Closes In:

"We got him. He's turning right onto Abdalla Zawawi, now left onto Abdul Rahman Ajiimi," a Technician calls out from the Mobile Command Post.

"Keep on him!" yells Max.

"Turning right on Muhammad Ibrahim Al Ghazzawi, left on Prince Sultan Road, right on Abdallah Batawil."

Max asks, "What's on that street? Is there anything with a parking structure?"

"Just a few markets, a school, and the University of Jeddah," the ISR Pilot reports, "Wait, he is slowing down. He is turning right into a parking lot. It's the Sheik Juffali Hotel, Sir."

The Sheik Juffali Hotel is a five-story luxury hotel built for parents of students at the University to stay at while visiting their children. The hotel was in operation for only two years before it had to be closed due to the subsidence of the ground beneath it. It was then sold to a multinational corporation to be used as storage and office space.

"Is this the place?" Max asks, "I need confirmation. I need to know what is in those containers."

As usual, Assim arrives for the first feedings of the day. He always has the same routine: he parks around the back of the hotel in a secluded area to avoid attracting attention. However, today, it most certainly has. Assim retrieves his cart from inside the building, walks back to his truck, and starts filling his 22 wooden buckets.

"Sir," shouts the ISR pilot, "I see corn, potatoes, and some kind of meat."

"Goddam! This is the place!" shouts Max, "Converge! Converge! Get me a fucking blueprint of this building now!"

Three Navy Seals exit the Command Center accompanied by Max and Ricky. In a matter of seconds, a silenced M5 rifle discharges a single 6.8mm round which pierces the back of Assim's head, just beneath the greater occipital lobe. It passes through the lesser occipital lobe, then the temporal lobe, before finally exiting through the frontal lobe in a spray of pink mist. By the time his body hits the ground, Assim is already dead. The two seals quickly drag his lifeless form to the back of the Toyota pickup, hefting him inside and covering him with a plain brown tarp.

"Okay," Max orders, "back off quietly."

They Are Here:

Something is different, Mike says to himself. The trio has been observing every facet of Shariek's operation for weeks. Today, Assim is late; Dumbass and Tiny have just finished their rounds, but Assim is nowhere to be seen. He is usually done with the first feeding before they see those two.

They're here, Mike thinks and says, "Okay, girls, this is it. Be ready when I call."

The Nurse enters the garage, and, this time, she isn't pushing her cart. Instead, she walks straight up to Mike's Cage and orders, "You two, come, we go now," pointing to Mike and Christina.

Stinky and Tiny open the Cage, pointing their cattle prods at Mike. "Come easy, yes?" Stinky asks.

"Yes, you have my word," Mike says, "Allah be praised." This disorients Stinky, but not for long.

Tiny removes Mike's chain from the wheel, and they drop to the ground. As he walks, the chains drag behind him.

"Follow me," barks the Nurse.

Mike looks back at Claire and Tami and mouths, *500;* they nod in acknowledgment. Christina walks closely behind Mike as they enter the hallway. He counts again: five feet to the first door on the right, thirty to the first on the left, and forty to...

"Ahh! You are back," Dr. Umar greets them, "Today is a big day for you both. Young lady, please take a seat on the exam table."

Tiny and Stinky are positioned outside the doorway, peering in. Mike is situated behind the Doctor in the room but nearer to Tiny and Stinky. Christina hoists herself onto the table and has to rotate so that the front of her body is pointing toward the doorway and the Doctor.

The Doctor writes something on a clipboard, places his gold pen under the clip, and then sets the clipboard and pen on the counter to his right.

"Put your feet into the stirrups," Dr. Umar motions to Christina.

Christina stares at Mike, her tight-clenched mouth and lips and her blue eyes burning a hole straight through his head. He quickly nods, *Keep going*, as she slowly puts one leg and then the other into the stirrups, never breaking her stare with Mike.

Christina feels mortified and enraged because of the positioning of the examination table. She is being forced to expose herself to all four men in the room. She desperately attempts to cover her body with her tunic but to no avail. She is consumed with the thought of exacting revenge on Mike for putting her in this uncomfortable situation. She swears to herself that she will make him pay for this.

"Doc," Mike states, "the Quran teaches us that all women must guard their modesty. I don't think Allah would be pleased with these two guards staring at her like this."

The Doctor looks at Christina, then back to the guards. He sees they are staring where they should not be. Then in Arabic, he pronounces, "In the

Name of God, the Most Gracious, the Most Merciful, you two close that door and stay outside," he looks at Christina and utters, "I am sorry, Miss."

It is true that Mike has just taken advantage of Christina, but it was necessary, and she will eventually come to terms with it. Mike will ensure the others pay the ultimate price for even so much as glancing in her direction.

"Please scoot to the edge of the table so we can see what is going on," requests Dr. Umar. He then opened a drawer under the table and removed a speculum.

Mike acts quickly, snapping the chains that have been binding his wrists. Freedom is his! He grabs the clipboard and tightly clutches the golden pen in his right hand. With one swift and decisive motion, he plunges the pen into the Doctor's back, between his seventh and eighth ribs, piercing his diaphragm and lodging itself in his right lung. This effectively silences the Doctor while he drowns in his own blood. The Doctor stumbles forward toward Christina and Mike in an effort to keep her quiet; touches his left index finger to his lips. He gently lays the Doctor down as blood trickles from his mouth and pools around his nose on the floor.

Mike tells Christina, "Stay behind me," as they move toward the door.

Suddenly, Mike stops. Thinking there is a real chance that they will both be killed in the coming seconds, he turns back to Christina, holds her face with both hands, and gives her the most passionate kiss of his life. Then he tells her, "I love you," and turns back to the door.

Stunned, Christina thinks, *What the hell was that?* She quickly snaps back to the current life-threatening situation and follows Mike to the door.

They wait at the door until they hear the guards yell in the hallway, "What is going on?" and "Come help! The two white whores are killing each other."

Tiny runs down the hallway and out the door into the garage.

Mike opens the door and seizes the single guard remaining outside. With one swift motion, Stinky is no more. He snaps his neck and pulls him into the examination room, and places his body next to the Doctor.

"Okay, out the door, go right, and take thirty steps. Then, go into the room on the right. Got it?" Mike instructs Christina.

"Yes, thirty steps; go right, got it," Christina answers.

"Let's go," Mike says.

Crouching and counting their steps, they make their way down the dark hallway to the room with the phone. Mike slowly opens the door; the space is empty. He grabs Christina's arm, pulls her inside, and shuts the door behind them.

"Sit in the corner," Mike tells her, "If anyone comes in, you hide under this desk and don't come out. No matter what you hear. You stay under that desk. Understand?"

Christina nods rapidly in acknowledgment.

He removes the handset from the wall and hears a dial tone. *Oh, thank God,* Mike thinks as he quickly dials.

The phone rings. "Go for Max."

"Max, it's me," Mike whispers.

Terri and Claire put on an incredible performance, with guards from all directions rushing in, yet not one intervenes. They seem happy to watch the two American Whores fight with each other. To add to the excitement,

Claire allows her tunic to slip off her shoulder, revealing her breast. Terri follows suit, letting her tunic fly up, exposing her lower half.

"I'm going to kill you, you bitch!" Terri roars.

"You're dead, you whore!" Claire counters.

Some of the guards and other prisoners begin yelling and cheering, bringing more guards to see what is happening. One of the head guards comes to the Cage and shouts, "Okay! Okay! Stop it now! Stop it! Get the fire hose!" He motions to Tiny.

Tiny runs into the hallway and doesn't see Stinky. He slows down as he approaches and calls out, "Husan, Husan!.... Husan, where are you?"

"Hang on, Max," Mike whispers, hearing Tiny calling for Stinky.

Mike opens the door slowly and sees Tiny walking toward the exam room. He looks both ways, up and down the hall, and carefully stalks Tiny.

"Aaaahhhh!" Tiny cries out in anguish as Mike clamps his hand over his mouth and snaps his neck with one swift, powerful movement. He firmly grasps Tiny and yanks him back into the room where the phone and Christina are.

As Mike snapped Tiny's neck, both of Tiny's eyes popped out of their sockets. When Mike enters the room and releases his body, Tiny's eyes break loose. They roll across the floor straight toward Christina, halting just inches away from her hiding spot. Christina's face suddenly drains of color, and she quickly brings her hands up to her mouth to muffle the scream that is about to escape her lips.

With Tiny taken care of, Mike picks up the phone, "Max, I need help. There are seventeen guards, some armed with AKs, but most have electronic cattle prods. There are three friendlies that we need to evacuate. I don't have the layout of this building, but I need to bring one Friendly out to you now," Mike informs him.

Max is relieved to hear Mike's voice and tells him, "I have the layout; you are in a hotel. There is only one parking garage. To the north, a long hallway leads to a receiving dock. We have people inside that dock waiting on your command. We have already neutralized six guards outside."

"I'm coming out now; make sure our men know I have one female Friendly in tow," Mike instructs, "Have my stuff ready."

"Roger that," Max replies.

Mike holds Christina by the shoulders and looks her in the eyes. He speaks in a clear and determined voice, "Christina, I'm getting you out of here right now. Do exactly what I tell you. When we go through that door, stay behind me, hold onto me, and don't let go until we are outside."

"What about Claire and Terri?" Christina worries, "We can't leave them here."

"We won't." Mike says, his voice hushed as he firmly grasps Christina's hand, "I'm taking you to a safe place, so just follow me." He opens the door cautiously, still hearing the commotion from Terri and Claire, "Come on, let's go." They quickly make their way down the hallway until they reach the door leading to the loading dock. Once Mike opens the door, the pungent smell of death permeates the air and fills their nostrils.

"Mike's coming out with one female Friendly in tow," Max directs over the radio, "Protect Mike at all costs. Keep your eyes open for snipers and sleepers hiding in the loading dock. CONFIRM ALL."

"Roger," each of the Navy Seals acknowledges.

Christina begins gagging due to the overwhelming stench. Mike sees a maze of dead bodies they need to negotiate and tells Christina, "Look at me, nothing else. Hold my hand, don't let go, and keep moving." She holds Mike's hand as tightly as she can, gagging and coughing as she tries to pull her tunic over her nose. Mike leads them through the bodies, watching for Shariek's guards and searching for his men. He spots a red laser waving back and forth on the wall to the east. He thinks, *Thank God, she will be safe, and I can return for Claire and Terri.*

"Sir, this is Alpha Four. I have him, Mike, and the girl."

As they approach Mike's men, he says with relief, "Glad to see you, boys!"

"Sir, this way," affirms Alpha five.

As they step over the last of the lifeless bodies they must cross to get to safety, Christina sees a heavyset woman whose face is obscured by her badly decomposed corpse. Upon recognizing her, Christina's eyes widened, and she let out a loud, gut-wrenching wail, tears streaming down her face as she screamed, "Mom! Mommy! MOM!"

"Grab her!" Mike orders the nearest Seal. Mike and the Seal pick up the overwhelmed and distraught Christina and take her outside to the waiting Marines.

"Sergeant!" Mike barks at Marine Sergeant Bill Hobbs, "Guard this woman with your life. Do you understand me?"

"Yes Sir!" responds Hobbs as he and another Marine carry Christina away, kicking and screaming.

Max and Ricky trot toward Mike. "Brother, it's good to see you," says Max.

"Boss," Ricky says.

Mike gets straight to the point, "There's no way Shariek doesn't know you're here by now. I have two female friendlies left inside; they're my top priority."

"All others?" asks Max.

"Captives are friendly but expendable if necessary. All others will not see the sun rise again," Mike explains.

"Understood," answer both men.

"Here are your tools Mike," Max says, handing Mike his M5 and spare magazines, a tool belt to hold the extra mags, and Mike's custom bowie knife.

Mike smiles at Christina, surrounded by four Marines in the back of a Humvee on the opposite side of the street. She looks at him, her eyes piercing through his soul as she silently mouths the words, *I love you too.*

Mike's smile slowly fades, and Christina gets a glimpse of a side of him she has never encountered before. His eyes become as dark as the midnight sky, and his face is emotionless. He looks like the very embodiment of death. In a low, menacing voice, he turns back to the garage and states once more, "No one else sees the sunrise."

Heeeeelp!:

"Shariek, there are U.S. Marines outside!" yells Shariek's personal assistant, Jaffe.

"Marines? What do you mean? Why are there Marines here? Where are they?" questions Shariek. He stands up from his desk and looks out the window. Shariek sees his Stallion talking with two men. Mike is handing off the brown-haired girl to a Marine. He grabs the phone on his desk and presses the intercom button, "Bring me the blond American girl, do it now!" he orders. Then he gives one more order, "Kill them all, now!"

Five heavily-armed guards run toward Mike's Cage. Claire and Terri have no idea what is happening. Suddenly, one of the guards swung the butt of his AK47, striking Claire in the face and sending her crumpling to the ground, lifeless. Terri attempts to come to her aid but is cruelly attacked by the same guard, the single violent blow to her head rendering her unconscious. The guards grab Claire's limp body and drag her away, leaving Terri on the floor.

Mike, Max, and Ricky enter the hallway in formation, with Mike in the lead, Max on his left, and Ricky holding the rear.

"Contact right," calls Max as Mike fires off one round, penetrating Dumbass's head and spreading his brains across the wall.

"SEALs on our six," Ricky states.

"You, you, and you," Mike instructs the SEALs, "clear each room starting on the ground floor. Max and Ricky, you're with me."

As they approach the door to the garage, Mike warns Max and Ricky, "Behind this door, there are Cages to the right and left. There are a total of 88 cages, each with an average of five people held captive. In one of the cages to the left, there are two white women; one of them is carrying my child," he explains.

"Then we get them out, Mike," Max declares.

"Hell ya, Boss!" Ricky exclaims.

Four heavily armed guards suddenly appear in the Cage area, having descended the south stairwell. Each of them is carrying an AK47 with a drum magazine attached. They immediately begin to fire into the Cages closest to them. The air fills with the sounds of gunshots, bullets, and the captive's screams of terror as the rounds rip through their skin, bone, and tissue. Desperately, they attempt to flee the onslaught of bullets, but there is nowhere for them to hide.

"Holy shit!" Mike bursts through the door, his gun blazing. He catches the first guard in the right cheek, the bullet piercing his teeth but not taking the man's life. The second round hit its mark, entering the guard's right eye, then exiting the back of his skull, leaving a hole the size of a softball. "One down."

Max quickly aims at the second guard and fires off a three-round burst that strikes him right in the chest. The guard falls to the ground, still squeezing the trigger of his rifle and shooting the third guard in the back of his head. "Thanks for the assist," Max says with a smirk, "Three down."

Ricky takes aim and fires a single shot, which strikes the final guard directly in the forehead. "Four down."

Mike runs toward his Cage, where he left Claire and Terri. Terri is on the floor, bleeding from the top of her head but Claire is not in the Cage. Mike grabs Terri to check for bullet wounds. "I'm not shot, Mike. They hit me on the head. I'll be okay," Terri tells him.

"Where is she, Terri? Where is Claire?" shouts Mike.

"They hit her over the head, picked her up, and then took her away. I tried to stop them, and that's when they hit me. I have no idea where they have taken her," Terri's voice trembles as she speaks, tears streaming down her face.

Mike calls out, "Max, take her outside. I have to find Claire."

Ricky shouts, "Boss, I am on your six!"

Mike is sure he knows where Claire is; that fucking coward Shariek has her in his office. He remembers when he was there looking out the window, only seeing the skyline, not the trees surrounding the building. "She must be on the top floor," he tells Ricky.

Mike and Ricky head up the south stairwell. "Call them out, Ricky!"

"Contact eleven o'clock," Mike takes aim, three shots to the chest, and quickly swaps out his Magazine for a new one. "Reloading... Ready," he announces. They move up the stairs cautiously and purposefully. Mike holds up his hand, "Hold," he commands. Suddenly, he hears a piercing scream from the floors above - it's Claire.

"Get away from me, you son of a bitch!" Claire screams as loudly as she can, "Heeeeelp!"

Mike's training and experience fly out the window as he runs up the stairs faster and faster, running past Shariek's armed guards firing at him.

Ricky hastily set up a spot to snipe at the men above. It isn't the best position for a sniper, but he has to protect Mike.

Mike swings his rifle behind his shoulder, grabs his knife, and runs directly into a guard, cutting him almost in half. The guards at the top of the stairs start shooting at him, pinning him down before he can reach the top floor.

"Ricky, I have two!" Mike shouts, "They have me pinned!"

Ricky, his nerves of steel on full display, cautiously moves into position as the guards shoot at Mike. He steadies his gun and fires two shots, both of which strike their targets and sends the men crashing to the ground.

"Got 'em, boss! Now, wait for me!" yells Ricky.

Mike doesn't wait; he can hear his Claire screaming. He hastily opens the door to Shariek's floor, pulls his rifle back around to the ready, and secures his knife.

Claire, please scream again! he thinks, not knowing exactly where she is. "Heeeelp!".... There it is; he hones in on Claire. *The last office on the right,* he edges closer to the door.

"Boss!" Ricky whispers, breathing heavily, as he runs up behind Mike.

Mike gestures to Ricky, *behind the double doors*. He then slowly crouched down and peered beneath them. His eyes caught sight of two sets of legs; one wearing white trousers and black shoes, and the other belonging to a much smaller person, with no shoes on - Claire's. Seeing nothing else, he cautiously opened the double doors.

A shot rings out from behind him. Ricky shoots across the doorway into Jaffe Shariek's assistant. Killing him instantly with one shot.

"Well, Big Man, here we are," Shariek asserts.

Shariek is firmly grasping Claire with the same scimitar he had used to brutally take her father's life. She can feel the sting of the blade against her neck and the trickle of her own blood running down her skin.

"Shariek, I will let you go, just release the girl, and you can leave," Mike says.

"Big Man. Mike, I do not think that will happen. No, I believe this is where I die and where your beautiful blond dies with me," Shariek proclaims.

"It doesn't have to be that way, Shariek. I give you my word; I will let you go," Mike tries to bargain.

"Your word. What does your word mean to me? Nothing. You are a filthy lying American pig," Shariek says with disdain.

Behind Mike, Ricky has Shariek's brainpan in his sights; he mumbles, "Locked."

Mike looks at Claire; she is trembling and scared. He is still barefoot and has a thought. All he says is, "Terri," as he taps his foot.

At first, Claire looks puzzled; then, like a bolt of lightning, she understands what Mike wants her to do. With all her might, she quickly raises her right leg and brings her heel down on Shariek's foot, who is not expecting this. He screams in pain and loosens his grip on Claire. She throws herself away from Shariek just as....

"Now!" Mike calls out to Ricky.

One single shot fires from Ricky's rifle and finds its mark, striking Shariek square in the nose and traveling through his head at an incredible 3215 feet per second before exiting his skull and shattering the window behind him. At that exact moment, Mike leaps forward to seize the Scimitar, which is still held close to Claire's neck. Everything has to be done with perfect timing......

Mike tightly enfolds Claire in his arms, his voice gentle and low as he whispers her name, "My Claire," and with just one touch from his beloved, the forbidding man who had just seconds ago appeared to be the embodiment of death has disappeared.

Ricky, We are Ghosts:

A week has passed, and Mike is meeting with his team at the U.S. Embassy in Jeddah. Mike intends to bring everyone responsible for what was done to Claire, Christina, Sammy, and Terri to justice, his kind of justice.

"Bro, I know; we will get them. You need to go back and rest for a while. Your body is broken Mike," Max implores his brother.

Mike just shook the comment off, "I'm fine. What do you have so far?" he demands.

Director Gray has ordered Mike to report back to the U.S. He has placed him on leave until further notice, pending Dr. Hansen's release to active duty. Dr. Hansen is the CIA doctor in charge of Field Agents.

Until he is given the 'All Clear', Mike is to remain at the Fort Sieb Military Hospital. That is where he and the three girls were taken for medical treatment. However, after his wounds were stitched up, and without a word to the girls, he left against medical advice and went off in search of his new 'Targets'.

"We have the name of his boss, Sheik Zubair Majeed," Ricky informs, "He is in hiding. Once he heard we were looking for him, he made like a ghost."

"Ricky, we are ghosts. He is a big fat fucking Sheik. How hard can it be to find that fucking guy?" Mike says with frustration.

Max tries to get through to him, "Mike, we understand, man. We have the entire CIA looking for him. I'm positive he will turn up. Now Bro, please, go see the girls. I'm sure they wonder where you have been."

"I'm going today," Mike says. "They don't know yet."

"Dude, you didn't tell them they were going back to the U.S. without you? I thought you like, kind of, love Claire?" Max asks.

"I do Max," Mike explains, "more than I have ever loved anyone in my life. I want to marry her. But the Mission comes first, you know that."

"Boss, there is no Mission. We were told to stand down, remember?" Ricky reminds him.

"Besides Bro, you're going to be a father. That is really important, Mike. Go back with them. Ricky and I will find this fucker. When we do, you will be the first call," Max assures him.

The telephone on Mike's desk begins to ring, and when he looks at the caller ID, he sees it is Director Albert Gray. Even though he has been expecting the call, Mike refuses to answer it.

"Boss, you have to talk to him. He'll just keep calling," says Ricky.

Mike can't speak to the man. He's angrier than he has ever been, and talking to Albert Gray will only make it worse. "Max, answer it," Mike motions to the phone.

Max shakes his head in response to Mike, not wanting to be the one to answer Gray's questions. But Mike insists, and Max gives in.

"Go for Max," he says as he picks up the phone.

"Max, what the Hell is going on there? Mike discharged himself from the hospital three days ago, and I only learned about it ten minutes ago. This is bullshit that I didn't know about this until now!"

Max turns his head towards Mike, Director Gray's voice is so loud that it carries to Mike and Ricky, allowing them to hear every single word that he is saying.

"I wasn't aware of that, Sir. I will try to find out where he is," Max lies.

"Max, you're full of shit! Ambassador Sorensen just told me Mike is in the office with you now. Hand him the God damn phone!" Gray shouts in anger.

Max looks at Mike, who responds with a nod before taking the phone from Max and saying, "Hello, Sir."

"Mike, I gave you a direct order - you must stay in the hospital or go directly home. What the Hell are you still doing in Saudi Arabia?" Gray demands.

"Sir, I am waiting for the girls to be released so I can take them home. Once they are, I will head straight to the U.S.," Mike promises.

"And when will that be, Mike?" Gray's voice gets angrier with each word.

Mike lies, "The Doctors say they will be released by tomorrow afternoon at the latest, Sir." He knows they will actually be discharged this evening, but if he tells Director Gray, he will have Mike and the women escorted back to the U.S. tonight. He is able to put the Director's mind at ease with his 'half-truths' allowing him to speak more openly.

"Mike, let me apologize again for not getting you out sooner. We had no idea that you would be sent to that place. We had assumed that you would be sent to some rich bastard to be used as a slave, and you could have escaped easily. Unfortunately, you ended up in that Hellhole. I am sorry

Mike. Sometimes the best-laid plans don't always work out," Gray says semi-apologetically.

Mike is angry about the fuck up, but that isn't why his rage is on the verge of boiling over. "I understand Sir. It is a good thing we destroyed that place, but you know they simply moved it to another location. We didn't destroy the whole Network,"

"Understood, Mike. We will take care of that, too. And as for the Sheik, I promise you we will get him. And When we do, I will ensure he can no longer hurt anyone. You have my word Mike," Gray says.

Albert Gray is mostly true to his word. He will try to find Sheik Zubair Majeed, but he will most certainly not kill the man. Gray will try to turn the Sheik for his contacts and let him return to his privileged life uninterrupted until Albert needs him again. For Mike, this outcome is unacceptable. He needs to find the Sheik and take care of him himself. The Sheik will not be allowed to live.

"Yes Sir. Thank you, Sir. I will go back to the States as soon as they are released. Please keep me informed," Mike asks.

"Mike, you know I will. Please take care of yourself. We need you to heal and be ready for your next Assignment," says Gray.

Mike slowly places the phone back onto its cradle, his expression gradually changing to one of deep contempt and disdain for the Director.

"What did he say Boss?" Ricky asks.

"Max, you and Ricky keep on the Sheik. We need to find him before Gray does," Mike directs, "I need to get the girls back to the States tonight."

"Bro, it will all work out. Just take them home, and let us find that fat fuck," assures Max.

I Would Have Beaten Around the Bush for Hours Before Asking:

Claire is sitting in a chair in her hospital room. She is tired of being in bed and is ready to leave. She isn't sure where she is going. Her parents are gone, murdered by that horrible man. She doesn't want to go back to Columbus, Ohio, but she now needs to think of what is best for her unborn child and Christina. For the first time in her life, she is the one in charge, no parents to fall back on. Claire has to make all the decisions about herself, Christina, and now a baby. It is a bit much for her to wrap her head around. Only a few months ago, she was a kid with no worries in the world. Claire had parents to take care of her, and being a mother was something in her future plans, not her present. On top of that, Mike, the father of her child, left the hospital a few days ago. And she hasn't heard from him since.

Christina is in the hospital room across from her sister. She has a slight infection and is on antibiotics. The Doctors also gave her some more concerning news, but she will keep that to herself for now. Claire is going to have a baby, and Christina thinks that is great. The sisters are only a year apart, but Claire's maturity is many years beyond Christina's. She knows Claire will take care of her and everything will be fine, which is as far ahead as she can see. Christina is not worried about where they will end up. She knows that wherever it is, they will be together.

Mike returns to the hospital that afternoon and makes his way to Terri's room first. Terri has already been released but is still in the room next door to Christina. She is sitting on the bed, ready to go home.

"Hey!" Mike says as he walks in.

"Hey, yourself. What happened to you? You were here one minute, and the next, you were gone," asks Terri.

"I needed to get some things in order before we all head home. How is your head?" Mike asks as he sits in the chair next to the bed.

"23 stitches! It will be a fun icebreaker at parties. I had to get 23 stitches in my head; want to know why?" Mike has a look of utter guilt on his face. Terri laughs a little and smiles, saying, "Look at your face! Mike, I'm fine. It's just my way of dealing with this whole thing, but really, I am fine. I want to thank you again for everything. I thought we would never make it out of that place."

"There is no reason to thank me. We were all in that Hell together. I can honestly say I had my doubts about us getting out. It took all of us to make it out, and thank God we did. I'm glad you're going to be okay," Mike says.

"I know that we planned on all heading home together, but I am leaving in a couple of hours. My parents want me back home as soon as possible. They called in a favor from our Congressman. He got me on a military flight to Germany. I want to see Sammy's friends while I'm there and tell them what happened to her," Terri tells Mike.

"That is great Terri. I think she would have appreciated that."

"What are your plans?" Terri asks, "You know Claire and Christina have no one now, right?"

"I want them to come home with me to San Diego; that is my plan anyway. I hope they will have me."

"I can almost guarantee that they both will. They are kind of a package deal, you know. Claire is overwhelmed at the moment. With her parents gone, this is her first time in the world without someone to fall back on if she needs anything. Suddenly, Claire has a lot of responsibility with Christina and a baby on the way. She needs you, that's for sure," says Terri.

Mike gives her a hug. She has to leave if she is going to make that transport.

"Again Mike, thank you so much for everything," Terri turns and walks out of the room.

Mike needs to talk to Claire, but first, he wants to see Christina. The way they left things has to be corrected. Mike should never have told her he loved her. He is going to have a child with her sister, and he plans on asking Claire to marry him as soon as the plane touches down in San Diego. That is if she agrees to go to San Diego with him.

He walks into Christina's hospital room. "Well, well, look what the cat dragged in. Where the hell have you been Mike?" Christina says as she is eating a pudding cup.

"Hey. Sorry, I had to check in with work after this whole thing, but I am back now."

"Ya, that whole 'I.T. thing,' right? Tell me again, what is it that you do?" smirks Christina.

"Internet Technology. I work for the State Department," Mike says.

"Right. And all those guys calling you Sir, like those Marines and stuff. Mr. I.T.," Christina laughs, puts her pudding down, and says, "I really don't care; I'm just glad you're back. After all, you're my sister's Baby Daddy," Mike cringes at that statement. He hated being called a Baby Daddy.

Mike starts, "I want to talk to you about that day," but Christina interrupts, "Mike, you and my sister are having a baby. What happened is in the past. Just go be with her. She will never admit it, but she is freaking out."

As he walks out the door, he says, "Thanks, Christina. I'll go see her now. By the way, would you be interested in staying with me for a while? I don't have a big house, but I want you and Claire to come home with me. My parents are really cool, and if you want to, you can stay with them. At least until you figure out what you want to do next."

"For now, I go where Claire goes. I think you need to talk to her first," says Christina.

Mike has a small apartment in San Diego. If that is what Claire wants, he needs to fit three people in it. He really isn't sure how Claire feels. Mike knows he loves Claire, but she hasn't said she loves him, not in those words, anyway. When he walks into her room, Claire shoots him the biggest smile of his life. She jumps up and hugs Mike with everything she has.

"I'm so glad you're back. I missed you so much," Claire says.

"I missed you Claire," Mike tentatively says, "Frankly, I thought you might be angry with me."

Claire tells Mike, "At first, I wondered if you had left for good, then your brother Max called and told me you would be back soon. He also told me you have difficulty telling people what is on your mind. So he let me in on what you are thinking."

Max, you son of a bitch Mike thinks. "Just so I'm part of all this, maybe you should tell me what Max said?" Mike asks.

"How about I just give you my answer? Yes, Christina and I will go home with you to San Diego. I will need to figure out what to do with our family home in Ohio. But yes, thank you for asking us to go with you," agrees Claire.

"That's great, Claire. Max is right. I would have beaten around the bush for hours before asking you. I am so happy you want to come home with me," Mike admits.

"When can we leave?" asks Claire.

"Now, if you're ready," Mike replies.

Gray the Politician:

Deputy Director Markus Delphy walks into Director Gray's office. The Director summoned him after his phone call with Mike.

"Sir, you wanted to speak to me?" asks Markus.

"Markus, you know Mike better than anyone. Is he blowing smoke up my ass when he says he will step back from this case?" Gray asks.

Markus is certain that Mike will stay on the Sheik; he has no doubts about that. "Well, Sir, Mike hasn't told anyone yet, but he is going to be a father. One of the women who were in his Cage with him is pregnant with his child. I don't know his plans, but I think he wants to spend some time with his new found love."

"Mike, a father. I thought I would never see the day Markus. Well, good for him."

"Yes Sir."

"Now, on to that bastard Sheik Majeed; where are we?" Gray asks.

"We tracked him to a port off the coast of Athens. He slipped our men, but we are on his trail. It's just a matter of time now, Sir."

"Markus, I want to talk to the man when you get him. Keep him on ice for me."

"Of course Sir. Your orders were very clear. No harm will come to Sheik Zubair Majeed," Markus acknowledges.

Home in San Diego:

Mike and the girls touch down at San Diego International Airport two days after their departure from Saudi Arabia. Mike told Claire and Christina about his family, how Max's parents adopted him, and what happened to his biological family. Now, the two girls find themselves in a similar situation, with no living family members apart from Mike and his adopted family. As they arrive at the airport, they are greeted by Mike's mother and father, Max Sr., and Rebecca Colburn.

"Mom, Dad, I want you to meet Claire and Christina Barnes," Mike introduces the girls.

"It's so nice to meet you both," Rebecca, Mike's mother, says, "I am Rebecca, and this is my husband, Max."

"You two are as beautiful as Mike described. It's good to meet you," Max Sr. says.

"Thank you both so much. I was just talking to Mike about how we are so happy to have a family to stay with," says Claire.

"Let me get your bags," offers Max Sr.

"Dad, we have nothing," Mike relays, "That's one of the first things the girls need to do: go shopping."

"Well then, you came to the right place. I will take you to Fashion Valley. You will love it there," Rebecca perks up.

The family piles in Max Sr.'s car and heads to Mike's apartment in downtown San Diego. His apartment is a small one-bedroom with a breathtaking view of San Diego Bay, not too far from the airport.

"Well, Mike is seldom home, but I come over and take care of whatever he needs," Rebecca tells the girls.

"Rebecca, you're a wonderful mother," Claire says, placing her hands on her stomach, "Mike talks about you all the time. I only hope that I will be as good a mother as you are."

Rebecca says, "Of course, you will be. Mike really loves you, Claire. He has never, I mean never, introduced us to even one of his girlfriends before. Well, once, when he was in the Navy, but that didn't last and never since."

Christina looks around the apartment. It is a total Bachelor pad, complete with men's magazines and a few other items she hasn't seen before.

"Umm... hey, I need to straighten up some things around here," Mike says to Christina. "Why don't you and my mom go shopping and buy some clothes for you and Claire? Is that okay with you, Claire?"

"Perfect. Christina, can you get me some sweats or something? I just need a few things right now, just until we can figure out what we are going to do," Claire says.

"Shopping? Aaa.....hello! Yes, of course, I want to go shopping," Christina reaches her hand out, palm up, and wiggles her fingers.

"Dad, I don't have my wallet. They haven't been able to replace it all yet. Can you take care of it for me?" asks Mike.

"Okay, come on ladies, let's do some shopping," Max Sr. put his arms around his wife and Christina, and he winks at Mike as he escorts the ladies out the door.

Mike and Claire are alone in Mike's apartment for the first time. Claire looks around, *it is small, very small,* she thinks to herself.

"Hey, this is just temporary. We will get a bigger place as soon as we can find one you like," Mike tells her.

"It's okay, Mike. I need to go home and get things situated there. I don't want to change your life. This is your home; there is no need to change anything for us," Claire says.

"Claire, my life is you now. That is if you will have me. I want us to get married," Mike says, a bit nervous.

Claire thinks about making Mike sweat a little. Of course, she will have him. "First, I am saying yes, but I want something more romantic before I pick a date; I want a grand gesture."

"Anything, I will do anything for you," Mike admits.

"Then take me to your bedroom. We can talk later. Right now, we are alone for the first time. Let's take advantage of it," says Claire.

As they walk to the bedroom, Claire says, "I just realized this will be my first time making love in a real bed."

My Financial Affairs Are in Great Shape:

While Claire is asleep and his mother and Christina are still shopping, Mike calls Max for a briefing, "Max, anything yet?"

"Bro, It's not the best news. Before he died, that little fuck Shrieks assistant shut down the entire database. We need it reactivated to get all the names. But the good news, well, not all good, is that Gray has already found the Sheik. I just received orders that Sheik Zubair Majeed is off limits," Max tells Mike.

"I figured as much. But I don't give a shit. Majeed dies."

"I knew you were going to say that, Bro. That's why I have Ricky tracking him now. When can you get to Turkey?"

"I will be on the first..." Mike looks at Claire sleeping in his bed, then corrects himself, "Scratch that. I'll be there soon. I have some things here that I need to take care of first. Just keep Ricky on him. He moves. I need to know. Understood?"

"You got it, Bro," Max says, "Ricky will stick to him like glue."

This is the first time in Mike's life that he has to think about someone other than himself before making a decision. Now, he has a family to think about. It's a huge change.

His family returns from Christina's shopping spree, and Mike's mom announces, "We have more bags in the car, Michael."

"Okay, Mom, I'm on my way," Mike walks out to help his father unload Christina's treasures. "Thanks, Dad. I needed a little alone time with Claire."

"I know you did, son. Why else would I go shopping?" Max Sr. replies.

"Dad, I asked Claire to marry me, and she said yes. Well, kind of, but yes."

"That's great son! Your mother and I think she is wonderful. And that Christina is a hoot. A real firecracker," Max Sr. laughs.

"I know; I want her to live with us, too. I hope Christina stays until she figures out what she wants to do with her life."

Mike isn't himself. His father, the person who knows him best, notices. "What's up, son? I can tell something is on your mind."

Mike confesses, "Dad, I don't know what to do. I love Claire with all my heart, but I have feelings for Christina too. I'm an idiot."

"Son, I only know what you've told me about what happened to you three. But I can understand your mixed-up emotions. The three of you were brought together in a way that most people, thankfully, will never understand. Listen to your heart. It will tell you the right thing to do."

"I know the right thing is to marry Claire. I truly love her, and of that, I have no doubt. But Christina, I'm just going to be here for her. If she stays, I can watch over her and keep her safe. She will make her own life. I just hope it's a life that makes her happy," Mike says.

"Son, I think I need to get your mother home. Let's take all these bags to the ladies so we can call it a night. We might take Christina home with us.

Your mom asked her to stay with us so you and Claire can have a little more time alone. Christina thinks it's a good idea, too," Max Sr. looks at him with a smile and wink.

"Fine with me, as long as Claire is okay with it. She is very protective of her little sister."

The men carry arms full of bags to the apartment and put them in the middle of the ladies. Mike's mom loves having girls to shop for. He looks around at his house full of women, shopping bags, and girly things and thinks, *I like this, all their stuff here. It's nice to see the girls happy.*

"So, did you get everything you need?" Mike asks Christina.

"Not even close! I would like to go back out tomorrow. I asked your mother if we could pick up Claire in the morning. Because I am going to stay with them tonight, and I think Claire should come and pick out her new wardrobe," Christina says.

"Christina, we don't have our finances in order yet. Max, Rebecca, thank you for the clothes. We will repay you as soon as we figure out where and how to get our parent's money," Claire insistently says.

"Don't worry about that. My parents help me manage my finances. I had my father use my cards to get you what you need. As far as money, you never have to worry about that again. My financial affairs are in great shape," Mike declares.

Claire looks around Mike's apartment. She is convinced that he doesn't have much; at least, his taste, or lack thereof, is telling her that. "Honey, I don't want to sound ungrateful, but this place is a bit small. I'm sure the government pays you well, but we can't take your money. Our parents were not super rich, but they were very smart about their finances. I think we will be fine."

Claire isn't aware of the substantial settlement Mike received after his parent's death. Max's parents made sure Mike's money was invested wisely when he was younger, and now he is worth millions, hundreds of millions. He likes this apartment, and it is just one of his apartments. Mike owns the entire building and most of the block. For now, he just assures Claire they will be fine.

Claire asks, "Christina, you said you are going with Mike's parents tonight. Why? You don't have to leave."

Christina starts grabbing clothes and putting them in her new bag as she explains to Claire, "Sis, you and Mike need to spend some 'alone' time together. It's Rebecca's idea, and she is right. Besides, there is only one bed here; I will have my own room at their house. We will be back in the morning to get you. You are going to love this mall."

Max Sr., Rebecca, and Christina say their goodbyes and hug and kiss Claire and Mike. After they leave, Mike and Claire sit on the couch together.

"Tomorrow, I will get you in touch with my friend, Dave Black. He is a lawyer and will help get your parent's affairs in order," says Mike.

"That would be great, Mike, thank you," Claire is relieved. "Now, I am going to clean up this mess Hurricane Christina just made of your apartment."

"Claire, this is our apartment now, not just mine," says Mike. "I want you both to feel at home here."

The Sheik is Back:

"Markus, thank you for coming in on such short notice. I usually don't make it a practice to work on Sunday, but I was just informed that Agent Perez is tailing Sheik Zubair Majeed," Director Gray says.

Director Albert Gray is talking with Markus Delphy in his office.

Gray has his own *'personal spies'* to monitor his most *'valuable assets,'* and it is these spies who alerted the Director to Ricky's presence.

"Sir, I don't know anything about that. I was told Agent Perez was still in Saudi mopping up Shariek's men," says Markus.

"Well, he is not! I need him off Majeed and back on his own cases immediately, if not sooner, Markus," roars Gray.

"Yes, Sir. I will contact him now, Sir," replies Markus.

Margaret is reading the paper and smoking as usual when Markus leaves the Director's office and passes by her.

"Hey, where is Mike?" Markus asks.

"Last I heard, he was in San Diego," Margaret says.

"Last you heard? What about his phone? 'Heard' anything there?" asks Markus.

Margaret has all of Mike's phones tapped. She can break into any conversation and is always listening. The only phone she can't access is Mike's 'Bat Phone,' as he calls it. That is a disposable phone that he replaces every week.

"Yes, I heard him talking to his lawyer friend this morning. There was a girl, I don't know her, who was calling to make airline reservations to Ohio. They are flying out in the morning. Other than that. Nothing," Margaret says.

"Please keep me posted. On second thought, I will meet them in Ohio. Margaret, please get me a commercial ticket to wherever they are going. I need to speak to Mike in person. Thank you," Markus says.

"You got it, Markus," Margaret replies.

Markus returns to his office; he needs to call Ricky off. The problem is that he is sure Mike is the one who put him on Majeed in the first place. Ricky and Mike are like brothers. He can't stop Ricky from doing anything Mike asks him to do alone. Markus will have to get Max to help.

"Max, we need to talk," Markus is talking to Max in Saudi Arabia.

"Of course, Markus; what can I do for you?" asks Max.

"Where is Ricky Max? And before you give me some line of bullshit, it's a rhetorical question," Markus says.

"He is tailing the Sheik," answers Max.

"Max, does Mike have Ricky doing this?" Markus asks.

"Yes Bro, he does," Max admits.

"No touch order Max! The Director of the CIA placed a no-touch order on the Sheik. Now you have one of the world's most proficient assassins following the man. What is wrong with you?" Markus says with authority.

"Markus, go meet those women. That is all I have to say. That guy needs to die, and brother, I support Mike on this one," Max says.

"Damn it, Max, you work for me! Call Ricky off immediately! I will take care of Mike. We will find a solution for the Sheik, but for the time being, he is strictly off limits!" exclaims Markus sternly.

Markus and the boys have been good friends for a long time, and he knows that asking Max to do this could strain his relationship with Mike. Despite this, Markus is sure this is the right decision. Max is willing to comply, at least for the time being.

"Ok, brother," Max says. "Ricky will be off the Sheik today. But you are telling Mike."

"I will; I'm going to see him tomorrow. I just hope he understands," Markus says.

After meeting with Director Gray, Sheik Zubair Majeed has wasted no time returning to his devious ways. In exchange for guaranteeing his safety, Majeed has supplied the Director with a wealth of 'information,' including the names of prominent figures such as Kings, U.S. Senators, Congressmen, and even a President or two. Director Gray values knowledge above all else. The intel he has obtained from the Sheik gives him a considerable advantage over those who would prefer to keep certain 'secrets' hidden. With the right amount of leverage in the right spot, Gray can move mountains, and sometimes, Congress can be as challenging as moving Mt. Everest.

Majeed finds himself 'untouchable' with the help of his new friend. He decides to double down on what is now 'his' Black Market Database of

Terror. Majeed quickly starts to rebuild his Sex Trade Empire. His deal with the Director includes him closing all the Baby Mills permanently. But now he has a new partner, in China, with products ready and available to sell. Majeed will be in the Sex Trade and Organ Removal / Replacement business, with the protection of the CIA. The world is his to conquer.

Max informs Ricky that he is to stop tailing Majeed. Even though Mike will be pissed; Max assures Ricky, Majeed will be taken care of in due time. He is no longer in hiding and will be easy to find. Max orders him to return to Saudi Arabia and help eliminate the remnants of Shariek's men. He also needs help shutting down all the Baby Mills in Shariek's former Network. The Director has instructed the men to follow every lead they can find and completely dismantle Shariek's Empire; however, Majeed and his people are not to be harmed or hindered in any way.

Home Again?:

The trio arrives at the girls' childhood home in Columbus, Ohio. Claire is the first to step over the threshold, with Christina close behind.

Claire thinks. *It's only been five months since I was here, but it feels like it was a lifetime ago.*

Christina rushes past Claire straight to her room to check out her things and jump onto her fluffy pink canopy bed. Mike, however, feels like an unwelcome intruder in the home without their parent's permission. Permission, under the circumstances, he will never be granted.

Claire slowly walks through the house, taking it all in. She pauses at the Baby Grand Piano, looking at pictures neatly placed on top. It is their whole life, her and Christina growing up, one of the family together around the backyard swing, a trip to the zoo, family vacations across the globe, their father with Congressman and Senators, and the one of him with President Bush. Claire's eyes fill with tears when she sees pictures of her mother pregnant with her. She feels overcome with emotion. Realizing she will never share the experience of being pregnant with either of her mothers makes her feel alone. Her parents are gone, and her child will never know them, but she is not alone; she has Mike and Christina. Claire glances back to see Mike standing in the doorway, almost like he is afraid to enter the house.

"Mike, what are you doing? Come inside; I want to show you around."

Mike walks into the house, still a bit apprehensive, even after the invitation from Claire. He scans the photos Claire is looking at; Mike is drawn to images of the girls when they were young. He walks to the pictures on the wall behind the piano. It is like watching a movie about the girl's life. He pulls one from the wall of Claire and Christina; they must have been about six and seven, and he wants a closer look. The image of them makes him smile.

Claire watches as he removes the photograph from the wall and steps closer to him. "My mother took that shot on the first day of school. I was in second grade, and Christina was in first."

Mike smiles ear to ear, looking at the picture and then at Claire, "I can't believe how much you still look like this girl, babe. Christina, too, those eyes. I couldn't miss them; you know it's her, for sure."

"I know; her eyes are the first thing you see when you look at her, except maybe when she is smiling. Christina's mom always said that from the day she was born, her eyes were huge, and when she looked at you, it was like she was looking right through you, into your soul."

Claire is looking at all the photographs. She gently traces her finger across a few of them and remembers her life before the Cage. Tears slowly trickle down her face. Her life has been divided into two parts; life before the Cage and life after. Memories flood her mind, and she realizes the life she once knew and loved is gone forever. This is no longer Claire's life and is no longer her home.

"Honey, are you ok? I know being here, with all the memories of your family, must be hard for you," Mike says as he pulls her closer.

She looks up at him and says, "It is difficult. It's also strange because I feel like I'm wandering through someone else's house. I grew up here, but this isn't my home anymore. It's a little hard to explain."

Mike understands what she is trying to say. He felt the same way when they were in his apartment. It is his past, and It isn't what he wants anymore. Mike doesn't want just an apartment or a house, and most definitely not a Bachelor Pad. He wants a place to share with his new family; he wants a home. He will call Dave when they finish here and have him find a home for his new family as soon as possible.

Christina slowly wanders through her cluttered room, admiring all the trophies and awards she has earned throughout her childhood. Track and Field, Softball, Field Hockey, Soccer, there were so many. As she straightens a few and takes her bra off one, a feeling washes over her; these things no longer mean anything to her. Everywhere she looks, everything is so very pink. Christina suddenly feels like she is a stranger in her own room. This house, her bedroom, her childhood home, they no longer feel like a place she can or even wants to call home anymore. Taking one last look around, leaving the child she once was inside, she closes the door behind her and sets off to find Claire and Mike.

Claire takes Mike by the hand, leads him down the hallway to her bedroom, and says, "I want to show you my room. No boy has ever been in here before, Mike. What do you think?"

Claire's room is nothing like Christina's. It is the room of a young woman, not a child. It has been this way since just before she turned ten when she declared to her parents, *I am no longer a child, I am a young person, and my room needs to reflect my aspirations.* Claire has always wanted to be 'big', and her bedroom is a testament to that. The walls are a subtle shade of white-gray, not the usual pink of most young girls, and adorned with delicate accents of pale yellow and dove gray. Claire has her academic achievements, trophies, and awards inside a trophy cabinet. Everything in her room is in perfect order; her desk is spotless, and the bed is made with military precision. Her books are arranged on their shelves, and not a single item is out of place. It is almost as if a decorator has designed the room for a young woman's first home, not a child's room, and it is ready for a magazine cover photo shoot.

Mike walks in and takes in his soon-to-be wife's neatly organized childhood. He immediately notices that it is not a little girl's room. Claire is mature well beyond the years she has been on this planet. She is an old soul.

"Wow, Claire. Look at all these awards! This is incredible. You are crazy smart, aren't you? First place in four Spelling Bees? Math Club President, Chess Club Founder, Debate Team, Valedictorian. So cool, I could never have obtained even one of these awards," Mike is so proud of his new love.

"Oh yea, she was a total Nerd, still is," Christina says as she walks into Claire's room and jumps on what was her picture-perfect made bed, grabbing one of the pillows and tossing it at Claire and grabbing another for herself.

Mike looks at Claire with a smile and says, "I wouldn't call your sister a Nerd."

"Christina is right; I was, and I still am, a nerd. But my little sister here is a tomboy, so she never lets anyone pick on me. She is lucky with boys too. I didn't have a date for my prom; Christina had two. For my prom, not hers, mine. For hers, I think she had her choice of every boy in school," Claire says as she smiles and laughs. She walks over to her bed to sit with her sister.

Mike can't imagine Claire not having boys chasing after her. She is such a beautiful and caring person. He is convinced guys must have swarmed around her, whether she was a nerd or not. He rolls the desk chair to the end of Claire's bed to sit near the ladies.

"Claire, not to embarrass you, but you're hot, and from all the pictures I just looked at, I can see you have pretty much always been hot," Mike says, "I can't believe you didn't have a lot of dates in high school."

Christina is more than happy to explain and jumps right in, "It's true, Mike, for a couple of reasons. First, some stupid boys are scared of my beautiful sister because Claire is so much smarter than all of them, but I think it is more because she wouldn't even kiss a boy until she was like 16. We also traveled a lot for our dad's job. When she finally decided she was old enough to be interested in boys and maybe, but just maybe, kiss one, we weren't here much. Most years, we were here for close to the entire school year. But we were only here a few months after I graduated last year. That isn't enough time for Claire. She needs to have a 'connection' with a guy before she even holds his hand. Guys our age are looking for a bit more than that, you know what I mean."

"What about you, Christina? You talk a lot about your sister. How was it for you with boys growing up?" asks Mike.

Claire finally has her chance to tell the story of her little sister, "Let me tell you about my little sister," she begins, "Christina has always been able to have any guy she wants, but she isn't interested in just any guy. She is saving herself for the right guy. Christina plays the game well, and all the boys know she is a 'tease,' but that doesn't stop them from trying to be the one she will finally give it all to. She will kiss the boys she dates, but that is it. She only pretends to be a wild child, but she is really a nice girl at heart. No one is ever good enough for her. After a few dates, Christina will let the guy kiss her, and then she comes in here, jumps into bed with me, and says, 'We broke up; he's not the right guy,' and she moves on without a second thought. Maybe someday, sis, you'll find the right guy, but I doubt it. You're way too picky."

"I found the right guy Claire," Christina leans across Claire, "he's in your bedroom now," she kisses Mike.

What can Mike say? He never wanted to be Christina's first, and it genuinely was life or death. Mike is not the "right guy" for her; he is about to marry her sister. Despite all this, he is still flattered and enjoys hearing that she believes he is the right one, even if she is dead wrong.

He slowly shifts from the chair to the bed, positioning himself between the two sisters. He wraps one arm around each of them, and they snuggle into him. "I am so sorry for the way that we all met and for the awful things that you both had to do to survive," he says, his voice full of remorse, "Christina, you deserved so much better than me, and what has happened to you. I know the right guy is out there for you, and I know you will find him. I promise," he looks at Claire and continues, "I know this may sound strange, but I am glad we met in that Cage. If it weren't for that horrible place, I would never have had the chance to meet either of you, and I can't imagine my life without you now. It's amazing how sometimes good things can come out of terrible situations. I think that's what has happened to us. We were meant to be together," Mike looks at the two women and thinks, *Having them both in my arms feels so right, but it is so wrong. I can't have them both. What is wrong with me?*

Markus Delphy, Deputy Director of the Central Intelligence Agency:

Markus lands at John Glenn Columbus International Airport in Ohio. He has Agent Tom Webber tracking Mike and his new friends. Markus needs to speak to Mike before he calls Ricky for an update. So far, Mike has been unable to get a hold of Ricky; he has no idea Markus is the reason.

"Mike's in the suburbs of Columbus, Fodor. It appears his friends have a house there; it belongs to a William Barnes. I think that was the father of the two girls. They are all three there now," Agent Webber reports.

"Take me there. I need to talk to Mike alone," says Markus.

Fodor, Ohio, is roughly 20 minutes from the airport. Webber drives Markus directly to the Barnes House. Markus has him stop right in front; he steps out of the car and makes his way up the driveway. Mike and the girls are inside, having just entered the kitchen. Markus doesn't call or send a text to say he is coming; he just shows up. They all see him at the same time. There is a breakfast nook in the kitchen with a large window stretching from the floor to the ceiling, giving a complete view of the front of the house. The girl's mother used to watch them leave for school through this window. That's where Markus is, walking up the driveway. Mike thinks to himself, *What is he doing here? I didn't think I had to start making up stories about my life to the girls yet, but I guess today is the day. Alright, Mike, be ready to answer their questions. They're about to start.*

Christina asks the first question about the man she doesn't recognize walking up their driveway. "Who is that?" she says as she watches Markus approaching the house.

"That is a co-worker of mine. He is working in the area this week. I told him I was here but never said anything about him coming to the house," Mike explains as he watches Markus. He turns to Claire and Christina and says, "Ladies, I need to talk to him for just a few minutes."

Claire puts her hand on Mike's arm, a bit confused about Markus being at their house, "What is he doing here? Wait, how did he know where the house was? Did you give him the address?" she asks.

"All Good questions, honey. I don't have the answers, but I will get them, be right back," Mike kisses Claire on the cheek and walks outside to meet Markus. He wants to get to him before he gets to the door, trying to head off more questions from the girls and find out why he is there at the same time.

Mike jumps in and asks, "What brings you here Markus? I haven't been able to get a hold of Ricky, and I haven't heard Margaret on the line the last few days, so I wasn't aware that you were coming," he shakes the Deputy Director's hand with more force than a simple greeting.

"Mike, good to see you too. You're looking good after what you have been through. Based on that handshake, I'm guessing you are healing up nicely," says Markus.

"Are you the reason I can't get a hold of Ricky, Markus?" Mike gets straight to the point again.

"As usual Mike, no small talk with you, just right to business. Yes, I am the reason. That is why I am here and what I need to talk to you about," Markus says.

Claire and Christina watch from the breakfast nook as the two men greet each other. It looks friendly from where they are, so they head to the front door and walk out into the yard. As the girls get closer to the two men, Claire, with her hand outstretched, says, "Well hello, my name is Claire Barnes, and this is my sister Christina. Mike said you're his work friend. Welcome to our home."

"Yes honey, this is Markus Delphy. He works for the Government too. He is working in the area and wanted to see how we were all doing," Mike says.

The second Mike says his name, Christina is on her new iPhone, looking him up. Mike had his dad pick up Claire and Christina, both new iPhones from the Apple Store in Fashion Valley, while Christina was shopping their first night in San Diego. Christina is almost always on her phone; it never leaves her side. "Markus Delphy, Deputy Director of the Central Intelligence Agency," Christina reads out loud.

Markus is caught off guard at first, "Ah yes, ma'am," he regains his composure, "Mike works for the State Department in the IT Division. I'm here working on a project that I could use Mike's help with. Just a few questions, do you mind if I steal him away for a few minutes?" asks Markus.

Mike turns to Claire, puts his arm around her, grabs Christina by the hand, and starts walking them back to the house. "It's okay, honey. He needs to run a couple of things by me for this project. It should only take a few minutes, and then I will be right in," says Mike.

Christina walks inside with her head in her phone, already moving on to Kate Spade, looking for a new case for her phone. Claire stops in the doorway and turns to Markus, "Markus, it was so nice meeting you. Maybe you can join us for dinner? We are talking about going out tonight," says Claire.

"Thank you ma'am; nice to meet you too. I'm not sure I can make dinner, but thank you for the invitation. After Mike and I finish up here, I'll check to see how late we are working on this project," Markus says.

Claire replies, "I hope you don't have to work too late. It would be nice to get to know one of Mike's friends. Please feel free to come inside to talk if you two would like," Claire kisses Mike on the cheek and closes the front door.

Mike walks back to Markus, turns away from the house, and they both get down to business.

"Mike, you disobeyed a direct order from the Director. You almost got Ricky wrapped up in your bad decision. I know it's shitty, but Sheik Zubair Majeed has a CIA Golden Ticket, given to him directly from Gray. You know damn well what that means. He is a No-Go, Do Not Touch, Do Not Even Look At Him. Do you understand, Mike?" Markus says sternly.

A CIA Golden Ticket is a form of clemency granted to certain criminals. It is essentially a "get out of jail free card" that allows criminals to avoid punishment for their crimes. The Golden Ticket is typically granted to persons who have provided valuable information or assistance to the Central Intelligence Agency and is seen as a reward for their cooperation. It is also sometimes used to encourage wrongdoers to provide information or assistance in the future.

"Markus, I want you to take a look inside that house. Do you see those girls? Just think of thousands more, just like them, who have been brutally taken away from their peaceful lives and destroyed by Sheik Zubair Majeed. He will not survive, Markus, and it will be by my own hand. Anyone who attempts to stand in my way will deeply regret it. I must bring this to an end. I WILL bring this to an end," Mike states.

Markus knows Mike will start this exact conversation and is ready for it. He pulls out the big guns and reminds Mike of who he is, what he did, and why.

"Mike, you promised loyalty and allegiance to the Central Intelligence Agency, your Government, and this Nation. This is a direct order. As your friend, one of your closest friends, the person who saved you from prison, I am asking you. Mike, please, let this one go, at least for the time being. If you don't, you will not only ruin yourself, but Max and Ricky will follow you straight to the depths of Hell, and you know it."

Despite the fact that Mike, like the rest of us, has his imperfections, it is his shortcomings that have enabled him to excel in his chosen field. It can be challenging for Mike to control his temper and rage, yet he generally manages to keep them in check. Mike's capacity to take a life without hesitation or regret is a great advantage in his profession, but it is still a major flaw in his personality. This might be beneficial in his line of work, but it is still a major deficiency in his character. The most significant shortcoming is his insatiable bloodlust. If he wants you dead, you will die, more likely than not, by his own hand. The depths of darkness within him are rarely revealed, but it's a source of power for him, longing to be fed, and the Sheik will make a perfect meal.

"What could Gray possibly want from that piece of human waste anyway? I'm sure it's something political. I tell you what... I'm willing to make a deal with you. I'll get whatever Gray wants from that piece of shit on the condition that he opens the season on the Sheik to me afterward."

"I am not sure what he wants, but I think I can make that work. Please, don't do anything until after I talk to Gray. I will find out what he needs from the Sheik and get him to agree to what you want. But you have to give me time to do it, just a few days, maybe a week. Tell me we have a deal?"

"Deal, brother," Mike agrees, "Now, come out to dinner with us. I want to introduce you to my fiancé and her sister officially. There is so much more to tell you about those two."

"Fiancé? That's great Mike. I wanted to say yes when Claire asked, but I wasn't sure you would want me there after we talked. I knew it could have gone the other way, and I'm glad it didn't."

"Me too, Markus," he laughs and points at the car Markus arrived in. "Since it seems like we are having a little party tonight, we should invite old Tom to join us for a drink now and see if he wants to go to dinner with us."

"How quickly did you know he was on you?" asks Markus.

Mike looks at his boss and friend; with a smirk spreading across his face and says, "We were still inside the airport terminal about three steps off the plane, Markus. You didn't think you could tail me without me knowing, did you? You did come here to see Mike McHaskell, not Mike, that guy who really does work in IT, right?"

Markus gives Tom a friendly wave, indicating that he should come inside as the two men walk to the house arm in arm, chatting about the two women inside.

I Couldn't Have Done It:

Max and Ricky are still in Saudi Arabia, where the ruling authorities have made the decision to demolish the Sheik Juffali Hotel to protect the country's reputation. Before the demolition can take place, the team needs to conduct one final sweep of the premises. As Ricky explores the Cages in the garage, Max searches Shariek's office for any information he can find on Mike and the girls. The office has been ransacked, and it is clear that Shariek's assistant has done an impressive job of destroying whatever he could. But Max is no ordinary investigator, and he is determined to find whatever evidence remains.

After going through so many Cages that all seem to be exactly the same, Ricky finds himself inside Mike's Cage. It is different from the others, standing out almost as if it was on a stage. Ricky thinks, *Shariek must have set it up this way so he could film it better; that guy was one sick bastard,* he takes in the terrible smell that is present, not nearly as pungent as when Mike and the girls were there, but it is still repulsive. Ricky observes the mattress, the buckets, and the two puddles of blood, one from Terri and the other from Claire; it is a somber moment. He grabs the metal bars tightly, just as Mike had so many times, and looks out over all the other Cages. He pictures himself in the same situation, chained up like an animal. Ricky releases his grip on the bars and steps out of Mike's Cage just as Max returns to the garage.

Max takes a deep breath of the air, shakes his head in disbelief, and looks around the area before he says, "Dude, can you imagine?"

"No way Max! I couldn't have done it. I'm still surprised that the Boss is alive," Ricky says, "I would have tried to escape by killing as many of them as possible, even though I know they would have killed me before I could make it out. There's no way I would have stayed here, not in this, not for anyone."

"Mike was in here, in that Cage, for almost two months, man. I couldn't have done it either; that's why he's the Boss Ricky," Max says.

"If that's what it takes to be the Boss, I never want to be the Boss. Did you find anything in the 'Shit Stains' office?" Ricky asks.

"I found what was left of the girl's records, not much, though. Most of the information is scrambled, but Shariek had some paper records. I found some on Claire and Christina, but almost nothing on that Sammy person and zip on Terri. We will have access to everything as soon as the system is back online."

"The Boss is a smart guy, you know. I would never have thought of using Gray's political bullshit. Getting him to help the Sheik reopen the Network is pure genius," says Ricky.

"Ricky, that has to stay between us. Markus can never know what Mike is up to. I think he just might pull a Boy Scout and fuck things up. Then we will never get what we need from that sick database."

"You got it, Max. You know I won't say shit."

The two men talk as they hear the sounds of crews drilling into the foundation of the building. Knowing that the structure is due to be demolished the following morning, the workers are in a rush to complete the necessary preparations.

Max looks around, then at Ricky, and says, "Let's get the hell out of this place, Bro. This place is giving me the creeps."

Ricky nods in agreement, "Right there with you dude. Let's go."

Dinner and a Show:

"Ok, so where do you want to go tonight?" Mike asks the girls.

Mike, Claire, and Christina are trying to figure out where to take Markus and Tom for dinner. "It's like herding cats," Mike tells Markus, "getting these two women to agree on anything is not easy." The sisters, who grew up in the same house with the same two parents, were incredibly different.

"Let's go to Alibaba. I love that place. The guys will love it too, the food is good, and you get a lot," Christina suggests.

"NO!" Claire almost jumps out of her skin and down Christina's throat. She takes a breath, smiles, and says, "I mean, Christina, I would rather go somewhere else if that's okay with you. Not everything, food-wise, agrees with me these days."

Mike sees Claire is visibly and uncharacteristically emotional when Christina mentions Alibaba. She yelled at Christina and she never does that. Then her face looks as if she is nauseous, even just thinking of going to that place. Claire, being Claire, just shakes it off, makes an excuse, and continues as if nothing has happened. But it did; Mike saw it and is all too familiar with what it is; *Shit, Claire is having PTSD flashbacks*, he thinks; *who could blame her.*

"Oh, sorry, Claire. If that's not good for you, how about that Japanese place, you know, where they cook your food right in front of you? That place is awesome," Christina suggests.

"Good idea, Christina," Claire says, "That sounds perfect. I'll call them now to make a reservation. If we're all going, we'll take up most of the table and need one. Is that okay with you, Mike?"

"Absolutely, Claire. Anything you want. We can meet Markus and Tom there. Make sure you give us at least an hour when you make the reservation so we can all have time to get there." Mike walks Markus and Tom to the door. He tells them he will get the women there as close to an hour from now as he can but asks them to hold their reservation just in case they are late. He has gifts for the girls he wants to give them before they leave.

After the men head out, Mike asks the ladies to come to the living room. "I have something for each of you."

The sisters enter the living room, where he has placed two boxes on the table in front of the couch. The boxes are wrapped in a luxurious, shimmering white paper, with a pale pink bow for Christina and a pristine white bow for Claire. The girls sit on the couch, instinctively, each sitting with her box in front of her, eagerly awaiting what Mike has in store for them.

Claire looks at the boxes and says, "I love gifts Mike. How thoughtful."

Christina tares into hers without a word, almost ripping it in half. Mike watches and chuckles. Christina's excitement and happiness are contagious. Mike thinks, *I love that about her.*

"OMG! Awesome! I have always wanted an Apple Watch. Thanks Mike! Claire, look, the band is kind of pink. So cool," Christina has it on her wrist and is modeling it for Mike and Claire in seconds. "Very cool. Is this pink gold?" she asks.

"Yes, it's gold. I know you like pink Christina, so yours is made of rose gold. I hope you like it," Mike says.

Claire opens her gift in a much more demure manner. "Mike, this is very nice of you. I've never had an electronic watch like this before," she says as she closes the box and sets it back on the table.

"Honey, your favorite color is white, so your band is white ceramic. The watch case is platinum so that you can wear it with everything. At least that's what the girl who helped me said. I hope she was right," says Mike.

Claire hasn't used the new phone that Mike purchased for her. He set it up, but she hasn't touched it since she got it. In fact, Mike had to bring it on this trip, Claire forgot to put it in her purse, and he saw it on the counter when they left for the airport.

Christina is the exact opposite of Claire; she is crazy about technology. Mike got them both the same phone in different colors, which is the newest iPhone model, and it won't even be available to the public for another four months. Christina is aware of this, but she assumes it is because he is a Tech Guy for the government. She is constantly on that phone. He also bought her the latest MacBook Pro and now this custom Apple watch. Christina thinks Mike is rich because she knows these items are very expensive.

Claire carefully removes the watch from its box, running her fingers along the band. She looks up at Mike with a smile and says, "This was so thoughtful of you. Getting one for each of us that perfectly matches our individual styles is really something special. I will wear it tomorrow."

Mike wants them both to put these watches on and never take them off again, but he will be happy if he can just get Claire to wear hers tonight.

"Honey, let me put it on for you. You see, it has all kinds of features. Of course, you can tell the time, but it can do so much more. You can talk to it, send messages, and track your steps; it will even check your heart rate. If you hold it here, it can do an ECG for you. I made sure it was as pretty as you are," Mike says as he places the watch on Claire's wrist and kisses her.

"It is very pretty Mike. I had no idea a watch could do all that and look like this. I will wear it tonight; even though I have no idea how to use it, I'm not sure I can even figure out how to tell time on it. But, if that will make you happy, it will make me happy to wear it," Claire says to Mike.

Christina is already wearing her new watch and is connecting it to her phone and laptop. She knows it can be used with both and is thrilled to set it all up, understanding that it is a miniature version of her phone. She says, "This is so unbelievably awesome! Look at all these faces I have to choose from. It's so cool! I can even open my laptop with it. Thanks Mike! I absolutely love this thing! I will wear it everyday."

He has a reason for gifting Claire and Christina these specific watches. They aren't typical Apple watches, but rather CIA tracking devices made to look just like the regular ones. As long as they keep them on their wrists, Mike can keep track of their locations and vital signs. He can even listen in on their conversations, but he will only do that if he absolutely needs to. Mike already knows that Christina will only take it off to charge it; that was the easy part. The challenge will be convincing Claire to wear the watch every day. He will start working on that tomorrow; for now, she has it on.

Mike grabs Christina's arm to prevent her from dashing away to play with her watch and computer together and says, "Don't go yet; I have something else for both of you," He received a package from Dave Black today; Dave shipped it Express Overnight yesterday. He opens the envelope and takes out three black credit cards. After inspecting each card, he gives them out, "Christina, this is for you, Claire; this is yours, and this one is mine."

Christina looks at the Black Card, "Holy shit! Claire, it has my name on it! Mike, thank you so much," she says as she jumps on him and gives him a kiss. Not like a sister-in-law, by the way. Mike thinks, *I will have to stop that from happening again.*

Claire stares at the card he hands her, and she looks at him and says, "Mike, this card says Claire McHaskell. I am Claire Barnes."

"I know, but I hope not for long honey," Mike says, "I just figured since we talked about it and you said yes, I would start the ball rolling. Don't worry; no one will ask for your ID with that card."

"But Mike, I'm afraid we don't have the means for credit cards right now. You know I spoke with your friend Dave yesterday, and he told me that settling everything from probate will take some time. We can't keep relying on your funds. I'm sure paying for three people instead of just one has been a financial burden on you, even with your parents' assistance," Claire's voice is filled with concern.

"Claire, do you know what a Black Card means? Because I do, so let me tell you, It means Mike is freaking rich!" Christina turns to Mike and adds, "Claire has 'instructed me' to keep track of what I spend with your parents so we can pay them back as quickly as possible. I was pretty sure I saw your Dad pay for stuff with a Black Card, but he would never let me near the register when we checked out. Who's rich Mike, you or your parents?"

Mike laughs, and a broad smile crosses his face before sitting beside Claire, warping his arm around her and gently taking her hand. He looks into her eyes and says, "Honey, don't worry about money. I have enough for us, for all of us", he says, looking towards Christina. "I gave the cards to my parents. It's my money; thanks to them, I have enough for us all, including them. We can talk about all this later if you still want to. For now, please, just take the card."

"So, how much are we talking, Mike? Like, as much as, say, Ariana Grande level? Or are you more on the Musk level?" asks Christina.

"Christina! That is none of our business. Mike, thank you for the card. We will respectfully," Claire gives Christina the 'Claire look,' "use them. Once I get our finances in order, we will repay you all we owe. Now, let's go to dinner, please."

Mike turns and gestures for the ladies to make their way to the door. Feeling extremely uneasy and wanting to end the conversation, Claire proceeds past him and out the door. Once Christina is sure that Claire is out of earshot, she grabs Mike's arm, stops him quietly, and utters in his ear, "So?"

Mike whispers, "Closer to Musk," smiles, and winks.

Christina's eyes widen in disbelief as she softly exclaims, "Holy shit, that's Awesome! I'm dying to know how that happened, but I guess I'll have to wait until Claire stops freaking out." She leans in and kisses him again, this time like she very much means it.

During the entire drive to the restaurant, Christina keeps asking Mike if Markus is like Jason Bourne, a fictional character in the movies who is a CIA agent. Mike relishes the thought of Christina interrogating Markus all night, so he eggs her on. Telling her, "Christina, when we arrive at the restaurant, I think you should ask Markus as many questions as you can think of so that we can all learn as much as possible about him."

Online Again:

"We are online!" announces Max. He and Ricky are back at the U.S. Embassy in Jeddah. Max calls Margaret as soon as Sheik Zubair Majeed reactivates the Network. Using Shariek's laptop they found in his office during the cleanup, Max can download all the information Mike needs.

"Margaret, I am going to send you a Target Package. Can you please prepare all the relevant Intel for Mike?" asks Max.

A CIA Target Package is comprehensive intelligence that helps an agent successfully carry out a Mission. It is a plan designed to minimize attention to the Mission and maximize the odds of completing the task at hand completely undetected. The Package also includes aliases with backgrounds and cover stories, transportation, communications and surveillance tools, weapons, and an exit strategy. The ultimate goal of the Target Package is to provide everything an Agent may need to carry out the Mission. Up to and including a kill. All without being caught or even raising suspicion among those around the operative or the target.

"Of course, I will start working on it right away," says Margaret.

"Sending it over now, and Margaret, this is for your eyes only. Markus and Al are out of the loop on this one; you okay with that?" asks Max.

Margaret says, "What Target Package? Max, you send me whatever Mike needs. And boys, you come home safe."

Margaret is Mike's assigned CIA Secretary. Mike is not her only assignment. He is, however, always her first priority, helping him in any way she can.

Margaret is Lead Secretary for the CIA. She assigns and oversees all CIA Secretaries to Agents and other Office Personnel as she sees fit. Margaret is not the Director's nor the Deputy Director's Secretary. She has someone else assigned to each of them. The Director still calls on her for almost everything, and so does Markus. But Mike is her primary concern. She reassigns most things the Director and Markus call her about to their secretaries. Margaret only personally handles things that have top priority or concern Mike. The other two men have no idea she does this. If someone were to take a closer look into operations, they would soon discover that nothing takes place without Margaret's knowledge. However, the same cannot be said for the Director.

She loves Mike like a son. She will do anything for him, and she has. Things that would end her career if anyone ever became aware. That is why going against the Director on this one doesn't take a second thought from her. Margaret knows Gray is on the wrong side of history this time, and Mike needs to fix it.

Max hangs up with Margaret and turns toward Ricky, "We have two people in Jeddah that we need to see; let's get rolling."

Soto Steakhouse:

The Soto Steakhouse is small and cramped, not Mike's kind of place. It's hard to have an exit plan in a place like this, but the girls wanted to have dinner here, so he went with it. He likes the atmosphere; it is lively and inviting and has cool Japanese decor. A grand koi pond is situated at the entrance, with a waterfall pouring into it on one side and a small stream flowing out of it on the other, then leading into the restaurant. It is a traditional Japanese restaurant with light bamboo floors and pale green Tatami Mats at very low set light bamboo tables, with golden bamboo and white Shoji Screens around them. Behind the tables, recessed areas provide the perfect space for an Itamae to stand and cook while simultaneously giving a captivating show to their audience. In the middle of the restaurant is an artificial blossoming Cherry Tree with branches reaching across the ceiling.

The restaurant offers a wide selection of Japanese cuisine, from tempura to noodles and Sushi. The Sushi Bar runs along the entire back wall, with at least sixteen stools. The enormous saltwater aquarium at the Sushi Bar is filled with a dazzling array of vibrant, exotic fish. As you dine at the Sushi Bar, you can enjoy the mesmerizing sight of the fish swimming beneath you while you savor your meal on top of the tank. Meandering through the restaurant, between all the different sections, are streams of water originating from the pond with its population of Koi in the front of the restaurant, complete with bridges to access all the different areas.

The staff at the restaurant is dressed in the traditional Japanese style, with the women wearing vibrant and beautiful kimonos in various colors and the men wearing the emerald green Samue and a black Maekake, both of which feature the restaurant's logo elegantly embroidered on them.

As they are seated at the table, the hostess asks each one if they would like a menu in English or Japanese. Mike and Markus both ask for one in Japanese to impress the ladies. Mike makes sure to have Claire on one side of him and Christina on the other next to Markus; he knows Christina is eager to start asking Markus all her questions.

Christina gets right to work finding out all she can about Markus. She doesn't even look at the menu. She asks Mike to order for her, turns to Markus, and begins her questions. She leans over and whispers, "Mr. CIA man, I am dying to know more about you," Christina stops whispering, "Do you fly your own plane or do you use different names? Or do you fly in private jets like James Bond? Do you have to go all over the world to bad places? Like, do you go to Russia or China? And...oh, oh, do you have to" whispering again "kill people?" Christina continues in a normal tone, "Just bad people, or do you have to kill good and bad people sometimes? Do you have crazy, super-secret weapons no one has ever seen? Do you have any of those with you now?" Christina is rapid-firing questions at Markus.

Mike and Tom love every second of this, laughing under their breath with each query. Mike is the Jason Bourne character here, all three men know that, but Mike and Tom will never help Markus out of this; it was too much fun for them to watch. Markus can't get a word in, even if he wants to. Christina never gives him a chance to answer, not even one question.

Claire tries to reign in her sister, "Christina, why don't you give Markus a break?" she asks, "He just wants to have dinner with us tonight. I'm sure he doesn't want to talk about his job."

"Thank you, Claire. Christina, those are all good questions. But sadly, I have a boring job. I work in a regular old office. The only exciting thing for me is when the clock hits five, and it's time to go home. I'm sorry to disappoint you. But I am more like the guy Jason Bourne walks past and ignores as he walks into his Boss's office," Markus remarks.

"Ahh, that's ok. I guess you all can't be like Jason Bourne. But hey, do you know him?" asks Christina.

Claire has no idea how to get her little sister to stop asking such silly questions, then the Chef shows up with the food, and Claire says, "Thank you, God. He's here to cook the food. Christina, please leave the man alone, and let's enjoy the show."

The Japanese Chef begins his demonstration, and Christina is enthralled, smiling ear to ear as he expertly tosses his knives and spatula around. Mike, however, is not watching the Chef; he is staring at Claire. He notices that Claire is flinching each time the knife or spatula makes contact with the metal. In a gesture of reassurance, he reaches for her hand and gently gives it a squeeze. Claire looks up at him and gives him a grateful smile. Mike thinks to himself, *She needed that. I am glad I am here for her.* The Chef puts on a terrific show, executing every move with finesse. He makes an Onion volcano, tosses a shrimp into his hat, and even shapes the rice into a heart that appears to be beating as he slides his spatula underneath it.

Mike looks at the girls; *It's nice to see them smiling.*

After the Chef serves each guest at the table, he finishes with a joke, "If you enjoyed the show, please come back again; I'll be here all week," They all laugh and applaud.

They begin to eat the masterpiece the Chef has just presented them with, and the food tastes as good as it looks. Mike needs to call Max; he thinks this is a good time to excuse himself. The girls are wearing their new watches, and Mike has done a visual sweep of the restaurant, so he knows the girls will be safe with Markus and Tom, safe enough for him to take a few minutes away anyway. "I will be right back; I'm just going to run to the restroom," he says as he leaves the table to call Max and get an update.

Markus can't help but notice how Christina looks at Mike. She follows his every move with her huge blue eyes, never blinking until he is well out of sight. Markus thinks, *Christina looks like a lost puppy searching for her master. I wondered if Mike knows she is in love with him.* Markus can see Claire loves Mike; that is obvious, and Claire freely shows how she feels. But Christina has got it bad for Mike. She is head over heels for the guy.

Tom leans over to Markus and whispers, "Do you think he knows?"

Markus replies, "I don't think he has any idea. I wish it were just my imagination, but if you saw it too...this could be bad Tom."

Mike makes his way past the restrooms and, after ensuring that no one has noticed him, he quickly exits the restaurant and calls Max.

"Go for Max."

"Where are we?" Mike gets right to the point.

Max reports, "The Network is up and running, and I have forwarded all the necessary details to Margaret. You can expect to receive the first Target Package in the morning."

"Good work Max, and our friends in Saudi?" Mike asks.

"Ricky and I will have them ready for you when you get here," Max says.

"Good, I will leave in the morning. I just need to set Claire and Christina up with security until I get back," Mike continues, "I can't run that request through Markus. Can you get me four agents here in Columbus?"

"Already done, Bro; they will be on the girls before you leave in the morning. Alvarez will be there also," Max informs Mike.

"Elena Alvarez? Huh, how does she look?" Mike says with a smile creeping across his face.

"Fucking hot man, fucking hot," Max has the same smile.

Mike catches himself, *What the hell Mike? You're engaged!* "Perfect Max, thanks. See you soon." He ends the call and returns to the restaurant. He slides into his seat at the table and cleans his plate. After everyone has eaten their fill, including dessert, the girls begin to feel the effects of the food coma. Christina feels it more than the others, probably because she ate three of the desserts brought to the table since no one else wanted them.

The night begins to wind down, and Mike knows he has to take a moment to speak with Markus in private. He is using Markus to keep Gray from discovering his true intentions, but Mike also considers him a friend and wants him to be at their wedding. On the way into the restaurant, Mike informed Claire that he would take Markus aside and ask him to be a part of their special day. After Tom says he will get the car, Claire heads to the restroom with Christina in tow and gives Mike a knowing wink, signaling he has enough time to talk to Markus.

Mike and Markus step out into the open air to await Tom and the girls. When they are alone, Mike pokes a little fun, "Markus, I'm glad you're here, even though you came without warning and attempted to have me followed. We have been friends for a long time, and I would be honored if you would stand with me at my wedding. Think you could show up for that?"

"Mike, again, sorry about having you tailed; I was trying to keep you out of trouble. You have more than just yourself to think about now. And, Yes, Of course, I would be honored to stand up for you and Claire; when is it?" asks Markus

Mike unsure, says, "In two weeks, I think, I hope. I proposed, and Claire said yes. But she wants some Grand Gesture thing before she picks a date. I have to figure out what that is, but the wedding is happening as soon as I do!"

"Mike, you know I think of you like a brother. So, I say this out of concern, nothing else; remember that. I'm not sure you can see this because you are so close to it, but Christina, Mike, she is in love with you, man. I mean, head over heels, she would defend you and say you were hungry if you started eating people kind of love. You have to do something before it causes a problem between two sisters; that could be bad," Markus tells him.

"I know. I see it, Markus, but she's young; she will get over me. Truth be told, and you're the only one, except my dad, I have told this to, but I love her too. It's crazy. I love Claire completely. I want her to be my wife, and she's having my baby. So that is what's going to happen. Christina will get over me when she goes to school or meets some guy her age. I just have to move her along on that path, and I will, as soon as I figure out this Grand Gesture thing, and marry Claire," Mike says.

"I'm glad you see it; even better, you have a plan. I'm a little worried about you having feelings for Christina, though. Use your training, stuff that down as far as you can, then move ahead with your life with Claire. I am happy you found her, messed up as it is how you found her, but I am still glad you found her. Let me know when she picks a date, and I will be there."

Markus's attitude shifts from that of a friend to that of a Commanding Superior. He stares Mike directly in the eyes and says, "Pay attention to me now. I am confident I can get Gray to sign on, but it may take a little while. I'm meeting with him tomorrow afternoon and will begin the process. You know I have to handle him carefully and make him believe the idea is his own."

"Ok, Markus, I will give you the time you need; just know the clock is ticking," Mike shakes Markus's hand, this time more firm than the first time of the day, "The clock is ticking."

The girls come out of the restaurant, say their goodbyes to Markus, and wave to Tom inside the car as Markus gets in. The men drive away, headed to the airport and back to D.C. Mike and the girls head back to the Barnes house.

Mike and Claire make themselves comfortable in Claire's room, a space that has never been inhabited by a boy before. But now, there is a man, a strong and handsome man, who is all hers. A man that Claire is snuggled up next to—a man who has every intention of remaining with her for the rest of their lives. Claire is pleased with the idea and soon drifts off to sleep, feeling a peacefulness she has never experienced before, enveloped in Mike's embrace.

Christina stays in her parents' room, feeling the emptiness that comes with their absence. She can still smell them in the room, bringing comfort to her. But Christina has a secret she is struggling to come to terms with and isn't sure what to do. She thinks that maybe if she sleeps in their room, she can feel what her mother will tell her to do. Christina doesn't want anything to disrupt Claire's happiness, and this secret just might.

Mrs. Claire McHaskell:

Claire and Mike lay in bed the following morning. Claire usually rises early, but she wants to stay with her love as long as she can this morning. She is holding the black credit card Mike gave her while he is reading on his phone.

Mrs. Claire McHaskell...Mr. and Ms. Michael McHaskell. Hello, my name is Claire...Claire McHaskell, it is nice to meet you, Claire was practicing her new last name in her head, and then she let one slip out, "Mrs. Mike McHaskell," Claire says very quietly, but Mike hears it.

He quickly responds, "Is that an invitation, honey?"

"Yes, Mr. and Ms. McHaskell cordially invite you to a dinner party at their home Saturday evening," Claire says, playing along with Mike.

He accepts the invitation, puts his phone down, and rolls to Claire in half a second.

"Yes, I need a Reservation," Claire is still pretending and trying to ignore Mike, but as soon as Mike is on top of her, she thinks, *Oh my! Every time, that thing is a surprise, every time,* Claire continues, "Yes, a reservation for...Mr. and Mrs...Mc...Haskell," Claire's voice changes pitch and tone as Mike accepts the invitation.

Mike stops and says, "Ok, Mrs. McHaskell, how about focusing on the job at hand?"

"You're right, Mike; I think I will just stay Claire Barnes," Claire smiles at him and starts to laugh.

"Funny," he says with a frown on his face.

Claire takes charge and says, "Flip over Mr. McHaskell. Mrs. McHaskell sent out the invitation to this party; it's my party this time."

Afterward, both Mike and Claire doze off; about an hour later, Claire suddenly springs out of bed and runs to the bathroom. Morning sickness can strike her at any moment. Some days, she is fine, but other times it comes on suddenly with a vengeance at any time of day or night. Mike can also hear Christina in the additional bathroom; it sounds like she is dealing with food poisoning. This makes sense, *that kid only eats junk food, and she had cleared her plate, Claire's plate, Markus's plate, and three desserts at the restaurant, and then she had two bowls of ice cream when we got home,* he thinks.

Mike has to leave in just a few minutes; Margaret has booked him on the 10:23 am flight to Minneapolis. So he dresses, grabs his phone, and heads for the bathroom door.

"Honey, I was called into work. It's only for the day, but I might be home pretty late," Mike says through the bathroom door.

"Oh, that's too bad. I was hoping you would be here today. I have a Realtor coming over at three o'clock to list the house," says Claire.

"I am sorry babe, but I need to get going. Are you okay in there? Do you think you're going to be a while? I would like to kiss you before I leave," Mike inquires.

Claire replies, "You better go; It might be a while. I think this baby learned to do back flips, it might be fun for a baby, but it sure isn't fun for me. I will see you when you get back."

"Okay, honey, I should be back late tonight. If anything changes, I will call you. By the way, Christina might be sick from all the crap she ate last night. I heard her in the bathroom earlier, and she's still there. That second bowl of ice cream, with everything she put on it, might have been too much."

"Okay, you go to work; I will check on her if I ever make it out of here. Oh no, not again, goodbye Mike," Claire says as she flushes the toilet again.

The Hush Puppies were Excellent:

Simon Johnson, a 'Hunter', lives alone in his one-bedroom apartment in the Near North Community of North Minneapolis. The area is known for its great food and ethnic fair. Simon woke up late this morning, too late for breakfast. No problem, he will grab the pulled pork special at the Squealin' Pig, a local BBQ hotspot. Still in bed, Simon looks at his phone, checking for new messages and missed calls, but nothing. Next, he checks for work notifications, "Score! Finally, some freakin' orders!" he says, scanning the current orders available to fill. His stomach growls. Simon stops scrolling, quickly gets dressed and heads out to pick up food. It's still early for lunch at the Squealin' Pig, and Simon gets his order right away, but the only place to sit is outside in the sun. It's hot this time of year in Minneapolis, and he doesn't have time to wait for a better seat. Simon has orders to fill, so he heads back to his air-conditioned apartment.

When Simon arrives at his apartment, he is immediately taken aback by the sound of his radio playing outside his door. *What the hell?* he thinks, *I know I didn't leave my radio on.* Simon slowly opens the door with a sense of caution and looks around. Seeing nothing out of the ordinary, he steps inside, trying to reassure himself, *Dude, don't be so paranoid; why would anyone be in your place*? Little does he know that someone is waiting for his return, waiting for Simon from behind the door. As he steps inside, he is struck hard on the back of his head. Simon falls to the ground and catches a glimpse of the unknown assailant's shoes; they are big shoes belonging to a huge man.

This single man's apartment is dark and dank, the walls are painted a deep purple, and the faded black carpet has seen better days. An army-style green jacket hangs from a hook on the wall, and posters of military vehicles are plastered around the room, with a lava lamp casting an eerie glow. Dirty dishes and crumbs litter the floor, and four bean bag chairs with headsets on top huddle around a ninety-inch TV. Chinese food cartons, pizza boxes, candy wrappers, and beer bottles are scattered throughout, and the pungent smell of marijuana fills the air. Model cars and a broken skateboard are on the kitchen counter, and unopened mail is strewn across the dining room table. This is the home of a total loser, the whole place reeks of despair and hopelessness.

Simon stirs, slowly coming to consciousness, and realizes he is in deep trouble. His arms and legs are bound tightly to the chair he is sitting in, his mouth sealed shut with tape, and a rope tied around his neck, hanging from the ceiling, making him feel off-kilter. He is completely immobilized and helpless, with no idea what will happen next.

Simon slowly surveyed his surroundings, cautiously moving only his eyes. His chair is perched atop his dining room table, teetering backward and appearing very unsteady. As he attempts to make sense of the situation, he notices a large man engulfing his pulled pork BBQ sandwich. He recalls the big feet he saw when he fell to the ground and now feels a throbbing in his head.

"Good, you're awake, but I'd be careful if I were you; you might not want to move," As Simon slowly turns his head towards the man addressing him, he can feel the rope around his neck tighten. He quickly turns back, more cautiously this time. "As I said, I wouldn't advise moving if I were you.

Now, please allow me to introduce myself. My name is Mike, and I think it's time we have a chat. Before we begin, I must say that this barbecue is the best I have ever tasted, and the hush puppies were excellent!"

Simon can not reply, his only response being a muffled scream as the chair he sits on begins to shake. His entire body is trembling as he looks up at the massive figure before him, talking to him as if they were old friends, discussing some fucking barbecue? He screams again, his voice filled with fear and desperation, "What do you want from me?"

"So, Mr. Johnson, because I really can't understand you, I need you to nod or shake your head yes or no while we talk. Pretty simple, right? Do you think you can do that? Again, I would do it slowly, but I need you to answer YES or NO, got it?" says Mike.

Simon slowly nods his head yes, and the chair starts to move; he learns quickly, correcting the movement by lifting his head.

"Fantastic, let's begin!" Mike takes a folder from the table and opens it, revealing pictures of young women of various ages, from around four or five to their mid-twenties. The photos appear to have been taken in a shopping mall or department store.

"Simon, I hope you don't mind that I call you by your first name. Simon, do you recognize these photos?" Mike shows Simon some of the pictures.

Simon moves his head very slowly and tries to say through the tape, "NO."

"That's too bad; it seems we're not getting off to a very good start. Simon, here's the deal; listen carefully now. You answer my questions truthfully and tell me all you know. If you do, after I get the information I need, I will only call the Police, nothing else. They can untie you if you don't fall before they get here. You might get to live. A fair deal, don't ya think? That's not all. Of course, they will find all this evidence here, tying you directly to these crimes, so you will probably end up in prison for a long time. But you're a big guy, and you should be able to handle it. At least you won't be dead, right?" Mike says as he gives him just a little pat on the shoulder.

When Mike touches him, Simon's eyes widen to the size of saucers, and he lets out a small squeak. Taking a moment to steady himself, he eventually nods, confirming his understanding.

Mike smiles at him and says, "Excellent, I think we are making progress. Simon, you see the young ladies in these pictures. Do you recognize any of them?" Mike's voice takes on a dark, almost angry, sinister quality as he continues his interrogation.

Simon's body trembles with fear as he hesitantly nods in agreement. He tries his best to stay calm, but the fear in his eyes speaks volumes. With a deep breath, he gives a single yet definitive nod, and tries to speak, confirming his answer, "yes."

"You see, that is better. I am glad we are getting along so well. You know, I really love this sandwich. I can't get over how good it is," Mike takes the last bite of Simon's lunch, "Where I come from, we are known for our Mexican food. We don't have BBQ like this. I mean, we have a few good places, but this is, hands down, better than any of them. I need to get more acquainted with BBQ. You know Simon, I feel I can talk to you, I am not sure why, but I feel like we could have been friends. Do you know why I need to get to know BBQ better?" Inquires Mike.

Simon slowly shook his head. "No," he thinks, *Why is this guy talking to me about BBQ? What the hell is going on?*

Mike continues talking to Simon, "Of course you don't; I am sorry. It's because while I was waiting for you to come back here, I bought a big ranch in Texas. My fiancé told me I have to make a Grand Gesture before she sets a date for the wedding. Do you know what a Grand Gesture is? I hope this is what she is looking for. If not, I am out of ideas."

Simon is confused, *Who the hell was this guy? Why is he telling me about his life?* He slowly shakes his head, "No."

"I don't think any guy knows what she's asking for. Let's hope this new ranch is it. Anyway, thanks for talking it out with me; now, back to business. This woman, do you remember her?" Mike shows Simon a photo of a redhead with very light freckled skin; it is a picture of Terri.

Simon starts sobbing and mutters, "Yes, but please, I was only..."

Mike strikes the table with his fists, Simon's chair shakes, and he screams as the chair starts to wobble, and the rope around his neck tightens again.

"Again, just a Yes or No, please." Mike says, "Okay, so now that we established you remember her, I need to know who your 'Finder' was for her. Are your 'Finders' in your phone?"

Mike reaches out and snatches Simon's phone, which is secured with a fingerprint scanner. He holds Simon's hand tightly and places his right index finger on the phone's sensor. In an instant, the phone unlocked.

"Good, are your 'Finders' in your phone?" Mike asks again.

Simon nods, "Yes."

"Okay, so I see a few people in your contacts. Only 25? Wow Simon, you need to get out more," Mike scrolls through Simon's texts, but nothing is of any interest. Mike thumbs through the rest of Simon's phone and opens an App called Seeker10. There he finds images of hundreds of women, children, and men. There is a list of daily requests and a history tab. Mike searches Simon's history until he finds Terri's picture attached to messages between Simon and CB.

"I believe I have identified the special request you were searching for: red hair, freckles, and a slim build. Absolutely perfect!" -CB

"Location?" -Simon

"Mega Mall" -CB

"Awesome, stay on her; I will be right down." -Simon

Mike becomes increasingly agitated as he reads the messages between Simon and CB.

"Simon, who is CB? Is this your Finder? The Finder for this girl?"

Simon again nods, "Yes."

"Simon, is CB working for you today?"

"Yes," mumbles Simon, then he remembers to nod.

"And is CB at the Mega Mall in Minneapolis today?"

"Yes," nods Simon.

"Okay Simon, good. Now, last question. Tell me the truth Simon, did you use anyone else to 'Acquire' this woman?" asks Mike.

Simon shakes his head. "NO."

"That's it. We're all finished with questions; thank you, Simon. Now see, that wasn't too hard, was it?" Mike asks, "But I need one more thing from you. And I'm afraid it will hurt, but I can't see any other option. Try not to move, okay."

Mike opens the black bag that he has with him. Inside is a roll of duct tape, a container of salt, rope, a box cutter, and a custom bowie knife. Mike pulls out the knife, and before Simon can react, he cuts off Simon's index finger with one smooth motion. Simon screams in pain but tries to keep his balance. "Careful now, you almost fell. I know that sucked, but I need to open your phone again, so...well, I have to take it with me. You understand, don't you?" asks Mike.

Mike gathers his things and repacks his bag. He again looks at the bag with the Squealin' Pig logo and says, "Great choice for a last meal," Simon's eyes fill with fear. Mike continues, "I mean, that was very good. Simon, thanks for Lunch. I got to go. I told my fiancé I would be home tonight, and I have one more stop to make before my flight."

Mike slowly pivots his head to meet Simon's gaze, and a wide grin spreads across his face as he gives his 'new friend' a hearty slap on the shoulder. The chair beneath Simon suddenly slides off the table, and Simon is crossed off of Mike's list.

The Very Least He Can Do:

Sergeant Harrison arrives at work a bit late today. He is just two weeks from retirement and in no hurry. Harrison took this 'Cush' job as Minneapolis Police Department Annex Managing Officer for the Mega Mall a year ago. Harrison intends to spend his last few days the same as he has each day of the last year, sitting on his ass. Leaving Mall Security to do all the "heavy lifting." Harrison sits in his chair and opens his lunch bag. "Awesome! Today I have a Cinnabon and a Twinkie for dessert." Harrison does the least, the very least, he can do and still get a paycheck. If the phone rings, he sends out anyone other than himself. Today they are short-staffed, but Harrison is prepared. He will push off any calls he receives until tomorrow. That's his best-laid plan, anyway.

Mike needs to find CB. He pulls out Simon's phone and uses his finger, which he brought along with him, to open the phone. He then opens the Seeker10 App. THE NEW MESSAGE tab is highlighted. Mike clicks on the tab. *Hey, look at this one. I think she is what you are looking for - CB.* Mike sees a photo of a young girl that can't be more than 16. The girl is in line in the food court at Moose Coffee. The timestamp was five minutes ago.

Mike surveys the area, looking for the food court. He walks towards the coffee shop, observing the people in the vicinity. Some are sitting at tables, talking, eating, and many are lining up to place their orders. Mike is determined to find the young girl he is looking for. After a few moments of searching, he finally spots her, sitting with four other girls around a table, drinking coffee, laughing, talking, and showing each other pictures and videos on their phones. Now for CB, *Where are you, you fucker?* Mike whispers to himself. He sends a message, asking if the girl is still at the Mall. He looks around and hears a 'ding' nearby. He notices a few kids making a 'TIC TOK' video, a woman with a baby in a stroller, and a Janitor mopping up a spilled soda.

The fucking Janitor, Mike mumbles, just as a reply dings on his phone. *What? How did he*? Mike looks down at his phone. *YES, I AM LOOKING AT HER NOW,* he looks back to the Janitor, who is still mopping.

Ok, so it's not him, Mike sends one more reply. *I am on my way; keep her in sight.*

'Ding'…. It's the lady with a baby. "You have to be fucking kidding me," Mike says.

"Mike?…Mike? Is that you?" Mike hears a familiar voice coming from behind him. He turns around to see Terri with an older man; she is smiling and walking toward him.

"I knew that was you; what are you doing here?" asks Terri.

Mike is shocked to see her and says, "Terri, it's good to see you. You look great."

Terri hugs Mike and returns to her question, "I thought you were in California. What are you doing in Minnesota?"

"I was in California. I'm just here doing some work at the capital in Saint Paul. The State Department sent me there for a day. I finished early and wanted to see this place. When they say Mega, they mean Mega," Mike says, "I didn't think you would ever come here again?"

"I didn't want to. Oh, sorry Mike, this is my Father, Dale," says Terri

"Mike, my daughter has told us all about you; you're the reason she is alive. Her mother and I owe you a debt of gratitude we can never repay. Thank you for bringing my baby home." Dale shakes Mike's hand, pulls him in, and hugs him. *Minnesota Nice,* Mike thinks.

"It wasn't just me; your daughter was amazing during everything. We worked hard as a team to get out of that place, Dale. I am so glad Terri got home safe to you; she's a great girl," says Mike.

"My dad is the reason I am here. He doesn't want me to be scared of the world, you know, after how we met and all. He thought it would be good for me to face my fears head-on, I agreed, and here we are. I will never come here alone, that is for sure. I probably won't go many places alone ever again," Terri says.

"I don't blame you. Your father is right; you shouldn't live in fear, but the world is not a very safe place. We know that firsthand. I'm glad to see you are taking control of your life and moving forward," While Mike is talking to Terri, He keeps one eye on the woman with the baby. They haven't moved, but the young girl and her friends look like they are getting ready to leave their table. The 'Finder', CB, takes notice as they gather their things.

"Terri, I'm so glad I got to see you. Crazy, we are both here today, at the same time and place, but I need to get going; I have a plane to catch," Mike says as he tries to walk away.

Terri grabs his arm and says, "Wait, Mike, how are Claire and Christina? Claire told me you asked her to marry you. That's terrific."

"I did, and she said yes. But she is looking for a Grand Gesture, whatever that means, before she picks a date. Any ideas what she means?" asks Mike.

"I haven't got a clue Mike," Terri answers, "Perhaps you should try asking Christina. They are so close I'm sure she has a good idea of what Claire wants."

Mike nods in agreement, with a smile widening across his face. Then looks back to the table of kids.

The girls and CB are on the move, and he needs to go now. Mike looks at his watch, gives Terri a quick hug, and says, "I will ask her; it was terrific seeing you again. I'm gonna be late for my flight," he quickly walks away but turns to say, "Maybe you could come to the wedding. I will have Claire call you," Then he quickly moves away in pursuit of CB.

With a heavy sigh, Sergeant Harrison grabs his radio in response to a call from one of the 'Mall Cop' Security Guards he has to deal with. His heart sinks when he hears that an abandoned baby has been found in the Children's Play Area. He is upset not for the baby but for himself. As per protocol, Harrison has to investigate the matter as a police officer. So he reluctantly leaves his Office, muttering under his breath the entire way. When Harrison finally arrives, three security guards are standing around a stroller, and one is speaking to the baby. Harrison knows he should have handed this off to the 'Mall Security Idiots', but protocol is protocol, so he has to answer the call himself.

"Sir, I was walking this area on my regular rounds and saw this baby sitting in the stroller alone. There wasn't anyone around her, so I stopped and watched until these guys got here. No one ever came for the kid. We've been looking but can't find the parents," reports one of the guards.

"Alright, I will take care of this," Harrison looks into the stroller, annoyed that now he has a baby to deal with. He sees a folder tucked behind the little girl. "What's that behind the kid?" he says.

"I don't know Sir, but we never touched the baby. We just stood guard and looked for the parents; everything is exactly how it was when we got here," says the guard.

Harrison removes a bulky file folder from behind the infant; it is tightly bound with a thick rubber band to ensure nothing slips out. He opens it to discover more than one hundred pictures of young girls from around the mall. On the photograph on the top of the stack, written in bold red ink, **"HEY GECKO 45 - DO YOUR FUCKING JOB!"**

The lifeless remains of Carly Bradford, or CB, is found 25 miles down the Mississippi River from the Mega Mall. Bloated and missing her head, her body has washed up on the shore of the North Mississippi National Wildlife Refuge, located downstream of St. Paul, Minnesota. When her pockets are searched, a note is discovered that reads, "Please, take better care of my daughter than I did of yours."

It Would be Faster if Christina Wasn't Here:

Mike didn't arrive back at the Barnes home until well after midnight. He is looking forward to getting some sleep; he has to be back on the road in the morning. But first, he needs to see his Claire. Mike is surprised that she is in the living room, curled up on the couch, half asleep, waiting for him.

Claire smiles at Mike the same way every time she sees him, with true love in her heart. "You're home late. Are you hungry? I can fix you something?" she says.

"You don't need to fix me anything; it's late, and seeing you is all I need," Mike continues, "How was your day, honey? Morning sickness last much longer after I left?"

"I was done with that about fifteen minutes later. Then I went on with my day. The Realtor says the house will sell fast. I want to get packed so we can go home as soon as possible. It would be faster if Christina wasn't here, but she is," Claire rarely says anything negative about her sister, but she is exhausted from packing, and her 'Baby Brain' takes over with that last statement.

Her words amuse Mike, and it makes him smile. Christina is a disruption, and there is no way around that; she is all-consuming. It's just who she is.

"So, how was your day Mike?" asks Claire.

"Fine, surprisingly... I saw Terri today; she looks good," Mike answers.

"You did? Where? I thought you were at work?" asks Claire.

Mike explained he wanted to see the Mega Mall, where Terri was "Acquired." Claire does not like the idea of Mike being there, making her stomach flip just hearing about it. Terri was stolen from that place, and it wasn't a safe place to be.

"I am glad you saw her and that she looks good. But Mike, I really don't want to hear about that place; it gives me the creeps. I can't believe Terri would ever want to go there again."

"It wasn't her idea; she was with her father. She was facing her fears head-on. I mean, good for her."

"Good for her, but I am exhausted. Mike, can we go to bed now and get some sleep, please?

"Of course, honey, let's go."

You Eat Like a Tiny Bird:

The following day Mike and Claire are in the midst of lovemaking when Mike abruptly stops.

"Honey, you're getting way too skinny," he says with concern, "Really, Claire, you're carrying our child and are more than two months along. Don't you think you should be gaining weight? Instead, you look even thinner than you did last week."

"Mike, we all lost weight in that Hellhole, and It's still early in my pregnancy, not to mention the morning sickness and the stress of moving. With all of that, how could anyone not be a little underweight?" Claire dismisses his concern.

"Or the fact you eat like a tiny bird. I'll tell you what, I have a project for Christina this week while I am gone. I will ask her to bring you burgers, fries, and pizza home. You know, her kind of 'food' that should fatten you up nicely."

"Ewww, yuk, Mike. I don't like greasy food, and right now, it doesn't like me at all. That would just make me sick, but I will try to eat healthier food, not what Christina eats."

"Good, because I can't wait to see what pregnant Claire's boobs will look like."

Claire holds up her breasts like they are in a push-up bra. "My ladies are fine just the way they are, Mike."

Mike smiles as he says, "Oh I know, but pregnant Claire will change those "C's" into at least D's."

Claire shakes her head, "Okay, fine. Now Mr. McHaskell, can we?... How did you put it?...get back to the task at hand, please?"

"Yes Ma'am, whatever you say, ma'am."

Mike has to get to the Airport. His flight to Germany leaves in a couple of hours. Before he goes, he needs to confirm that Christina will be on his 'Mission Team' to find Claire the perfect engagement ring.

Christina is excited to help him, "Mike, this will be so much fun. I know her taste, and you know I love to shop. Thanks for asking me to do it; I am so excited for you guys to get married. I need to grab my phone and order a ride; then, I can get you the perfect ring for her."

"I have another plan, and it includes a ride for you. My friend Elena is in town. She will be here soon to pick you up and take you shopping," he tells her.

"Who is this, Elena, Mike?" Looking at him with her eyebrows raised and both hands on her hips, Mike knows he better have a good explanation for this "friend" being a woman.

He says calmly, "Christina, relax. Elena is just an old friend, nothing like what you're imagining. Plus, Max has a thing for her. I told her about your 'Mission'; she's eager to lend a hand."

"Ok then, I'll go with her. Hey, I know you have bought me a lot already, but..."

"Get yourself something too. Whatever you want." Mike bends over to kiss Christina on the forehead; she has other ideas and quickly positions herself and gets a real kiss.

Christina runs off to get ready, "Thanks, Mike; I will get her something really special. Claire will love it!"

That kid, Mike says under his breath.

Jürgen and Lina Hoffmann:

Mike's next two 'Targets' are located in Trier, Germany. The city is known to be the oldest in the country, with its foundations laid by the Romans in the first century AD.

Before being 'Acquired' and spending the short remainder of her life in that 'Hellhole', Sammy was in Trier, Germany. Mike's latest mission involves an unlikely duo - Jürgen and Lina Hoffmann. While in Germany, Sammy and the Hoffmanns were 'friends', providing her a place to stay and being her club-mates. What Sammy didn't know, and Mike has since discovered, is that the Hoffmanns were part of Shariek's Network of Terror.

Mike steps into GHOST Nightclub in Trier, a popular Techno Disco converted from an old stone-lined cellar. The room is only 25 feet wide and 100 feet long, with three-foot-thick arches randomly placed and extending up to ten feet into the room, creating a labyrinthine atmosphere. Ten of these arches transform into small bars, from which a continuous stream of fog pours out from behind and above. The remaining arches are used as seating areas, with high tables and stools for patrons and a few VIP Areas featuring white leather couches and mirrored tables. The nightclub is beaming with pink and blue neon lights; some follow the arches, others on the ceiling, and still more on the walls, along with a maze of black lights. In the middle of GHOST is a thirty-foot section with no arches; this is where the DJ's stage and dance floor are. Four 6' tall platforms anchor the dance floor, each with a Cage on top and a scantily dressed person inside dancing. The DJ controls the music and the lights; a giant disco ball and lights cover every inch of the ceiling over the dance floor, all connecting to the DJ's computer. The DJ's music also includes an incredible light show that illuminates the entire Club and creates an atmosphere of excitement and energy.

The music is loud, with the Techno thump, and it is much too crowded. *I hate these places*, Mike thinks as he searches the crowd for his soon-to-be new friends.

"Hey, you're a handsome big boy. Do you want to dance with me?" asks a woman dressed in nothing but a neon mesh mini dress and knee-high boots.

Mike thanks the young woman but politely declines her offer; he is meeting with some "friends." Taking two steps away, Mike thinks to himself, *Holy Shit! She is naked!* Suddenly, the woman wraps her arms around him, pressing her body against his back and grabbing his manhood. Mike pulls her arms off, looks at her, still holding her by the arms, and repeats his refusal. He gently but firmly pushes her away as she speaks something to him in German. However, Mike is not interested in what she is saying as he has spotted his "new friends" at the bar behind him. "Bingo Fuckers," Mike exclaims, and he quickly makes his way over to them.

"Well hello, you are a beautiful man," says Lina Hoffmann as Mike brushes against her to make himself a space at the bar.

Lina Hoffmann is a tall, blond woman, standing at 5' 7", with piercing blue eyes and a slender physique. Mike can't help but think, *She's the perfect example of a Hitler Youth and a bit young to be in her line of work.*

"Thank you. You are magnificent, and I'm a lucky man to be so close to such a beautiful woman," Mike smiles at Lina and touches her arm.

Lina laps up his compliment, then puts one hand on Mike's arm and the other on her husband and introduces him, "This is my husband, Jürgen, but we don't get hung up on titles."

"Jürgen," he sticks out his hand, "I'm Mike."

Jürgen grasped Mike's hand, not shaking it but simply holding it. He examines Mike from head to toe as if he were a fabulous piece of meat, "You are a real mountain of a man, aren't you, Mike? I bet you have an enormous cock don't you?"

Fucking Germans, Mike thinks as he smiles and pulls his hand away, placing it on Lina's back, "Well, maybe you can find out. I am very interested in your wife" he looks Lina up and down, giving her the same treatment he had just received from Jürgen.

"That can be arranged. Lina, what do you think?" asked Jürgen.

"I am very interested, Jürgen; I think I need to see it," Lina gently caresses Mike starting at his thigh and working her way up his zipper. She pauses with her hand over his little soldier waking it to attention, and says, "Yes, very interested indeed." Then she makes her way to the button on his pants, sliding two fingers inside and pulling on his waist.

Mike takes her hand, looks her in the eyes, and says, "Then how about I get us a couple of drinks, and you can grab us a table? What will you have?"

"Himbeergeist, for me, Jürgen will have a Jägermeister," Lina kisses Mike on the cheek, and she and Jürgen walk to the table behind them that has just emptied.

"I will get us all a double; don't go anywhere," Mike turns and quietly says, *Fucking Dumbasses, they have no tastebuds*, before he orders their drinks.

The bartender hands Mike the glasses with a knowing wink, to which Mike responds with a broad smile. He discreetly drops a few pills into the drinks and stirs them with his finger before blowing the bartender a kiss. The man blushes, mouthing, *call me,* with his right hand held to his ear. Mike gives him another wink before heading off to the table with his 'special drinks' for Jürgen and Lina.

Lina says, "Thank you, Mike," and kisses him again as Mike hands them their drinks.

"Prost!" Mike says, Lina and Jürgen join him "Prost"

The new trio of friends knocks back their drinks with one swift gulp; now, Lina wants to dance! Mike, playing his part, takes them both by the hand, and they head to the dance floor. He is the meat in a Lina, Jürgen sandwich. The two degenerates are getting more and more handsy as time goes by. They are openly grabbing Mike and rubbing themselves all over his body, including his 'enormous cock' as they both keep exclaiming. He takes it, waiting for the drugs to kick in. Twenty long minutes later, Mike's 'Hell' ends.

"Whoo, buddy," Mike says, "I think you both had too much to drink. Maybe, I should take you two home?"

"Yes, take us home, Big Man, we are going to rock your wor…" Lina passes out mid-sentence, and Jürgen is right behind her. Mike thinks, *Finally, these Germans drink so much the drugs took way too long to work; I thought they were both gonna try to mount me on the dance floor.*

Mike carries his new friends out of the Nightclub. The crowd cheers as he slaps Lina's butt on the way out. "Go get 'em, tiger," says one of the women in the club. Mike turns and winks at the woman, then deposits his prey into his waiting car.

Love is Love:

Jürgen slowly opens his eyes, finding himself hanging upside down, his hands bound together. He is in a state of disorientation and confusion as he surveys his surroundings. It is a tunnel, and it seems to be very old. The walls are made of stones or bricks but are almost entirely covered in cobwebs and spiders. The flickering torches affixed to the walls create an eerie light that illuminates the sinister and hellish atmosphere. He could smell the dirty water, like a thick sludge laced with excrement, slowly moving beneath him. Turning his head, he sees the gorgeous Mountain of a Man with the delectable cock from GHOST, sitting on a chair to his right-hand side. For a moment, he thinks, *I must be on a crazed LSD-induced trip, but I don't remember taking anything.* However, as he begins to feel the pain from being suspended upside down, he realizes this is no LSD trip. This is real. He is actually hanging from his feet in an ancient sewer.

Panic sets in, and Jürgen yells, "What the fuck is going on here?"

Mike is surprised when he hears Jürgen's voice, having been seated there for a while and preoccupied with Lina's phone. But when Jürgen finally stirs, Mike is set to start interrogating the man.

"Finally! You're awake. I don't know what Doc Hansen has in those pills I gave you, but I guess it is pretty strong," Mike says, smiling, "You were out so long, I had to go get a chair."

"What is this place? Why am I hanging here? Upside down?" Jürgen cries out.

As Mike speaks, scrolling through Lina's phone without looking at Jürgen, he points out the remarkable feat of engineering in this old Roman sewer. "Think of the history here, Jürgen," he says, "The Romans built this place a thousand years ago, and it has withstood two World Wars and countless ground battles in your shit hole of a country; amazingly, it's still standing. Who knows, there could still be some Roman shit down here, literally!"

"What do you want from me?" asks Jürgen as he struggles to untie himself, but it's useless.

"First, Jürgen, why are there so many photos of your wife screwing other men?" asks Mike as he shoves Lina's phone toward Jürgen's face.

As Jürgen struggles, he begins twirling around, causing Mike to let out a stifled chuckle of amusement.

"We have an open marriage; she can see whomever she wants," yells Jürgen; his face begins to show signs he is getting dizzy and queasy.

Mike steps back to be safe, no need to add this guy's sludge to his shoes, and asks, "And you? Can you see whoever you want?"

"Yes, of course I can. Now tell me, Why are we here?" Jürgen exclaims.

"I am getting to that, but doesn't she get jealous? I mean, if you're screwing other women, or maybe men, doesn't she get upset about that?"

"You're American, right? We don't have the same victorian principles you have. Love is love; if we want more than one partner, we have more. There is no reason for there to be jealousy. You Americans only believe in monogamy; this is why your marriages do not work. Here our divorce rate is less than half of yours. Is that why I am here? What do you want from me?"

"Hmmm, that's certainly something to think about, Jürgen. You know, not too long ago, I would have taken your wife back to your place and had my way with her before I drugged you both. Needless to say, you wouldn't have been invited. But times have changed. I'm getting married soon, and I don't think my fiancée would be too happy if I were to provide your wife with the kind of satisfaction you can't. So, I guess we'll have to move on from here."

Mike takes a step back; on the ground next to him is Lina. Jürgen notices her body and that she is not moving. "What have you done to Lina?"

"I was beginning to think you would never notice. You have an extremely self-centered attitude for someone who claims to have such a strong marriage," Mike glances at his watch, "It took you seven minutes after you woke up to realize she was lying on the ground beside me. I don't think that will get you the title of Husband of the Year, even if you did allow her to fuck anyone she wanted. But anyway, she's dead; I guess the drugs were too strong for her," Mike says matter-of-factly, "You see, total rigger..." he gives Lina's stiff, lifeless body a kick.

Jürgen starts to scream, "Help!!!... Madman!!!... Murderer!!!... HELP!"

"Jürgen, my man, we are thirty feet below the surface. This tunnel runs for miles, and no one can hear you, so if you want to spend your last few moments on earth screaming, then be my guest. But I have other matters that we need to discuss," Mike takes out his knife and slices through the first one of the two ropes suspending Jürgen above the murky sludge. Jürgen's head plunges into the water, which is far deeper and more disgusting than it appears or smells. He manages to pull himself up as if he were doing a sit-up.

"Good, excellent, Jürgen. I hope you have been working out. Just try to keep your head above that water. Who knows what kind of diseases are running through that stuff," Mike starts rummaging through a folder, "here it is; this makes me sad," he pulls out a photo of Sammy.

Jürgen struggles to keep his head out of the sludge, "Help me; I am going to drown!"

"Yes, that's the idea, you're beginning to understand,...now, do you know this woman?" Mike shows Jürgen the picture of Sammy.

Jürgen decides not to answer; he struggles to keep his head above the water, and this *bastard American is going to let him drown*.

"Okay, so you need some help then?" Mike stands over the man just as he has done to many other men before and punches Jürgen in the stomach.

Jürgen suddenly finds himself plummeting back into the murky sludge, unable to keep himself above it. Mike reacted slowly, grabbing hold of him and lifting him out of the water, giving Jürgen enough time under the water to understand the situation. Mike needs answers, and Jürgen must start talking.

"Jürgen, once more, do you recognize this woman?" Mike is now holding him up out of the water with his right hand, and in his left, the photographs of Sammy are directly in front of Jürgen's face. Mike's gaze is intense, and he is awaiting Jürgen's response.

"Yes, her name is Sammy," Jürgen yells through the pain and gasps for air.

"Correction! Her name was Sammy, Jürgen; she is dead."

"Yes, I know. Well, I knew her. Sammy's friend visited us a few weeks ago to tell us what happened to her," Jürgen is struggling to breathe and having a tough time talking. Still, he wants to live, and he thinks telling this madman what he wants to know might save his life.

"Yes, I know she did; she's a nice girl. She wanted to make sure you knew what happened to your friend. Let's get back to your first question. Sammy is why you are here and also why you are going to die tonight," Mike releases Jürgen forcing him to hold himself up again. He splashes into the water, then back out again a few times. Jürgen can no longer hold himself up and sucks the filthy water into his lungs. Mike says, "I don't think you should get that shit in your mouth. You should try to stay out of that water."

Using all his might, Jürgen pulls up and holds himself out of the water long enough to beg for his life, "Why?" Jürgen asks, coughing and choking, "Why must I die? What did we do? Nothing! We had nothing to do with her death!"

Mike grabs Jürgen, holds him up, turns Lina's phone towards him, and shows him the App on the screen. Sucher10 (Seeker10), Registerkarte Geschichte (History Tab), there is a photo of Sammy, "This is why Jürgen, this is why."

Jürgen watches in horror as Mike goes through the App and finds Sammy; Mike knows everything. Jürgen and Lina are both 'Hunters' and 'Finders' in Sammy's capture. They are why she was 'Acquired' and ultimately died, in that Baby Mill and Mike knows all of this.

Mike releases his grip on Jürgen, standing by until the man can no longer remain above the sludge. Submerging his head in the water for the final time, Jürgen holds his breath for as long as he can. This time, however, he is too weak to pull himself out of the water far enough to take a breath. Inhaling the putrid sewer sludge, Jürgen's body begins to shake and convulse in agony. Mike watches as Jürgen's movements gradually weaken until they eventually cease. "Four down," Mike mutters to himself as he walks away.

A Woman Emerges:

Christina is having the absolute time of her life, shopping for Mike and Claire. She has carefully selected the perfect ring for Claire; not too big, not too small, with a 1.03-carat VVS1 Cushion-cut yellow diamond Halo Engagement Ring in platinum with a matching .34-carat infinity band. Mike has not asked her to get a band, but Christina thought the set would be something that Claire would have chosen for herself; if only for a few moments, she could forget about the cost. She tries on the set one more time before it is wrapped in the signature blue box. Though she secretly wishes the rings were for her, she reminds herself that Claire is Mike's fiancé, and she is not. Mike did tell her to get something for herself, so Christina points to her new rose gold apple watch and tells the clerk at Tiffany & Co., "I would like to see a bracelet and ring that will match my new watch," She is delighted with the 4mm Tiffany & Co. band she will wear on her right middle finger and the iconic Tiffany Heart Tag bracelet for her right wrist, both in rose gold. She is more than pleased with her purchases and is sure that Mike and Claire will be thrilled with her rings.

Mike assigns Agent Elena Alvarez to look after Christina while she is shopping. Mike and Elena have been friends for years. After spending the night together a couple of years ago, Elena thinks they can become something more. However, since that night, there is always a certain distance between them that Elena cannot bridge. She tries to get closer to Mike for a year but can never find a way. It feels like he might be seeing someone else, so she asks him if that is the case, but he denies it. The truth is Mike's true mistress is his job; he always puts it above everything else and is unwilling to choose between his career and a woman. Unfortunately for Elena, now that Mike is getting married and having a baby, it looks like they will remain just friends.

Elena is enjoying her shopping excursion with Christina and getting to know her better. She thinks, *Christina is a delightful, adorable, and stunning young lady, but she still dresses like a teenager. I think I can help her transform into an amazing woman.*

Many women in this world think they are attractive and work hard to demonstrate it to everyone. However, some women are confident in their beauty and do not feel the need to prove anything to anyone. Elena is a perfect example of this, radiating an air of assurance and composure. She is aware of her beauty and remarkable character, which is evident in her clothing, makeup, hair, and general attitude. She expects to be seen and treated in the same way she sees and treats herself, and she deserves nothing less.

"Christina, you are stunningly beautiful and have such an incredible figure, but your appearance is still quite young. With just a few tweaks, you can wrap any man you desire around your little finger. It won't take much effort. We can update your style and give you a makeover. Mike told me to get you whatever you want after you select Claire's ring. What do you think? Would you be interested in making a few changes?"

Christina responded with appreciation, "Thank you so much Elena. Do you honestly believe I can do that with just a makeover? Your style and appearance are absolutely stunning, and I would love it if you could help me to look more like you."

"Christina, sweetie, I am so excited to help you with your transformation. I'm sure that when we're done, Claire and Mike won't even recognize you. We'll leave the 'little sister' here, and you'll be returning home as an amazing woman. Let's begin with some new clothes and then head to a salon I know of nearby. I'll make an appointment while we shop, and don't worry about spending too much of Mike's money. He has more than enough, and I'm sure that when we're done, he will be absolutely stunned by the results."

Christina is determined to make an impression on Mike, and she thinks, *Maybe Elena is right; I've been wearing the same clothes since I was twelve. I'm an adult now, and I think it's time to start dressing and behaving like one.* She is eager to make a change and show Mike and Claire that she is capable of being mature and sophisticated.

The two women are on their way to Michael Koss to begin Christina's transformation into a stunning woman. They choose a fawn Marilyn large color-block Saffiano leather satchel and a coordinating soft pink large pebbled leather tri-fold wallet to replace the mini backpack she is using as her purse. After that, they move on to the basics of her new wardrobe. Elena selects a cerise crepe boyfriend blazer, a black bibbed knit one-shoulder cropped top, a black logo leather waist belt, and a pair of black Imani patent leather sandals to complete the look. The outfit was perfect on her, so Elena asked the salesgirl to wrap up the same outfit in navy with a white belt and shoes. Next, they picked a stretch crepe belted utility dress, a gold metallic stretch viscose tank dress, a fun turquoise logo jacquard tank dress, a midnight satin halter jumpsuit, and a merlot Georgette tie-neck romper. To add to her wardrobe, they also chose five pairs of denim boot cut jeans, Gwen black leather boots, linen belted shorts, pleated stretch crepe shorts, logo tee shirts, linen front tie shirts, one brown and one white Sasha T-strap sandal, and a cotton belted trench coat. This creates the perfect base for the wardrobe for Christina's transformation.

They popped into Kendra Scott for a few accessories. Nothing fancy, just something for every day that would match her growing rose gold collection, Mike started with her phone. They find an Elisa 14k rose gold open frame pendant necklace and Lee matching earrings with white diamonds.

Louis Vuitton was next for two pairs of My Monogram Cat Eye sunglasses, one in black and one in light pink, and just a few more. A pair of LV X YK painted dots jeans, a white ribbed knit crop top, a black Technical Gabardine blazer, black Territory Flat Ranger boots, and black flame platform ankle boots. Just to be sure she has enough clothes and will not need to wear those kid clothes again, jogging pants with matching tops, open ankle loungewear pants and matching pullovers, and a hand full of casual tops while they were there.

Elena and Christina end their shopping spree, for today, at Kate Spade for just a few more things. Both rustic brown and black Willow Wedge Booties, Leandra Loafers in blazer blue and black, and Lift Sneakers in optic white. Just before they check out, they see a great cardigan that is the perfect color for Christina and another that is made for Elena. They stumble upon a color-block phone case at the register that matches Christina's new MK bag and wallet.

Everything they buy is sent to the Valet Station and loaded into the car for them. Before heading to the Salon, the only thing left is Cosmetics and Fragrances at Neiman Marcus. They had just enough time for the lovely lady at the Chanel counter to match Christina's coloring and wrap up everything, including Christina's new timeless fragrance, Chanel No.5, quite the jump from The Body Shop Mango Body Mist she use to wear.

It is almost time for the appointment Elena made, and they will just barely make it on time. As they make their way to the Salon, the two women discuss Mike, Claire, and the baby. Elena is attempting to guide Christina in the right direction, helping her to find her own path. She is aware that the sisters have a strong bond, and the recent events have only reinforced it, but she also knows that Mike and Claire will need some time to grow their relationship. Christina's constant presence might make that more difficult. Elena is beginning to think of Christina as a younger sister and wants to do whatever she can to help her make the most of her life.

When they arrive at the Salon, Elena gives very precise instructions about how she wants Christina to look - wanting her to be the most beautiful woman anyone has ever seen. Initially, Christina is a bit apprehensive about all the attention she receives, but after a few moments, she settles down and begins to relax and enjoy her transformation—every detail of her look changes, from her hair and makeup to her outfit. When Christina steps out of the beauty salon, she is an entirely different person. She leaves her old self behind and is now the woman all other women aspire to be.

"My goodness, Christina, you are absolutely stunning!" Elena says in awe, her eyes traveling from head to toe. "If I were into women, I would be all over that!" she continues, unable to take her eyes off Christina's beauty. Elena is entirely mesmerized by the woman standing before her.

"Really?" Christina spins around, striking a pose as if walking the runway in Paris. Her movements are graceful, and her expression is one of pure joy and confidence. She feels like she is in a world created just for her. It is a moment she will never forget.

"Oh my God, yes honey, you are exquisite. I could tell you were an attractive girl before, but I had no idea you were concealing this remarkable woman," Elena says.

Christina is a stunningly beautiful woman, and as she and Elena stroll through the mall, heads turn to admire them both. She has always been able to attract boys' attention, but now, grown men are gazing at her with admiration. Christina is thrilled that all these people are not just looking at her companion but at her as well. She feels truly amazing.

Elena wants Christina to experience her new Superpower. "Let's go get some lunch; just follow my lead."

The two women step into Smith & Wollensky, and all eyes are upon them. Ahead of them, a couple is talking with the Hostess, "I'm afraid it will be about fifty minutes before I can get you a table. Would you like to wait?" the Hostess inquires. "We anticipated a wait, so that will be fine," they reply, sitting down to begin their fifty-minute sentence.

Hearing how long the wait will be, Christina turns to Elena, "I am starving and don't want to wait that long. Let's go somewhere else."

Elena grabs Christina's arm, spins her around to face the Hostess, and says in a confident voice, "Come on, gorgeous. We don't wait. Smile and ask for a table. I promise you will not be disappointed."

Christina is nervous; she knows there are no tables available. She just heard the Hostess tell the people before them that the wait was almost an hour.

"Good afternoon. Are you ladies here to join us for lunch?" asks the Hostess.

Christina smiles and does as Elena tells her, "Yes, my friend and I would like a table for two."

"Okay, there is a..." the Hostess is interrupted by her Manager.

"Welcome, ladies! I have a delightful table for two right by the window. If you will kindly follow me, I can show you to your seats right away," The Manager says with a smile.

Christina is absolutely stunned as she looks toward Elena, her eyes wide with disbelief.

"We don't wait," Elena says again. She smiles, takes Christina by the arm, and follows the man to their table.

Back to Saudi:

"Okay, Max, where too next?" Mike is ready for the next 'Target Package'.

Mike is overcome with a powerful desire to abandon his Mission and return home to Claire and Christina. He knows that his Mission must come first, but the thought of being with them is so intense. *Come on Man,* he thinks, *Finish the Mission, and then you can be with them. You can do this.* He is determined to fulfill his Mission and reunite with the two people he now cares for more than anyone else in the world.

Max and Ricky have Mike's next 'Targets' in their care.

"You have a midnight flight to Jeddah. This one will be easy," says Max, "Ricky has already softened them up for you, Bro."

"Good, make sure they are still alive when I get there. I need to look into their eyes as the life drains out of them."

"Of course, Bro; what do you have planned?" asks Max.

"This one is pure genius, Max. Ricky is going to enjoy it."

Mike steps onto the plane, feeling the weight of his beloved's absence like a heavy burden. He is almost paralyzed by the sheer amount of time that seems to pass as if seconds were being stretched into hours, then days. His heart aches for home, but a deep, dark hunger stirs, reminding him of its presence. His thoughts slowly return to reality, and he whispers, *Yes...Yes, more must pay...* He knows that he has to keep going, even though it feels like an eternity will pass before he is reunited with his beloved.

As soon as the plane touches down, Mike is out of his seat. His heart pounds intensely with exhilaration and anticipation. He has come to this place with one goal: to take revenge on the men who captured the love 's' of his life. His palms are trembling as he watches the other passengers disembark the plane, and with a less-than-polite "Please excuse me," Mike pushes his way off the aircraft. Max is waiting for him at the ramp, ready to help him with his 'Mission of Retribution'.

"Max, let's go," Mike rushes past him, never slowing down, hurrying his pace as he speeds through the Airport, almost sprinting as Max struggles to keep up. His strides are long and determined, not missing a single beat.

With Max trailing behind him, Mike manages to make it out of the Airport and into the U.S. Embassy limousine waiting for them. With urgency in his voice, Mike shouts to the driver, "Drive!" As soon as Max closes the door, the driver quickly sets off.

The Limousine speeds away towards the Embassy, and Mike can take a break for the next fifteen minutes. However, it is far from a relaxing experience. He is preoccupied with the men responsible for 'Acquiring' Claire and Christina and is eager to take revenge.

"Hey Max! How have you been, Max? Great to see you Max. Yes, I am getting married Max. Would you be my best man Max?" Max sarcastically carries on.

Mike glances across at his brother and can't help but chuckle. "I get it; sorry, brother. How are you, Max?"

"Good Bro, and you? Although I know how you are,"

"I am good, and yes, will you be my best man?"

"Of course I will. How are the girls?"

"Good, really good. This is so strange for me; I have such a strong urge to get back home to them that it's driving me crazy. I can't seem to get them out of my head."

"I figured Bro. At least we have a surprise for you. Not only did we get the 'Hunters', yes, two of them. But Ricky also located the 'Finder.'"

Mike declares confidently, "Awesome, Max! Are you certain that's everyone? Every single one of them has to be eliminated. If there's anyone else out there, I must come face-to-face with them."

"No one else so far. I did find the orders for all of the girls except for Claire. Maybe she was just with Christina, and they took her like a bonus? I don't know," says Max.

"So, who ordered Christina?" asks Mike.

"Shariek, that Fucker had her down to the size of her ass, man."

"Shit! I wish we could kill him again. I would take longer this time and make him suffer more for what he did" Mike can see they are drawing near the embassy, and his body starts to tense with anticipation. His heart begins to race, and his hands start to tremble.

Finally, the limousine pulls up to the U.S. Embassy. Mike jumps out of the car and runs inside, leaving Max behind. He shows his identification to the guards and rushes into the elevator, pressing the 'B' button impatiently. "Come on! Come on!" he growls as Max hurriedly follows him into the elevator.

"So, not going to wait for me then?" Max says, shaking his head at Mike.

As the elevator descends, Mike stares at the doors; his eyes turn black and void of emotion, as the darkness takes control. When the elevator doors open, Mike is transformed into a different person and marches directly toward the holding cells. Ricky is seated on top of a desk in front of one of the cells, holding three metal keys. He looks up as Mike approaches, and his expression matches Mike's. Cold, dark, and ominous.

"Which one is the 'Finder' Rick?" Mike asks, not looking anywhere but at the three men in the cells.

"The one on the left in the blue shirt," Ricky answers.

Unlike Max, Ricky understands what Mike is feeling. The same darkness flows through both men; no small talk is required. He does as the Boss asks.

"Open the door Rick!" Mike orders.

Ricky inserts the key into the lock and slowly twists it until they hear a 'click'. With unwavering determination, Mike grabs the door and throws it open. He rushes forward without hesitation; his hands clasp around the neck of the man in the blue shirt. Mike stares into the man's eyes and feels his life slowly draining away from him. Mike's darkness grows with each passing second, and his grip tightens as he yells, "LOOK AT ME! LOOK AT ME!" The man's body goes limp and hangs in Mike's hands like a rag doll. The other men in the cell are filled with terror and scream in fear, pushing themselves as far back into the corner of the cell as they can. Mike's grip does not relent, crushing flesh and bones until the man's neck eventually gives way.

"Okay Bro, okay, he's dead," Max tries to pull Mike off the man.

As Mike slowly lowers the dead body to the ground, "Leave me alone, Max!" Mike shouts, his voice rising with each word. His hands are shaking, his grip tightening until he can no longer continue, and they give out. He turns to the other occupants of the cell, their eyes wide with fear as they attempt to scramble through the bars that confine them.

The men see the Mike you never want to meet, the cold face of death looking right through them. "You two won't be getting off so easily," Mike speaks, his eyes never leaving the two men. "Ricky, is the chopper ready?"

Ricky answers, "Yes Boss, ready when you are."

Emotions and Food:

The Barnes house is in the final stages of packing. Claire, being Claire, never takes a break. This includes eating; the entire day goes by without a bite of food. Her emotions are all over the place tonight. One minute she is happy. The next, she finds herself crying hysterically.

While Christina is away from the house, Claire goes through her mother's jewelry, but nothing particularly stands out - that is, until she finds her great-grandmother's brooch. This piece of jewelry has been passed down through three generations to her birth mother, and her father had presented it to his second wife on their tenth wedding anniversary. Claire knows her mother always intended for her to be the fourth generation to possess the brooch. She will keep it close to her heart until she hopefully someday has the joy of passing it to her daughter, making it a five-generation heirloom.

Claire is almost done packing up the entire house, and her parent's bedroom is the last room she tackles. She carefully takes their clothes off the hangers. She puts them into boxes to donate to charity, ensuring they can help someone in need. As she is carefully folding one of his sports coats, she stumbles upon a letter tucked away in the pocket. Upon closer inspection, she realizes it is a letter from her birth mother to her father. She is drawn to the idea of reading the letter, yet she knows it would be inappropriate to do so. She respects her father's wishes and leaves the letter unopened, just as he had done. Claire intends to keep it this way.

The House is slowly but surely becoming more sparsely populated. The Moving Company has provided Pods, which are located on the driveway, to store all of the boxes and any furniture that Claire wishes to keep. Mike is determined to make sure that Claire does not lift or carry anything; he has hired men to assist with the moving process, and they are present all day, carefully and diligently taking the boxes out of the house as Claire packs them.

When Christina returns to the house, she is loaded with shopping bags from opulent stores like Louis Vuitton and Michael Kors, a departure from her usual haunts of Forever 21 and H&M. She has a few small blue boxes that she is keeping hidden from Claire, a surprise from Mike. As Christina enters the living room, she finds Claire sitting on the couch, browsing through family photos.

"Wow! Christina, you look amazing," Claire says as Christina walks in.

"Thank you. Elena is great; this was all her. She helped me pick out clothes and arranged a total makeover for me. Do you like it?"

"Christina, you look beautiful. Really, I almost can't believe you're the same girl who left here this morning."

"That's because I am a woman Claire, not just your baby sister."

Claire's eyes fill with tears as she realizes Christina is right; she is no longer a child but a grown woman.

"Oh, come on, I'm still Christina. But I'm really enjoying dressing like this, so there's no need to keep any of my old clothes, they're all going to Goodwill. This is the new me now," Christina declares, spreading her arms out to her sides, "Also, we had lunch at a nice restaurant. Oh, I have food for you, and you must 'eat it all.' Those are instructions from Mike. But we had the greatest lunch. Our table was by the window, and it seemed like every man who passed by stopped to look in at us. It was almost like we were in a movie! Old men, young men, men alone, men with someone else - they all stopped. To top it all off, the Manager came over and tore up our bill right in front of us. It was absolutely insane!"

Claire has been overwhelmed with emotion all day, and when she finally gets to hug her sister, she can't help but let out a flood of tears, "I love you so much," she sobs, "I just love you so much."

Christina shakes her head and says, "Okay, okay. Now, it's time for you to eat, mommy."

It's kind of Like Barbecue for Jeffery Dahmer:

The average temperature in the Rub' al-Khali desert in Saudi Arabia in August is an incredible 110.5°. However, today it is even hotter at 115°—the sand spiking at 145°. Mike orders the U.S. Navy Blackhawk Pilot, Capitan John Crawshaw, to drop his passengers approximately 100 kilometers into the sand dunes. Mike and Ricky took turns undressing and removing from the helicopter two Arab men. Both men are unceremoniously dropped from a height of 50'. This is done to ensure that their legs are broken upon impact. Then Mike and Ricky will land on top of the highest dune they can find to watch the men in the sand below.

The human body is remarkable, capable of withstanding some of the most extreme conditions on the planet as long as the necessary equipment and supplies are present. This includes shelter from the sun, food, and plenty of water. None of these are available for the two 'Hunters' except one water canteen. Mike and Ricky, on the other hand, are prepared. Ricky set up a shade tent; Mike brought two lounge chairs, five gallons of fresh water, and a cooler of ice. Ricky also brought snacks, so the two men could comfortably watch the 'Show'. Mike sends the Blackhawk back to base; he will radio when they need a ride back.

With a cooked egg in his canteen cup, Ricky treks up the dune towards Mike, who is waiting for him in the shade tent, "Boss, it really works!" he exclaims with a smile.

"Look. It cooked, no shit, it cooked," says Ricky. "look at this."

"Wow, I thought that was a myth; very cool Rick," answers Mike.

Mike and Ricky are keeping a close eye on the 'Hunters', roughly 500 yards away. Mike believes this is the most awful way to die, and if there were a worse one, it would be happening to the 'Hunters' at this very moment. The sun is beating down on the sand, which has been heated to an unbearable temperature of over 140° - more than enough to roast the 'Hunters' alive. Taking turns, Mike and Ricky use the scopes of their rifles to observe the men, who are gradually succumbing to the heat of the desert. Human skin cannot tolerate temperatures higher than 130°, and the 'Hunters' are well beyond that limit.

"Gees boss, that one on the right. His feet are coming apart; I think I see bone!" Ricky says.

Mike peers through his scope; his brow furrows in concentration. "I think you're right; it's fascinating that we can still hear them. I had assumed they would be much quieter by now, considering it's been almost eight hours and that one's tongue is the size of a dead fish in his mouth."

"What's even more unbelievable is that they still haven't gone for the water," says Ricky, "I guess the bacon on the canteen is like their Kryptonite."

At this moment, Mike hears the men shouting out to Allah, imploring for his permission to consume the unclean bacon water, but of course, there is no response.

"Ricky, $20 says you can't hit that canteen from here."

"$20? Shit, make it $50, Boss!"

"Okay, but a few rules. One shot and no range finder," says Mike.

"It's a bet; let's see the green," Ricky rubs his fingers together in anticipation.

Mike removes $50 from his wallet and places it in the sand in front of Ricky.

Ricky's laughter echoes throughout the air as he trains his sights on the canteen. The second most lethal assassin in the world steadies his breathing, inhaling deeply before slowly exhaling. His right thumb flicks the safety off, and his right index finger applies pressure to the trigger, gradually tightening his grip.

Ricky stops and turns towards Mike, "Boss, how did you do it?"

"What's that, Ricky?"

"Max and I, we were in that garage. I went into your Cage and looked out. I couldn't stay in there for more than five minutes, and it wasn't even locked. Boss, how did you make it out alive?"

"Ricky, I don't know. All I can say is that the girls saved my life. So many times I wanted to… I mean, Ricky, I almost gave up a few times. I wouldn't be here right now if it wasn't for Claire. That's how I know."

"How you know what, Boss?"

"That's how I know she is my soulmate, Rick. That's how I know I need her in my life for the rest of my life."

"That's cool Boss!" Ricky spins around, and without hesitation, he fires his rifle. The canteen flies up into the air, then Ricky takes another shot. This time, the bullet split the canteen in two, sending water flying in all directions, turning it into a fine mist in the air.

"Fuckin' showoff," says Mike.

"Nice doing business with you Boss!" Ricky picked up the fifty.

The 'Hunters' scream out in anger toward Mike and Ricky. Their blistered arms waved with clenched fists.

"Boss, it's been a long day; maybe we cut it short?" asks Ricky.

"Let's, give them a few more minutes. Hey, where did you get this fruit? It's delicious," asks Mike.

"Ya, it is; I went into town yesterday. You know Boss, Saudi is really upping their food game. All this stuff is grown here now. Look at these grapes and those oranges. Much better than ten years ago."

"Well, good for them."

Ricky peers through his scope at the 'Hunters' with a disgusted expression and says, "Yuck Boss! That guy's leg looks cooked like a piece of BBQ beef."

Mike says, "Hey, talking about BBQ, I am moving to Texas when I get back."

"Texas? Whereabouts, Boss?"

"Just north of Dallas, a place called Caddo Mills," Mike says, peering through his scope at the men in the sand.

"Cool; my uncle had a place near there when I was a kid. Small town Boss, really small."

"I know, Rick, that is why I'm moving there. I want to start a life there; I hope Claire wants more kids. Because I want a bunch, maybe five."

"That's Cool Boss; it's good to see you moving on with your life," says Ricky.

"Yep. Okay, let's end this; I want to go home," says Mike.

"I got the left.........." says Ricky.

"Okay, I got the right....." says Mike.

Two shots ring out..................

Best for Us Sir?:

Markus Delphy still hopes to obtain the Director's approval for Mike's plan. He is scheduled to meet with Director Gray to discuss Mike's proposal again.

"Markus, I don't know when I will need Sheik Majeed's assistance. It could be next week, next month, or next year. Unfortunately, what Mike is proposing is not a viable option. I apologize, Markus. I understand that Mike is eager to eliminate this person for what he has done. Still, the Sheik is too valuable for us to risk losing him."

"To us Sir? Or to you?" asks Markus.

"It is one and the same, Mr. Deputy Director," Gray utters definitively, making it abundantly clear to Markus that he is, in fact, Director Gray's employee and not the other way around.

"Yes Sir, did you know that Majeed has relaunched his database? This means that women around the world are once again vulnerable to the horror of being abducted and sold by him. We certainly don't want that to happen Sir," Markus says solemnly.

"I am aware Markus, and if Mike has his way, the system will be down permanently. But that is the price I am willing to pay for the information from the Sheik. It's worth it, Markus," explains Gray.

"Sir, I highly doubt that any of the parents of those girls will deem it to be worthwhile," Markus expresses.

The Director releases a heavy sigh, his expression one of anguish. "Markus, I know that one day you will have to make difficult decisions such as this one. It will weigh heavily on your conscience, and I'm sure you will be up all night, just like I am right now. I can assure you that this is not an easy decision, but the end justifies the means. Plus, the Sheik has agreed to close down all the Baby Mills in the Network, and we have teams working hard to take out the remainder of Shariek's men. We should look at this as a victory, Mike, should look at this as a victory."

"Yes Sir," Markus replies, "I will let him know."

Gray looks at Markus intently, his expression conveying the gravity of the situation, "I know this may be difficult for Mike to accept, but I am certain that this is the best choice for us," he declares with absolute certainty.

Two Dozen Roses:

Two days later, Mike arrives at the Barnes girls' home, his arms filled with two dozen roses and two heart-shaped boxes of chocolates. Inside one of the boxes is a key to their new ranch in Texas, which Mike has bought as a Grand Gesture to convince Claire to set a date. All he has to do is make sure he doesn't mix up the boxes. Taking a deep breath, Mike steps through the door, "Hey, I am back," he yells as he opens the front door.

Claire is almost finished packing, and the house seems mostly empty, apart from a few pieces of furniture and a few boxes. She spots Mike coming in and rushes to him, giving him a warm hug and a passionate kiss, "Hey sweetheart, I'm so glad you're back," she says with a smile.

"These are for you," Mike hands Claire one of the bouquets of roses and a box of chocolates, "Where is Christina?" he asks.

Claire places the bouquet of roses and the box of chocolates on the table and says, "She heard you drive up; she'll be right in. Christina has a surprise for you."

Christina walks down the hallway toward Mike. At first, he wonders who the girls have at the house. He doesn't think they have any friends over, *but who is walking down the hallway?* Suddenly he realizes.... *Oh my God, it's Christina.* Mike has a powerful surge of affection and fondness wash over him. Christina is not just beautiful but a radiant presence with an aura of elegance and grace that instantly captivates his soul. He is in awe and maybe in love. Mike can't take his eyes off her.

"Wow! Christina, you look incredible," Mike turns to Claire, "Claire, what happened to our little Christina? She turned into a woman while I was gone," He is still taking in every bit of this new Christina.

Christina can tell Mike likes what he sees, making her smile. Elena has taught her well during their short lesson, and she uses her new knowledge on him. "Thank you Mike," she tries to take the roses and the chocolates from Mike's hands, "Are these for me?"

"Ah…..Ah ya, yes, these are for you," Mike stumbles over his words, still in shock over the change. He looks down at his hands and lets Christina take the roses and chocolates, "I hope you like them," he says, standing in place, not knowing what to do next.

"Mike, you know how much I love junk food; I can't wait to try one," Christina opens the box and sees a key in the middle of the chocolates; she looks at him confused, "What is this?" she asks.

Mike finally snaps out of it and whispers, "Oh shit! Hey, give me that box," He grabs the box and rushes back to Claire, discovering the unopened chocolates on a table near where she is working. *Thank God. She hasn't opened it yet.* He tells himself, *you have to get your shit together. Claire is your fiancé! Christina looks great, but she is her sister, and you must get this Grand Gesture thing locked down.* He switches the boxes and tries to get Claire to stop working long enough to open them, "Claire, you haven't opened the box yet?" Mike asks.

"No, not yet; I am not very hungry, but I will Mike, thank you," Claire says.

With his head straight and the correct box in hand, he walks back to Christina. She is smiling at him and laughing a little too. She loves seeing him get all worked up over Claire; it is obvious how much he loves her sister.

Mike hands the correct box to Christina and says, "I'm sorry, I gave you the wrong box. I mean, you are getting a key also, but I hope this is the Grand Gesture Claire is looking for. I need her to stop what she is doing long enough to open it," he says quietly. Mike turned his attention back to Claire and her box. He picks up the box holding it out to Claire. "Open them Honey…"

Claire stops what she is doing and looks up at Mike, *Okay, what's up?* she says to herself. Christina is now behind Mike, smiling at Claire. *These two look guilty as sin. She* asks, "Okay you two, what's going on?"

"Honey, please just open it," Mike asks, wiggling the box toward Claire.

"Alright, I will open it," Claire takes the box from him and opens it, "What is this?" she removes the key and holds it up, dangling it in front of Mike and Christina.

"I bought us a house!" Mike says with excitement, "Not just a house, a home, a big ranch in Texas. I know I didn't ask you first, but I saw it and knew it was the place for us. It's where I want to raise our family; I hope you are okay with it. Please be okay with it; you're okay with it, right?"

"Hmm… Well, I like Texas. A ranch you say…Then I guess we are Ranchers," Claire throws her arms around Mike and kisses him.

Mike embraces Claire and then looks at Christina, saying, "We would be delighted if you decided to come with us to Texas. I'm sure Claire would be overjoyed to have you there with us, and I think it would be perfect to have us there altogether. What do you think? Would you be willing to come to Texas with us?"

"Texas? Well, I have never been to Texas. There are Cowboys in Texas, and I'm a big fan of Cowboys!" Christina already knows she will go with them, but it is fun to make Mike squirm, "I'm just messing with you, I go where Claire goes, and I bet she will love raising her kids on a big Texas Ranch!"

Mike embraces Christina and pulls her into the hug with Claire, "I'm sure you two will love the Ranch. I'm so excited to get there and begin our new life together," Mike looks over to Claire, his eyes twinkling with anticipation, "So, is this the Grand Gesture you were hoping for? Can we finally tie the knot now? Please?"

Claire smiles and pats Mike on the Chest, "No honey, it's not."

"No?" Mike is deflated and confused.

"Mike, it's wonderful. I truly love the idea of raising our family there. But it's not the gesture I am looking for," says Claire.

Mike throws his hands up in confusion and says, "Really, Claire? Really?" He is entirely perplexed, *What else can I do? What does she want?* Mike asks himself.

Christina sees Mike's frustration and Claire's unwillingness to tell him what she wants. She knows Claire wants Mike to figure this out on his own. That is not happening today, and they all need a break after Mike's failure.

"Ok, guys. Mike can figure it out later. Right now, I have something I want to ask you to do tonight. It's our last night in Columbus. My father always promised to take me dancing at the Supper Club after I turned 18, but he never had the chance. Before we leave, I would like to share one night there with you two, please," Christina looks at Mike. If he is on board, Claire should be too.

Mike is happy to have something to do other than figure out what Claire wants from him. He is able to deconstruct the most intricate, diabolical, evil madman's Network with ease. Still, he cannot for the life of him, figure out what Claire wants. At least he can give Christina this one thing her father could not, and he enthusiastically agrees, "I'm game, Claire?"

Claire says, "The two of you should go without me. Christina is already dressed and ready to go. If I go too, you will have to wait while I shower, get dressed, and get made up for a night out, and I am not very hungry."

"Mike, it's almost 7:00 pm, and Claire hasn't eaten anything all day. I have been keeping a close eye on her, so don't let her tell you otherwise," Christina says.

"What? Claire, you're going!" Mike insists, "I'm buying you the biggest steak they have, and you're going to eat the entire steak and all the fixing that come with it. After we eat, I will dance with my two best girls. Don't even try to say no. Just head down that hallway and get yourself ready; we're all going."

Claire tries to think of a way to stay home, but she sees the look in Mike's eyes. She cannot make any excuse that he would agree with; she is going. "Fine. I have to shower first. I'll be ready in a few minutes."

"Shower? Can I join? It's been a long week, you know," Mike never passes up an opportunity.

Claire grabs his hand and gives it a tug, urging him to come along. "Come on, stud," she says with a playful smile.

Christina laughs and says, "Don't take too long. I am starving, especially after hearing Mike talk about a big steak."

Mike looks back toward Christina, "You better grab yourself a snack; I'm hungry too," and winks.

After Mike and Claire close the door, Christina sits on a chair surrounded by boxes. She gently places her hand on her stomach and quietly says, *Hey little one, your Daddy is home. I guess we are moving to Texas. So, you're going to be born a Texan. I am sorry I haven't told them about you yet. But, I need your Aunt Claire to marry your Daddy first, then I promise I will tell them both. And don't worry; I will find you a great stepdad. Like I had, and if you're a boy, I will name you William after your grandfather.*

Mike hollars through the door of the bathroom, "Hey, Christina! Can you please bring us towels? Claire packed them in a box labeled, "Towels," whispers Claire, "Towels. Just open the door and throw them on the counter; we are jumping in the shower now. Thank you!"

Christina shouts back down the hall, "I will find them. You two have fun but be quick, don't forget I'm waiting for you, and I'm hungry."

Okay, little one, I need to help them, like always. I love you, my baby. I can't wait to meet you. Christina gets up and searches for the box marked Towels.

Ladies, Change of Plans:

Max has been grinding away for the past few days on Mike's project, yet he hasn't been able to open Claire's file. All the other files have successfully been opened, and Mike's file is printed out and sitting on Max's desk. The CIA initially planned to plant Mike into the Network so he could destroy from within. Mike was meant to be purchased by a wealthy widow in Sochi, Russia. But Shariek had other ideas and hijacked Mike, transferring him to the Baby Mill. The paperwork indicated almost everything, but the transfer itself was missing.

"That's it; Mike was hijacked. His transfer from the 'Hunters' to the 'Buyer' was changed at the intake center," says Max, "It must have happened after they took his blood sample. Shariek needed Mike for his Baby Mill, so he pulled him out of the stream before he could be transferred as originally planned."

Mike's file indicates he passed away during the 'Acquired' stage. After the Intake and Exam stage, he was re-added to the Network. Max employs the same criteria to try and locate Claire. He uses the same matrix, searching for her up to the 'Acquired' stage and again after the Intake and Exam stage. The same discrepancies are present.

Max yells out loud, "Holy Shit !" I was wrong. Claire was a Target."

Mike is loading the rental car for their final trip to the airport. The movers have packed everything, and the house is empty. They have the address and are on the road to a storage facility in Caddo Mills, Texas. "Hey ladies," He calls out as he pokes his head in through the front door, "We need to get moving if we're going to make our flight. It does leave in just over an hour!"

Hand in hand, Claire and Christina stroll through their childhood home for the last time, their hearts filled with excitement for their new lives to begin. Claire is confident and content; she will be a mother and live with Mike at the Ranch for the rest of her life. Christina, however, is still determining her future. She is relocating to Texas and living at the Ranch, but many things in her life need to be discussed and sorted out. But they can wait; Claire and Mike need to get married first.

"Christina, you know you can live with us for the rest of your life if you want to. Please don't worry about that; I always want you with me. Besides, I bet you meet a guy in a month, fall in love, and get married. Then we can raise all our kids together, almost like they are siblings," says Claire.

"I know it's all going to be okay, and I want to be near you too, but raising 'all' our kids together, the way you say it, sounds like a lot of kids, Claire. Let's fatten you up with this one first," They smile, laugh, rub Claire's too-small pregnant belly, and walk through the rest of the house, saying goodbye to their childhood and their parents.

When his phone rings, Mike is leaning on the car, waiting for the girls. It's Dave Black; "Hello Dave."

"Mike, I received your message. Gabby and I are thrilled you're visiting us today. However, I don't think we can enter the house. I rented it back to the previous owners for the next two weeks while you renovate the property," Dave says, "they needed extra time to move into their new home. Nevertheless, I'm sure it'll be alright to look around the rest of the property."

"That's fine; I want to show the girls the Ranch. Did you get the Suburban for Claire?"

"Sure did; it's just as you requested. Dark blue, all leather, seats eight, 4x4, and everything else you requested has been customized. I will pick you all up in it at the airport and take you to the Ranch."

"Good Dave, Thanks."

"Mike, there is one more thing that I need to bring to your attention, Christina. She has spent more than forty thousand dollars this week, which is enormous. What should I do in response? Should I put a stop on her card?"

"No, Dave. Whatever she wants, I want her to have. 40K isn't bad; I asked her to pick out Claire's engagement ring and a few other things."

Dave revealed that, besides the already considerable sum of $40,000, he had a separate charge for Tiffany & Co. that amounted to an additional $75,000.

"Wow. No, it's fine Dave; leave it alone. Christina is finding herself. Elena took her out for a makeover, and it takes some money, that's all. Besides, they will come into some of their own correct?"

"Yes, I received an offer from Durant, but I turned it down. They will be back," says Dave.

Dave filed a wrongful death lawsuit against Durant Energy for the deaths of the girl's parents and the suffering they had endured. William Barnes was an executive at Durant Energy, and the company did not provide proper security for him or his family while they were in Saudi, which is why Shariek was able to grab them all. In light of the tragedy of losing their parents, Dave demands $100 million to compensate for the immense loss and suffering the women have endured. He is seeking fifty million dollars for the loss of their parents and an additional fifty million dollars for the anguish they experienced and may continue to experience from being in that Hellhole in Saudi.

"Being injected with drugs and treated like livestock will not be well-received by a Jury. The company will fold like a cheap suit, fearing a Jury will reward far more than I am asking for," Dave explains.

"Dave, thank you for looking out for them. They deserve every penny that company makes for the rest of its existence. What you are asking for will set them up for the rest of their lives, with or without me. I have a call coming in that I need to take. See you in a few hours," Mike clicks over to Max.

"Hey, Bro, we are just leaving the house in Ohio. I am taking the girls to see the new Ranch in Texas. What's up?" asks Mike.

"Mike, I have some new information. It's about Claire's abduction," says Max.

"What kind of information, Max?" Mike's demeanor changes immediately.

"Mike, Claire was ordered, from her head right down to her toes. I found the bastard that ordered her, and Mike, he just placed a replacement order."

Mike and Max speak for a few more minutes until the girls finally walk out of the house.

"Okay Max, I will find out; send me the photo. Let's get Ricky on the guy. I am not sure how soon I can break away again, but I will, for this, I most definitely will," Mike hangs up the phone, smiles, and says, "Ladies, change of plans."

Özdemir Motors:

"For over 150 years, Özdemir Motors has been a symbol of style, elegance, dependability, safety, and affordability. It all began with my great-great-grandfather, who started Özdemir Works and sold wooden carts and wagons. As the industrial revolution gained momentum, Özdemir Works transformed into Özdemir Motors and began manufacturing high-quality automobiles. Despite wars, famines, and pandemics that have occurred throughout the years, Özdemir Motors has remained a reliable source of quality at an affordable price. We have never wavered in our commitment to providing our customers with the best products and services available. Today I am delighted to share the news that Özdemir Motors is making its debut in the United States, marking a major milestone in the company's history. This is the first time that Özdemir Motors has entered the U.S. Market, and we are confident that our innovative products and services will be well-received by customers across the country. We look forward to providing the highest quality of service and the most advanced technology to our customers in the U.S.."

Emree Özdemir is presenting at this year's Geneva International Motor Show in Geneva, Switzerland. Emree, son of Mustafa Özdemir, is the last remaining heir to the Özdemir motors fortune. Emree's company is striking out into the American auto space. Today he will announce Özdemir Motors USA.

"In conclusion, I express my sincere gratitude to the wonderful people of my beloved homeland, Turkey. Without your unwavering support, Özdemir Motors would not be the successful company it is today....So, what do you think, Cahill?" asks Emree Özdemir.

"Sir, it is brilliant, just brilliant. You will have them eating out of the palm of your hand," says Cahill.

Cahill Kaplan has been with Özdemir Motors most of his life. He started forty years ago working for Emree's father, Mustafa Özdemir as a stock boy in the parts department. Now Cahill has worked his way up to management. Cahill is in charge of anything that pertains to Emree's needs. *He is more than just an assistant. Cahill is more like family,* Emree tells everyone. But in actuality, he is Emree's enabler. It was Emree that ordered Claire Barnes, and Cahill facilitated that transaction. Emree isn't finished with his orders. He wants a complete stable of women, all of them just like Claire and Cahill will do his best to fill his stable. There is one thing Cahill doesn't know, Emree knows Claire. In fact, he has known Claire and her family her entire life.

"This is a big week Cahill. Today, Europe, tomorrow America. We are unstoppable now."

"Yes Sir, you have brought Özdemir Motors to the brink of greatness. Your father would be so proud of you Sir," says Cahill.

"I think you are right, Cahill; too bad he is not here to witness this today. But no use dwelling in the past. Forward is the only path for us now. Onward, Cahill, time to conquer America!"

Uncle Em:

After Max calls Mike, the plan changes; Mike and the girls fly back to San Diego, not Texas. Mike wants to show them the Ranch, but unfortunately, something at work requires his undivided attention. Claire is understanding, she doesn't like that Mike has to leave, and she can't hide her sadness. Claire knows he will have to be gone for work often, and she will need to get used to this. She also knows Mike will always come home to her.

The following morning Mike is running late, his flight is leaving in just over an hour, but he needs to talk to Christina first. He walks out of his bedroom. Claire is still sleeping, *She is tuckered out,* he says to himself as he walks into the living room. Christina is on the couch. She is already awake and on her phone, as always. "Good morning," He says.

"Hey Mike. Are you going somewhere?" Christina notices he is dressed and has his overnight case in his left hand.

"Yes, I have to go to work again. I shouldn't be gone long, just a few days at most."

"You sure do travel a lot Mike," Christina says, looking back at her phone.

He kneels in front of Christina. She looks up at him. He is holding a brand new, rose gold iPad in a pale pink Michael Kors case. Christina puts her phone down and looks at Mike suspiciously, "Okay?"

"Before I hand this iPad over to you, I need two things from you," Mike says. "First, I want to show you a picture. If you recognize the person, I need you to tell me. Still, you can't ask me any questions about why I want to know, none at all, and you must forget I asked anything about the person. If you agree, the iPad is yours. Do we have a deal?"

"Alright, let me make sure I understand this correctly. You want to ask me a question, and if I don't ask any in return, you'll give me that iPad. But if I do, then what? No iPad? Mike, come on. You clearly bought that iPad for me, specifically. They don't make them in rose gold, and the one you have is rose gold, and it is in a Michael Kors case that matches all my other things. They also don't make them with my name engraved on it, yet there it is," she points to her name in a beautiful font, "So, do you honestly think I don't know it is already mine, even if I don't do what you ask?" Christina reaches for her personalized iPad.

Mike hands Christina her new iPad. "Okay, but I need your help, and you can never tell Claire anything about what I will show you. And when we are finished, please, try to forget about it, okay?"

"That's better," says Christina, "you could have just asked Mike. You didn't have to bribe me with an iPad, but thank you. I really wanted one. So, where is this picture you want me to look at?"

Mike pulls out his phone, scrolls to the photo, and turns his phone to show Christina, "This guy. Do you know who he is? Have you ever seen him before?"

"Yes, that's Uncle Em," says Christina. As soon as she answers his question, she's already moved on from the photo like Mike asked, and she is opening her new iPad.

"Uncle Em. Christina, can you give me a little more than that, please?" Mike says, shocked by her response.

"Sure, I was just trying to do what you asked me to. He isn't really our Uncle. He is a friend of my dad's from way back. Dad worked for an oil company when they met, and Uncle Em, I think, is like a used car salesman or something. They had a race car together somewhere. I don't remember where. Claire and I saw them race in Europe when we were just kids. When he came to the U.S., he's not from here; Uncle Em would come to the house and stay with us. He didn't have a family and always showed up with gifts for Claire and me. I haven't seen him in a few years, at least. So, what's with the questions about Uncle Em?"

"Now it's time for you to forget that I showed you this picture or asked you anything about it, remember?" Mike says.

"Okay, I totally don't care about that guy anyway. I always thought Uncle Em was a total creeper, so whatever," Christina is already on her new iPad, and Mike is just a disturbance.

"Thank you, Christina; I need to go," says Mike.

Christina looks up from the iPad. She has time; it is pairing with her watch and phone. "You said two things Mike."

"Two things?......Oh ya. Your sister wants a Grand Gesture from me. For the life of me, I can't figure out what this Grand Gesture is that she wants. Do you have any ideas?"

"For me, a Grand Gesture could be something like an iPad, some choco-lates, or jewelry - you get the idea. But for Claire, who is a hopeless roman-tic, a Grand Gesture could be something as simple as a handwritten note or as big as fireworks on the beach. Anything that comes from the heart is what matters to Claire. Regardless of the size or cost, it's the thought that counts to her."

"Well, I will keep trying, I thought the ranch would be it, but I was wrong... again."

Mike is even more stumped than before, but it will have to wait; he has a new 'Target' to meet.

"You will figure something out. See you in a few days Mike," Christina is deep into her new iPad. She looks up at him again, "Anything else?"

Mike is staring at her, looking her up and down...again. *She smells so good,* he thinks. *And she is glowing; I mean glowing....Mike, what the hell is wrong with you? Claire is no more than 20 feet away in* **YOUR BED,** *you asshole. Stop undressing Christina in your mind.* He speaks, "Nothing Christina; I will see you in a few days," Mike gets off his knees and leaves the apartment.

The Golden Ticket has Expired:

Markus Delphy is deep in thought, reflecting on his conversation with Director Gray. His desk is littered with images of young girls who have all vanished. He asked Margaret to assemble a report of missing people from the past few days. The file she gives him contains over a thousand beautiful young girls reported missing in the United States and Europe. Markus is a loyal 'Company Man' for the most part; following orders separates the United States from the Banana Republics in the world. *He has to adhere to the Director's orders, doesn't he?*

As he flips through the images, his heart begins to ache. He says to himself, This isn't right; I have to do something. Oh my God, this one is just a child; Gray is wrong. Markus pushes the intercom on his phone, "Margaret, would you come in here, please."

"Yes Sir, I will be right in," answers Margaret.

A few seconds later, in walks the sixty-something woman smoking a cigarette. "What can I do for you, Markus?" says, Margaret.

"You know you can't smoke here, right?" Markus says as the smoke slowly bellows out of Margaret's mouth.

"Yep," Margaret blows the remaining smoke from her mouth into the air. "Did you need something?"

Markus shakes his head in disbelief, staring at the photographs in his hands. "Are all these girls part of Majeed's new Network?" he asks, his voice tinged with dismay. He is trying hard to comprehend the magnitude of the tragedy before him and that the director is "*okay*" with this.

"We believe so; some may just be runaways or even worse. But yes, most likely, the majority of them are now part of the sex industry," comments Margaret.

Markus can't take another second of this; it is time to unleash his pit bull. "We must take action, Margaret. Get Mike on the line immediately. He is off the bench, as of now," he declares.

"Yes Sir, right away," says Margaret.

After attempting to reach Mike, Margaret tells Markus, "Mike is on a flight to Switzerland. He can't be reached for the next twelve hours. However Markus, I have the next best thing - Max - on line 2."

"Max, where is Mike?" barks Markus.

"Not sure Boss; why?" asks Max.

"Because Max, it's time for Mike to meet the Sheik," Markus says.

"Fuck ya Markus! It's about time," says Max.

"Get Ricky on him now; we do this without the Director's knowledge. The Sheik's Golden Ticket has just expired!" orders Markus.

Granola...This Stuff is Shit:

Claire was utterly exhausted from the week-long packing in Ohio, causing her to rise later than usual. Looking around Mike's apartment, she quickly realizes that the task ahead of her is daunting. Taking a deep breath, Claire sighs, surveying all the items that must be packed. With a determined expression on her face, she gets to work.

Christina is sitting at the dining table. The last remaining bowl of cereal is in front of her. She takes a spoonful and utters a disgruntled "Granola... This stuff is shit," in a loud voice ensuring Claire will hear.

Claire is entirely immersed in her task this morning; packing. She opens a drawer in Mike's bedroom. While removing items and filling a box, she stumbles upon a stack of Gentleman's magazines. She begins flipping through the pages, taking in the images and articles that fill them.

This is the first time Claire has ever actually looked at one of these magazines. Christina has been trying to show her things like this for a while now, but Claire has only ever taken a quick glance and then moved on. Today, however, she is intently studying the photos, deep in thought. Mike is her first everything; she has only ever barely kissed a boy before him. Yes, she had a childhood crush and a peck on the cheek, but that was it. Claire is filled with anxiety, as Mike has been involved with many more experienced women. She worries that he will become bored and lose interest in her if she doesn't do enough for him. All these thoughts and fears are running through her mind this morning as she looks over at her sister.

"Christina, I need to ask you something. And please don't laugh at me," Claire says as she walks into the dining room.

"Wow! You set that one up Sis, but okay, I won't laugh. What's up?" Christina says as she notices what Claire is holding and knows this will be fun, for her at least.

"You, um, you have done some of these things, haven't you?" Claire shows Christina some of the pages she has dogeared in the magazine.

"Claire, you know I have. But not actual sex; I never had full-on sex before Mike," Christina clarifies.

"Yes Mr. Clinton," Claire says, pointing to one of the pages, "this is also considered sex."

"Who is Mr. Clinton?" Christina asks.

"Oh, never mind," Claire walks away deflated and shaking her head.

Christina says, "Hey, come back! What's going on Claire?"

Claire wants to talk to Christina. She has questions she can only ask her sister, so she walks back into the kitchen, determined to ask her questions. Showing Christina one of the pages, she says, "Is this hard to do? I mean, I never have, but do guys like this?"

"Sis, why are you asking me about all this? Did Mike say something? Christina is worried about her sister.

Claire puts her embarrassment aside, "No, not yet, but he will; I really don't know what I'm doing. I just know he's going to get bored with me.

He's been with women who are definitely more experienced than I am and know how to do these things. I don't even know what you call them."

"That is absolutely absurd; it's just your anxieties talking. Mike adores you; he won't ever get bored with you. He has made it abundantly clear that he loves you and wants to be with you for the long haul," Christina tries to assure Claire.

"Then why does he have these magazines if he doesn't want these things done to him?"

"I can't speak for Mike, but I have had these kinds of magazines before. That doesn't mean I want to do all these things."

"You didn't? Really?" asks Claire, a little relieved.

"Okay I did, but that doesn't mean Mike needs those things to keep from getting bored with you," Christina says.

"Christina, please, let's just say that he does. Do men like all these kinds of things?" Claire flips through the magazine.

"Fine Claire. Yes. Men really do like this, and this, and this," Christina points to the people on the pages, doing all sorts of different things to each other.

"Have you done these things?" asks Claire.

"Yes. Some of them, anyway. Claire, you might be a little embarrassed at first, but you need to ask Mike what he likes. I don't know if I am the best person to talk to about all this. I have only had 'real' sex one time. You definitely have me beat there."

"What if I hurt him or something? What if I choke?" Claire is working herself into a panic.

"Claire, take a breath. I don't think any of that will happen. It's something you can do, Sis. It will come naturally; talk with Mike when he gets home. He can tell you what he likes. I'm sure there are things he wants to do with you too, and you might even enjoy some of them," Christina tries to be as encouraging as possible.

Still fumbling through the magazine with an apprehensive look, Claire says, "Okay, I will try one thing at a time until I figure it out. Thanks, Christina; I appreciate you not making fun of me."

"It's cool. Now Claire, let's get some food. This stuff sucks!"

"You go; I am not hungry."

"Claire, you are way too thin again! You are pregnant, and you shouldn't be this skinny. That baby needs food to grow. You keep saying you aren't hungry, but what about your baby? You're not just hurting yourself this time; you're also hurting your unborn child. Please, Claire, don't do this again," Christina begs, "especially with a helpless baby to think about. Mike would be devastated if anything happened to you or his child. Please, can we go get something for you to eat?"

Surviving with only minimal food while they were in the Cage was easier for Claire than the others. She suffers from Anorexia and has for most of her life. Going without food isn't new for Claire. She is used to skipping meals or going an entire day, if not longer, without eating a thing. That awful place put her back into a cycle she had worked so hard to overcome. Anorexia is self-imposed starvation that some say can only be put into remission and never be completely cured. Symptoms can include appearing very thin, having a below-normal body weight, denial of hunger, and fixation with food preparation. Traumatic events can often push a person who has seemingly won this fight right back into the awful cycle. Since their return from Saudi Arabia, Claire is showing all of these signs, and this time she is pregnant.

Christina knows all about Claire's condition, but she is sworn to secrecy and hasn't told anyone. After Claire was hospitalized when she was 16, Christina vowed never to let this happen to her sister again.

"You're right, Christina. I have to get a handle on this. I don't want anything to happen to my baby. I'm sorry; I don't want you to be scared. We've had enough fear in our lives. I will take control of this right now. Let's go out and get something to eat; that granola looks awful."

"Claire, thank God you agree. Let's go," Christina suddenly stopped, grabbed Claire by the shoulders, and looked into her eyes, "You promise you'll eat enough for you and the baby, right? An entire meal, not just a few bites?"

"Sister Swear," Claire says, and then hugs Christina tightly.

I Just Need the Boss and a Brunette:

Ricky is at the Auto Show, taking notes about the venue and looking for all the exits, security cameras, guards, elevators, ramps, back doors, stairs, walkways, and anything else that is important. This place is way too public for Mike's plan. Ricky says to himself, *Mike won't want to hear it, but it's true: Emree Özdemir will have to be dealt with the old-fashioned way. By sniper action or poison, Mike isn't going to be able to engage this guy 'hand-to-hand'. Not here, anyway.* Ricky continues his reconnaissance.

Max is on his way to Switzerland; the team will be on this together. Max has good news for Mike; he has the green light on the Sheik. Not that it matters. The Sheik is going down, green light or not. Mike will 'meet' everyone involved, and the Sheik will be the grand finale.

Ricky finds their 'Target'. Emree Özdemir is drinking with his old friend Gabriel Toussaint at the bar.

Gabriel Toussaint is a high-end fashion designer whose designs are seen on the Red Carpet, worn by First Ladies, Presidents, and the rich and famous for the past 15 years. Born in Paris, Toussaint has homes in Europe, Asia, and the U.S. Unlike Emree, Toussaint is bisexual. He slightly prefers men, but he is flexible on his sexual partners, as long as it is hard and rough. Ricky moves closer to better hear the conversation between Emree and Gabriel.

"I have a few new girls coming in tonight. You are welcome to join us. We will be at my Villa in Cologne." says Emree.

"All your girls look the same, blond, skinny, light eyes. You need some diversity in your flock; they say variety is the spice of life," Gabriel insists.

"What can I say? I have a type, Gabriel. Shall we order something special for the party? What do you think?" Emree asks.

"Doesn't that take a while?" asks Gabriel.

"Not any longer; there are 'Acquired' items in stock now. Zubair is running the business, and the inventory is improving. I bet I can get someone here tonight for you; it will be my treat. I will make you a deal, my friend. Not only will I pay, but I will also allow you to pick one out for me," says Emree.

"Seriously? I can pick out anyone I choose for you. Maybe a curvy brunette with dark eyes?" asks Gabriel.

"Yes. Order whatever you wish, and I will pick someone for you. I think a big man, one that can last for hours. A dumb but suckable man, just for you, my friend."

"Well, Mon Ami, you have a deal. I'm excited to see what you have in mind for me. But sadly, I cannot be there tonight. I have something else I must do. I am available tomorrow night. I'll look into our options in the morning," Gabriel promises.

"I am excited as well. Cahill will place the order for us. Just tell him what you want for me, and I will do the same for you," Emree says.

Ricky is already working on a plan, *This is good,* he thinks, *Now I just need the boss and a brunette.*

Well, It's Not Taco John's, That's for sure:

Agent Elena Alvarez has been watching over Claire and Christina. She wants to talk to them before she leaves on her new Mission. Agent Perez has just called Elena away. She will head to Switzerland to meet with Mike and the Team. Elena will not be coming back; she has requested a transfer out of the U.S. and onto the European Team. Elena has become attached to Christina; she likes having a surrogate little sister and wants to say goodbye.

Christina and Claire sit in a roped-off, pink patent leather, high-back booth with a chandelier hanging over it. The pale blue walls were adorned with crazy face masks and pictures of huge men wrestling. While waiting for their food in this unique place, Christina looks at the pink logo magnet the guy who took their order gave her. Christina looks up the *Lucia Libre Gourmet Taco Shop* on her phone and reads about it. A huge smile crosses her face as she reads, *if you have a special occasion to celebrate, you should be sure to reserve the Champions Booth at least 24 hours in advance.* Christina thinks, *Elena was so right. We don't have to wait and don't need a reservation. The guy who took our order sat us here without me even asking. I love this!*

"This isn't Taco John's, that's for sure," says Claire as she looks down at her breakfast burrito.

Christina says, "I got the California burrito. It's a Carne Asada burrito with french fries in it."

This is the first time the girls have ever had authentic Mexican food; Columbus, Ohio, isn't known for its Mexican cuisine. This is San Diego-style Mexican, and it is delicious.

Agent Alvarez enters the restaurant and sees Claire and Christina sitting in the Champions booth.

"Elena? Hi! What are you doing here?" asks Christina.

"Hi Christina. Hi Claire, it's nice to see you both. I see you're having some real Mexican food, and Christina, nice job getting the Champions booth!"

"Wow. First Ohio, now here! What are you doing here, Elena?" Claire is perplexed to see her here.

"I live here, just across the street from Mike's apartment building," says Elena.

"Huh, I wonder why Mike's never mentioned that?" Claire remarks as she smiles at Elena. "But it's good to see you again. Have you ever eaten here before? It's delicious; it's called Mexican food."

"Yes, I know it is; I am Mexican, Claire."

"Oh, I'm sorry, of course you are. But this is really delicious. Would you like some?" Claire offers.

"No, thank you Claire. I'm good. I love this place; it's one of the best in San Diego. They've won awards for their Surf N' Turf burrito. Enough about the food; I'm glad you're both here; I wanted to say goodbye."

"Good-bye? What do you mean?" asks Christina.

"I've been transferred. I'm going to work at the U.S. Embassy in Paris," Elena explains.

"Oh, that's great Elena! I love Paris, the City of Lights, the Eiffel Tower, and great coffee. You will love it there," says Claire.

Christina is not as happy with this news, "Well, that sucks! I'm going to miss you. Have you heard we're moving? We're heading to Texas as soon as Mike gets home."

"Texas, that's great! Mike will love the BBQ there; it's the best," says Elena.

I didn't know Mike liked barbecue, Claire thinks, now worried that she didn't know this small detail about him. "Just another one of Mike's mysteries I don't know about, I guess," she says.

Claire's reaction surprises Elena; she feels like she has just revealed a huge secret Mike has been keeping. But it is just BBQ! "Um, well, Mike is a great guy, Claire. I'm happy he found you, that you found each other. I know you will both be very happy together."

As Christina sits quietly eating her burrito, observing the interaction between Elena and Claire, she thinks, *Maybe there's more to Elena and Mike than he has admitted. This is fun to watch.*

Before Christina can take another bite, Claire begins talking to Elena again, "Thank you, I'm sure we will be. It's been a tough few months, but things are finally coming together. Did you know we just cleared out our parent's house, and we're selling it? Then, there's the new place in Texas, which isn't a Grand Gesture, by the way. Today, I am packing Mike's apartment, including his Nudie magazines and sex toys. Mike's family is the only family my sister and I have now. Have you met them? I think they're great."

Claire is winding up, getting increasingly frantic with each word, "Hopefully, we are getting married in a couple of days, but Mike, he's always gone, somewhere? Who knows where? Do you know where? I don't know where. And just a few days ago, Christina suddenly became this amazing, beautiful woman, with men sniffing around her all day. You helped her become this woman, not me; thank you for that, by the way. Then there is Mike not telling me that the world's most beautiful woman, that's you in case you are not aware, lives across the street from him. Now, I find out he likes BBQ - just one more thing I don't know about him. To top it all off, I am pregnant, such a happy thing. I have crazy hormones raging through my body, trying to take control all the time, oh, oh, oh, and...and I haven't even given Mike a blow job yet, not just him; I have never given anyone a blow job. But yes, you are absolutely right; we will be happy, I am sure of it..."

Elena is standing in front of the booth, her eyes growing wider with each word Claire speaks. When she stops and takes a breath, Elena manages to get out four words: "I am sorry, what?"

While Claire tries to compose herself, Christina explains, "Elena, what you just witnessed has only been confirmed a few times in my lifetime. You just saw something that has been seen fewer times than confirmed Bigfoot sightings. You have just found yourself in the middle of, and the target of, a Claire-ism. It will pass, but for right now, 'Nessie' a.k.a the Loch Ness Monster, has just made her appearance. It is best to let her be for a while. She will dive back under the water without another word."

"I'm sorry. I've been under a lot of stress lately and didn't mean to take it out on you. It's just that everything seems to be hitting me all at once," says Claire.

"Claire, I completely understand; I would feel overwhelmed too. I just wanted to see you both before I left and say goodbye. I have to get going; my flight leaves in about an hour. Christina, you look great. Keep it up. And Claire, things will get better. I know it all seems overwhelming right now, but you can handle it. Just trust in yourself, and you will be fine," Elena says.

Claire has one more question for Elena before she leaves, "Elena, could I ask you one thing before you go? You and Mike...were you, you know, did you?"

"I have to go, ladies," Elena says, backing away from the table. "I don't want to miss my flight. You're going to love Texas."

I Don't Think I Can do it Without Staring at Her:

Ricky and Max await Mike's arrival; his flight touched down thirty minutes ago, and he is on his way to meet them. The two men are staying at the hotel directly across from the Convention Center and Auto Show. Ricky has been busy devising a plan to get Mike and Elena closer to Emree Özdemir. He has also come to believe that Gabriel Toussaint should be taken care of at the same time.

"The guy is a freak Max! We should at least look into him. Maybe I'm wrong, but I think he should be removed from the equation," says Ricky.

"I will look into him, but the 'Target' is Özdemir. Elena will get close to him, and then Mike can move in to finish the job," says Max.

Mike walks into the room and says, "Hello, boys! Miss me?"

"Boss, Max and I were just working on a plan. I think we can get you and Agent Alvarez into Özdemir's house here in Cologne," says Ricky.

"Max already filled me in Ricky. You have a good plan. I'm proud of you Rick. That shows initiative and great leadership skill," says Mike.

"Thanks, Boss. With you getting married and about to become a dad, I want to work on my skills so that someday I can lead my own team," Ricky says.

"Looks like you're well on your way, brother," says Mike, "Now Max, can you get me back on the Network?"

"Sure can Bro," says Max, "I have a 'Hunter' account. I'll post you as an 'Acquired' in inventory. I'll use your old photos from Shariek."

"I really don't want Elena in that system, even if it's only for a few hours. Look what happened to me. What can we do to protect her after we upload her?" asks Mike.

"Bro, you know the system is spread out all over the world. Majeed set up multiple servers to guarantee that nothing would ever be completely erased. I'm afraid once we upload, it's out there to stay," says Max.

"Then we leave it up to Elena; it will be her call," says Mike.

"Boss, about the money: you know Elena will go for some big bucks. Can we maybe?" asks Ricky.

"Spoils, boys. Take what you need, then the rest goes to the usual places," says Mike.

The Central Intelligence Agency is primarily funded by the "Spoils" of its Missions. Congress holds tight to the purse strings on taxpayer funds, making it difficult for the CIA to carry out off-the-books operations with the necessary transparency requirements. As a result, an unofficial policy of obtaining money from criminals and depositing it into secret accounts was established. The Agents refer to it as "Spoils of War." It is also not unheard of for Agents to set aside some of the "Spoils" to compensate for the additional expenses they incur while on assignment. After all, it can be hard to ask for reimbursement for certain costs when one is an Assassin.

"Thanks Boss," says Ricky. "I'm starting to get a little tapped out. We really need our own plane; those commercial airline tickets are getting crazy expensive."

"When will she be here?" asks Mike.

Max says, "Elena is on a flight that left just after yours. I hope it's cool; she's staying here with us. I didn't want to get more than one room."

"Come on, Max, we know you're still hoping for a rendezvous with Elena. I have bad news, Bro: she's not interested," Mike says.

"Dude! You hit that and just let it go. You may not be interested anymore, but I am; it's my turn to take a shot," says Max.

Mike smiles at Max and says, "Let's not make her uncomfortable, okay, boys? I'm beat. Wake me when she gets here." He then moved off to the bedroom, leaving the guys to work on the particulars of the Mission.

"Max, dude, you shouldn't try anything with Elena. The Boss still has a thing for her," says Ricky.

"I know Bro, I won't," says Max. "but she is still nice to look at, and you know how much I like to mess with my brother."

"Fuck ya, she is," says Ricky.

Agent Elena Alvarez arrives in Geneva and makes her way to the hotel. As she walks into the room, Ricky passes her, and they exchange a nod. Ricky is heading to Emree Özdemir's Chateau in Cologne for recon. Elena knows Max has feelings for her, but tonight they have to take some "candid" photographs to upload. She is not particularly concerned with Max's emotions; however, they could potentially distract from the Mission. If that were to happen, Mike would not be happy.

"Hey Max, how have you been?" asks Elena.

"Elena, it's been a while, a few years, right?" says Max, "I'm doing well, and you look great as always."

"Thanks, Max. You look good yourself. So, where is Mike?" she asks.

Max gets up and begins to make his way to the bedroom. "He is in there. I have a robe in there for you to change into. I will go in and wake him up so you can...."

"No problem, I'll take care of it," Elena interjects, cutting Max off. She walks straight into the bedroom. Mike is still awake, and he sees her enter the room.

"Hey, I will step outside so you can get undressed," says Mike.

Elena replies, "Don't bother; you both will be getting a show tonight."

"Elena, before we do this, I need to make sure you understand the entire plan and all the risks involved," says Mike.

The plan is relatively straightforward: Mike and Elena will be delivered to Emree's Château for the party. Mike will do whatever he has to with the 'little Frenchmen' and then make his way to Elena and Emree. Elena needs to delay Emree for as long as possible, giving Mike the time he needs to reach them. If need be, she will do whatever Emree wants, up to and including having sex with the creepy, disgusting guy. Mike is insistent that if her life is in danger or Emree is going to hurt her in any way, she must take action and not let that happen. After Mike has dealt with Emree, the two of them will slip out of the house under cover of darkness, right past Emree's guards.

Mike goes over the plan with Elena multiple times; it is a good one, but they can make changes if she feels uncomfortable in any way. Understanding the Mission and knowing her limitations, Elena agrees.

"Mike, do you remember what we learned at the farm? 'Anything for the Mission.' Now let's get these fuckers," Elena says as she starts undressing.

For the database, Elena needs to have photos taken of her body, complete with measurements and sizes. Elena knows what is required of her and will complete her Mission.

"I will be outside when you're ready," says Mike as he leaves the room.

"Max, are you going to be okay here? I don't want her to feel uncomfortable," Mike says. "If you need to leave and have me take the photos, I can do it."

"Bro, I hate to say this, but could you do it? I don't think I can without staring at her," Max admits.

"Of course, Max; why don't you go with Ricky and ensure everything is in place?"

Max thanks Mike again; he knows that Elena is a pipe dream for him, and seeing her naked will only make things worse. As for Mike, he has seen her before, and Elena will be more comfortable with just him there.

"So, where do you want me?" Elena walks out of the bedroom. Mike points to the makeshift exam table. They need to make the photos look like they were taken in one of the intake facilities. Mike will use pictures of other women for more personal images. Still, he needs Elena for the full-body photos.

"Just lie down on the table and relax as much as you can; you need to look like you're drugged," Mike tells her.

Elena removes her robe and starts to get into place. Mike has forgotten how incredible Elena's body is; he is in awe but tries not to show it. *This is a Mission, an important Mission. Claire is my only concern. Getting the man that 'ordered' my Claire, that is the Mission.* He keeps repeating this in his head, but his body has a different plan, and it shows.

Elena cracks a smile as she observes Mike's physical response to her naked body. She is not uncomfortable being naked in front of him and acts no differently than if she is fully clothed. "I talked to your fiancée this morning; she seems a bit stressed," she says.

"I know; I forget how young she is," Mike says as he snaps photos of her arms with a tape measure to show her exact measurements.

"Claire is a nice girl, but she's very young, Mike. What is she, half your age?" Elena says in jest.

"Shit, Elena! How old do you think I am? She's only about fifteen years younger than me."

Elena laughs and says, "Oh, only fifteen years? That's all? Well then, no problem, I can see with that. You know you're a cradle robber, right?"

Mike tries to ignore what Elena is saying and continues with the photo shoot, "Okay, now turn to your side; I need to get your profile."

"I really like them, Mike. Claire and Christina are very nice girls."

"I hear I have you to thank for Christina's new look?" Mike lifts her right arm for the next picture on the list.

"I admit it was my idea. After all you guys went through, she needed to stop looking like such a kid. Christina is incredibly beautiful and would have done it herself soon enough. I enjoyed helping her do it right."

"You also enjoy spending my money, but you did a good thing for her. Thanks," Mike raises his eyebrows and focuses on the next shot, "We're almost finished. Turn over, and now you're drugged; remember, eyes closed."

Elena rolls over on her back and closes her eyes, and plays drugged.

"This is going to be cold," Mike says as he takes a chest measurement and photos.

"You know the last time you saw me naked was almost three years ago, Mike," Elena reminds him.

Mike feels guilty about how things ended with Elena, "I know. I'm sorry it didn't work out. It wasn't you; it was me."

"Don't use that line on me, Mike. What was it then? I was all in, 100%, but it was like you were determined to make it not work. I wanted us to work; I really did. Why didn't you?" Elena demands.

Mike stops what he is doing and looks into Elena's eyes, "Elena, that was one of the best nights of my life."

"Seriously Mike, I'm baffled! If we both had such a great time, tell me, what happened?" Elena is angry and a little hurt at the same time.

Mike tries to explain, "I wanted more than just that one night and more than we could have ever had. I pictured us getting married and moving to a bigger place; you know I have always wanted children. But I didn't want a CIA Agent for a wife. I couldn't bring myself to ask you to give that up; I wouldn't even consider asking."

"So you just took that decision right out of my hands?" Elena says, irritated, sitting up on the table.

Mike knows the answers, but he asks the questions to allow Elena to see for herself. "Let me ask you then, would you give all this up? Would you have given up all the work you put in, all the obstacles you overcame, to become a Field Agent just for the promise of a life with me? Not knowing if it would work out or if I would return from a Mission? All this, and you would have chosen us over your career?"

Elena never thought of it in that way. The truth is, no; she wouldn't have given up her life in the CIA, not for anyone. She has worked too hard to achieve her position to give it up for anything.

"I guess, at the time, you knew me better than I knew myself. You are right Mike; I wouldn't have given up the CIA for you, not for us, not for anyone."

"Neither would I, not then anyway, but I would today. Claire has no idea what we really do, and I hope she never finds out, but I would walk away and never look back if she asked me to." Mike confesses.

"Mike, I'm truly grateful for this conversation with you. I never thought of things from your perspective. I think it will help us better understand one another, and I am sure we will benefit from this. Now, let's upload these photos; we have a serious bad guy to put an end to."

That's Why He is The Boss:

Max and Ricky are surveilling Emree Özdemir Château, where security is incredibly tight. In order to rescue Mike and Elena when the time is right, they need to find a way to gain access.

"Two on the south side, four on the north," Ricky reports.

Max inquires, "Alright, the driveway has guards stationed at five different points, all the entrances are being monitored, and the garages too. Have you checked out the west alleyway yet?"

"All covered, Max. I can't see any other way in. The only thing I can think of is the back of the house, but it's a sheer cliff that plunges down at least a thousand feet to the water below."

"I don't know; Mike and Elena will be a bit impaired. Climbing down that might be a problem. What about the basement?" asks Max.

"No go, Max, just no entrances uncovered," Ricky says.

"Ok, let's get back to the hotel and tell them what we learned. Mike will figure something out. That's why he's the Boss," says Max.

You Have The Poor Guy Stumped:

Claire works hard all day to get Mike's apartment packed up, and surprisingly, Christina even lends a hand for a while. Everywhere she looks, Claire sees empty shelves, closets, and drawers; the only things remaining are the furniture and a few essential items. As usual, Christina sits on the couch with her head buried in her iPad.

"Hey, thank you for your help today; I am beat," Claire sits next to Christina on the couch, "But we made good progress, don't you think?"

Christina says, "We sure did; we make a good team," She was still looking down at her new iPad.

Christina is engrossed with her iPad for the majority of the day. It seems like she is investigating something, but every time Claire attempts to peek at the display, Christina quickly switches it off.

Claire is concerned about how Christina is acting, "Sis, are you okay? I see you looking a bit sad lately, and you have been sick a few times this week."

"I'm okay. I have been kind of sad, but it will pass," Christina knows that Claire won't let this go that easily.

"Why? Is it because we're moving to Texas? I thought you were excited about the move. I know I am; it's a fresh start for us all."

"It's not that Claire. Texas should be fun."

"So what is it?" Claire isn't giving up.

Christina has to try to explain in a way that Claire will drop it, "It's hard to explain. I feel like I'm in limbo. Like my life isn't moving forward like yours is. You and Mike have a plan; I am just following along."

"Oh, Christina. Your life is moving forward, just not the same way, but it is, believe me," Claire says.

"I guess you're right. I've been wondering, have you picked out any baby names yet?" Christina tries to change the subject and move on, but Claire isn't finished with her yet.

"Not so fast," Claire says, "I also asked you why you are not feeling well. What's going on with you?"

"Yeah, well, I'm feeling much better now. I think it was all the junk food I ate. You know how much I love it. I tried a bunch of new things all at once, and I think I went a bit overboard. But I'm doing much better now," Christina has been feeling off for a couple of weeks, but she isn't ready to tell Claire the real reason why. Not yet.

"Okay, good; I was thinking I might need to take you to the doctor if you didn't get better soon."

"I figured it was about time for 'Mother Claire' to appear. I'm fine; stop worrying so much about me. You have enough to worry about. Now I have a question for you. Why are you driving Mike crazy with this whole Grand Gesture thing? You have the poor guy stumped. He can't figure out what you want. You have me stumped too. What do you want him to do?"

"He knows; he just doesn't know he knows."

Christina looks confused, "Okay, now you've ventured into crazy talk. He doesn't know he knows? Because I can assure you, he doesn't know Claire."

"Yes he does," Claire insists, "Mike just has to think about it. Even if he doesn't figure it out, it's okay. As soon as Mike returns, I want to get married, but don't tell him that, please. I want to see if he can figure out the Gesture, and I hope he does."

Christina looks Claire in the eyes and says, "You're nuts! You know that, right? Poor Mike, the guy has no idea what he's getting himself into."

The Upload:

Elena observes Max as he uploads her nude photos to Majeed's database. It appears that Max is taking great pleasure in the task. "Are you having a good time, Max?"

"I am sorry, Elena. It's just; you are so attractive, you know," Max apologizes.

Ricky chimes in, "Ya Elena, if I was into Hispanic chicks, I would totally be after you."

"Does Tu Madre know that about you, Enrique?" Elena teases.

"Ahhh, hell no! She would kill me. She wants a bunch of fat Mexican grand-babies."

Elena laughs at Ricky's answer and then turns to Max. "Hey, Max, I was just razzing you. It's okay, enjoy yourself, and thank you for the compliment," she says, running her hands down her sides and smiling.

Mike has had enough of the junior high antics, "Max, Ricky come on, I told you not to go there. Elena, I'm sorry, my brothers here are assholes and can't help themselves. Max, please close the program. Nothing is going to happen until tomorrow. Let's all get some sleep."

Mike can't sleep. He pours over the pictures Max and Ricky took of Emree's Château. He hasn't found his escape route yet but has a plan.

Early the following morning, Mike is intently staring at the computer monitor. All of the images of Claire and Christina from the Intake Facility are still on the Network, and he has one of Christina's photographs on the screen. He reflects on something he heard in the tunnel in Germany, and a more 'unconventional' idea has come to him. Suddenly, Elena emerges from the bedroom and notices Mike lost in his thoughts.

Elena seeing what he is staring at, speaks in a concerned tone, "Mike, what are you doing? That's not ok!"

Mike quickly closes the window on the computer, "I know, I'm really messed up, Elena."

Elena sits beside him and asks, "Ok, tell me what's happening. Christina is also 'messed up' about you. Fill me in."

Mike glances at the boys to ensure they are still sleeping; then, he turns back to Elena. "I haven't told the boys or anybody else yet. But Christina and I, when we were in the Baby Mill... Let's just say we have some unresolved issues because of what we had to do."

"You didn't? Really Mike! What about Claire?" Elena is in shock.

Mike attempts to explain, "It was something we had to do; the doctor was going to examine her. He was going to figure out that we hadn't done it, which would have put her life in danger and mine. We had no other option at the time, but I was hooked after that. I love them both, and now, I don't know what to do about it."

Elena does not understand this at all, "You need to figure this out. Mike, you are about to get married to one of them. Are you in love with Claire?"

Mike doesn't even have to consider his response, "More than anything," looking at Elena, he feels remorseful for his insensitivity towards her, "I am so sorry, that was insensitive."

Despite Mike's remark, Elena is unfazed, at least she appears to be. She is trying to comprehend how he can be in love, not with just two women at the same time, but with sisters, at the exact same time.

"Don't worry about me. I am worried about what you just said. I'm trying to figure out how it's possible for you to love both Claire and Christina simultaneously."

"Hear me out for a second; why can't I? Is it really so wrong to have both? I remember this guy saying to me, "love is love," and if you love more than one person, why not? Is that really so far-fetched?"

Elena is astonished; she can't believe her ears. *Has Mike lost his mind?* she thinks to herself; *this is bat shit crazy!* She speaks to him in no uncertain terms. "What on earth are you talking about Mike? There's no way you can have two women. That is in no way acceptable."

Mike sees the look on Elena's face, and he realizes that he is on the losing side of this discussion. It is time to move on, "Alright Elena, you're probably right. Thanks for your help."

"I'm sure I'm right," Elena says firmly, ensuring she is as straightforward as possible, "Mike, you can not keep looking at Christina's pictures. It's not fair to Claire, and it's not fair to Christina either. She needs to move on from you, and I understand how difficult that can be. You have to put some distance between the two of you, and it has to be a lot of distance. That's the only way she can handle this. You have to get right in your head about this and make it happen."

"Hey Boss, Elena. I need some coffee; anyone else want some?" Ricky was awake and heard the entire conversation.

Mike was thankful for the interruption, "Yes Rick, the usual; Elena, you want anything?"

"The biggest they have with cream and sugar. Thanks Ricky."

Ricky feels partially responsible for everything that happened while Mike and the girls were Caged, "Boss, I am sorry for what happened in there; it was all really fucked up. We tried to find you sooner, Bro. We really tried."

"I know, brother. We can't change what happened, but we can serve up the consequences." Mike wants Ricky to know it wasn't his fault.

At 6:00 am, the auction for Mike and Elena will begin, and by noon the auction will end. Max can narrow Cahill's options to just a few women. Elena will be the only one who does not have blond hair, light eyes, a fair complexion, and a very slim figure. Ricky, who had overheard Gabriel at the bar, knows he is looking for a curvy brunette for Özdemir. Elena is the only one in the search results with the desired 'attributes.' The team is confident that Gabriel will place a bid on her.

Mike is not as confident that he will be chosen in the auction. Most of the men in the auction are so much alike, almost identical clones. Mike wants to make sure he is the one that Özdemir will pick. He asks Max for help, "Max, we need to reduce the number of other men that Cahill can bid on. We can't risk him not selecting me."

Elena scrolled through the images of Mike's intake, shaking her head in amazement. "Mike, I'm sure the little Frenchman will be more than happy to be with you. I can guarantee it!" she exclaims. As she keeps scrolling, she comes across the more intimate pictures. "Wow, these are really detailed! Everything is on camera! Daaaammmn! Oof, I remember that very well."

"Hey, why are we looking at the Boss's junk?" Ricky walks in with coffee for the team.

"What!?" Mike exclaims, staring at Elena's computer screen in disbelief. "Come on, Elena, really?"

Elena can't help but chuckle as she closes the windows displaying Mike's very personal pictures, "I am sorry Mike. But I had to do it. After all, turnabout is fair play, right?"

Mike tries to ignore the distraction and refocus everyone's attention, saying, "Okay, let's get to work, everyone. The bidding for Elena has just begun, so Max, why don't you start it off with a million-dollar bid and get the ball rolling?"

Max enters the first bid, "One million dollars for Miss Elena. Done Boss!"

Mike stared out the window, sipping his steaming cup of black coffee, as he murmured, *And now, we wait.*

It didn't take long for the scheme to start to come together. Max is ecstatic, "Dude, Cahill is online. Just as I predicted, Elena, you're now at 2 million bucks. I can't wait to see how much you'll go for!"

Elena's gaze is fixed on the screen, expressing discontent and uncertainty. *I'm not sure if I should be offended or take it as a compliment,* she mutters.

Gabriel Toussaint arrives at the Özdemir Château before the sun has even risen, filled with anticipation for the day's events. Unfortunately, Emree is not present, but he has left Cahill in charge of selecting the perfect man for Gabriel. Emree has specified that the man must be incredibly large, capable of easily overpowering Gabriel, "big enough to break him in half," and "quite handsome." This plays right into Mike's hands; Max has ensured that he is the only 'Acquired' that fits this description.

"Do you want to see what Emree bought for you?" Cahill asks Gabriel.

"Yes, I am very excited," Gabriel looks at the computer screen and sees a mountain of a man, "Oh my, he is a big boy."

"You have no idea, Gabriel. Let me show you the rest of the mountain," Cahill clicked on the photos of Mike's manhood.

Gabriel claps his hands and shouts, grinning ear to ear, "Eurêka! C'est énorme!"

"And here we have the perfect girl for Emree; she fits your description perfectly. I am sure he will be pleased with the change," Cahill clicks on Elena's pictures, admiring her beauty.

Gabriel is astonished, exclaiming in awe, "She is absolutely Magnifique, a true masterpiece! She is a wise decision; purchase her at any cost."

As expected, the auction concludes with Cahill as the highest bidder for Mike and Elena. Everything is proceeding according to plan.

"And that's it; we have been sold," Mike says as he steps away from the computer, looking satisfied.

Elena's gaze remains fixed on the computer screen; her expression is utter disgust. "It's appalling," she states, "to think people are being bought and sold like livestock. It's disgusting."

"You went for some big bucks, Elena. $12 million; I mean, that's pretty damn good! Disturbing, but wow, impressive at the same time," Ricky is smiling ear to ear.

Max couldn't help but get a dig in on his brother, "Mike, you didn't do too bad, I guess. Five million is good for a hunk of meat like you. You didn't come close to Elena, but you are just not in the same class as her. Still respectable, I guess."

"Hilarious Max. It's not a contest. We were both purchased by that degenerate; that was the plan. I am just glad the Mission is still on target."

Elena knows that she has to take part in the fun, or else she will succumb to the shadows of being purchased. "It's alright, Mike; five million isn't anything to sneeze at. I mean, I ended up getting more than double what you did. Then again, it is for all of this," she says, striking a pose like a game show model and gracefully running her hands down her body to emphasize that she was the prize that had just been won.

Mike growled. "Let's get ready."

Most 'Acquired' are conditioned before being sold, with drugs used as part of the process. After they are taken in, they are placed in holding areas and given potent narcotics to keep them quiet and compliant for delivery to the 'Buyers.' Sometimes, the 'Acquired' need to be stored for a few days. They are usually sedated upon delivery, although not to an excessive degree. Mike and Elena need to be sedated today to maintain the illusion. Still, Mike must remain alert and protect Elena from whatever Emree has in store for her.

For this reason, he is on the phone with Dr. Hansen, "Doc, I need to have full function as soon as possible without raising suspicion. Nothing like what you gave me in Germany, that stuff was way too strong. Make the dosage even less for Elena. She will be with a very dangerous man and must be able to take care of herself if things go wrong."

Dr. Hansen assures Mike, "It's just a mild sedative, I promise."

"Doc, if I pass out or Elena gets hurt because I can't help her," Mike was interrupted by Dr. Hansen."

"Mike, I understand the game plan here, trust me. Low.... grade.... sedative, nothing more," the doctor assures.

"You better have this right doc," says Mike.

The Sheik is Here?:

Ricky and Max closely watch Emree Özdemir at the Geneva International Motor Show. Mike is adamant that this will be Emree Özdemir's final night on earth, and he warns the guys not to "*Fuck this up*." He makes it clear that they must ensure that everything goes according to plan and that there is no room for mistakes.

"Hey, did you hear the Boss this morning? He is really messed up," Ricky says.

"Yeah, I did," Max says, "two women? I mean, if anyone can make that work, it's Mike. But yeah, he's really in a bad way man."

The two men stare as the 'Prey' arrives, their eyes fixed upon the figures as they slowly approach.

Emree Özdemir and Gabriel Toussaint are standing close to the main stage of the Car Show, and Emree declares that the 'prizes' will be delivered this evening, no later than 6:00 pm. Today is the day that Özdemir Motors will be making its grand international announcement to the world.

Gabriel grabs his friend's arm, "Yes, Emree, I know. I am very excited."

Emree looks at his friend, "You should be a little scared, Gabriel. That big man is going to break you in half, I am sure of it. Did you see the photos of him?"

Gabriel winks, "In my wildest dreams, Emree. I hope he does."

Max and Ricky casually wander near the main stage watching the two men.

"So what happens to Özdemir Motors tomorrow when this guy doesn't exist anymore?" Ricky nods toward Emree.

Max looks at Ricky, shaking his head, "I don't know, he's just one dude. So the company keeps going. That's what they say in business, right? No one is irreplaceable. Someone else will take over, hopefully not someone as fucked up as him."

Ricky runs his hands along an Ascari Blue metallic Audi R8 Quattro Coupe. "I wonder Bro, what would happen if we got into the car business?"

Max watches as Ricky practically makes love to the car, "What do you mean by 'car business'?"

Ricky places both hands on the car's roof and proposes, "What if we took control of that little shits company?"

Max laughs, "Sure, from Hit-man to Car-man...that works."

Ricky glances back at Emree, "I was just thinking, that's all. We got $17 million from that prick today. Why shouldn't we pocket it all?"

"Nah Bro, we only got $12 million. That Sheik dude takes the rest as fees," he watches as the convention center gradually becomes crowded with onlookers as Ricky is "envisioning" a different reality. Max's attention is drawn to an unexpected guest, Sheik Zubair Majeed.

"Son of a bitch! Ricky, look who we have here," Max nods to Majeed.

"Hoo-ly shit! We need to tell the Boss," Ricky grabs his cell phone to call Mike, but Max stops him.

"No, wait Rick, today our Mission is Özdemir. We will get Majeed, but not tonight; he is not our 'Target'."

"Max, Bro, Mike needs to make that decision, not you. We have to tell him; you have to tell him."

Ricky is right, and Max knows it. Max also knows Mike better than anyone alive. If Mike knows the Sheik is here, the Mission changes, not necessarily for the better.

"Majeed, it is nice to see you." Özdemir greets him with open arms, "I did not know you were coming to see my launch."

Majeed and Özdemir embrace, "Of course my friend, I would not miss it."

Özdemir introduces the men, "Zubair, this is my friend, Gabriel Toussaint. Gabriel, this is Sheik Zubair Majeed."

Gabriel places his hand across his chest, "It's nice to meet you, Monsieur Majeed. We were just talking about you."

Majeed stands tall and proud of himself, "Yes, of course, you were. I have heard of your most recent purchases; excellent choices, very excellent."

"Zubair, I hope you can join us tonight," says Özdemir.

The Sheik places his hand on Özdemir's shoulder, "Ahhh, Emree! I wish I could, but I am meeting with a very important man from the United States of America today. I guess you can call him my partner in my latest venture."

"Invite him to join us; the more, the merrier, my friend. I have plenty of girls for all of us to enjoy." Emree is trying to impress the Sheik.

The Sheik enjoys a good time as much as any man, "That is very thought-ful. I will ask my new American friend; I am not sure it is his type of party. I, on the other hand, would not miss it."

Mr. Özdemir to the main stage, please, is announced over the PA.

Emree lights up as he hears his name above the crowd's noise, "I hope to see you at the celebration with your American. Gentleman, I must be going. It appears to be my time on the main stage."

The Shit Show to end all Shit Shows:

Mike and Elena are busily making the final adjustments to their plan, going over it one last time when Max and Ricky enter the room. Max tells Mike about the Sheik, letting him know that he is likely to be at the party tonight and that he will also bring his guards along.

Mike clinches his jaw, "That Fucking guy is here..." The plan to take Emree after the party is off. Now Mike needs Max and Ricky's help.

Elena is listening to Max but is entirely in the dark about who the Sheik is and what any of it means. "So Mike, could you please explain what this all means?"

Mike is conflicted; he needs to take the Sheik's life, feel it drain from his body, and witness the terror in his eyes as it happens, yet he also has to do the same to Emree. He will have to adjust his strategy on the fly.

"Okay, I need your help guys," Mike says, "I haven't told you everything Elena," he turns to Max, "Can you fill her in please?" Mike's mind is racing, and the darkness is starting to wash over him and take control.

"Elena, Emree Özdemir isn't just some random pervert. He's known the Barnes family for years and was a close friend of the girl's father. They call the guy Uncle Em. He even stayed at their house when they were kids. For years, he's been purchasing girls who look like Claire, but this time, he orders Claire herself. When Claire turned 19, Emree decided to buy her so she could carry his children. That piece of shit even sent a photo of her to the 'Hunters' in Saudi. During her intake, Shariek Blon Mosomid decides he has other plans, and he makes it look like she's killed in a struggle during her capture. Shariek sent her to the Baby Mill with her sister and Mike. Özdemir has no idea she's alive; he still believes she died in Saudi."

Elena turns to Mike, "So you're conflicted on who to get first?"

Mike is trying to devise a new plan that will allow him to get the Sheik and Özdemir. "If I take out the Sheik, Özdemir will go underground, knowing something is up. If I take Özdemir first, the Sheik will disappear."

Elena can't understand why Mike wants to, needs to, have them both die by his hands, "Why not just split up and take them all tonight? I'll take Özdemir, and you take the Sheik."

Ricky explains, "The Boss must be there to look into the eyes of those two leaving this world as they take their last breath. I understand this better than anyone else."

"That is completely ridiculous," Elena says, her voice filled with disbelief. "Mike, you are a trained assassin, not just a cold-blooded murderer. Just do your job. What you're saying, it sounds like you're a monster, not the Mike I know and love." Elena quickly realizes the implications of her words and adds, "I'm sorry. I didn't mean it like that."

Mike understands what she is trying to tell him, but it doesn't change his mind. There is a burning desire driving him to face both men. "I hear you Elena, and I know you're right, but I have to do this. Ricky and Max, I need you both tonight."

Max is adamant, "No Mike, we have to stick to Ricky's plan. If we rush in recklessly, it will spell disaster. There are women in there that need us to rescue them. Let's take Emree first, and then we'll get the Sheik. Let him go after the party and stay on Mission."

Mike has already decided, "Mission changed Max. Elena, you're off the hook. Ricky, get our stuff ready."

"Roger that, Boss. I have our 'tools' in the van; I'll be right back." With that, Ricky exits the hotel room.

"This is not good Mike; Elena, please try to talk some sense into him. You two stay here; I'll be right back." Max quickly heads into the hallway, searching for a place to call Markus. *This whole thing is turning into the Shit Show to end all Shit Shows.*

Elena sits beside Mike on the bed and gently places her hand on his. "Mike, Max is right," she said, her voice calm and reassuring. "We need to regroup and focus on Özdemir. We'll all help you get the Sheik afterward. It won't take long, I promise."

Mike slowly turns to face Elena, and she can see the fury in his eyes. She reaches out and tenderly moves the hair away from his ear. He takes a deep breath as a wave of calm washes over him. However, the moment is fleeting, and Mike's darkness soon returns.

Mike tries to make her understand, "Elena, I must do this. I understand you don't know why, but I have to be there as they take their last breath. This could be our only chance to get them both."

Elena tenderly holds his face in her hand, kisses him, and stares into his eyes. She is looking for the kind compassionate man she knows is hidden behind those eyes, now as dark as a starless night. She speaks gently, trying to soothe his rage, "I understand; I just know you're not thinking clearly. You and Ricky will cause a lot of destruction if you go there. You won't be able to control yourself. Mike, there are innocent people there, young women who have been purchased by this creep, who don't deserve your vengeance."

Mike is intently listening to her, taking in every word she utters. He realizes now he has another problem to deal with, Elena.

He takes Elena's hands into his own, gently placing them in her lap. His voice is steady and firm as he says, "I'm sorry Elena, but you need to go now, please. I must do this."

Max is on his phone, waiting for Markus to answer, "Come on Margaret Where the fuck is he...."

"Hello, Max; how are things going there?" asks Markus.

"Not good Boss. Things here are about to become a total disaster!" Max explains to Markus about the Sheik and Özdemir.

"Sounds like we can get two birds with one stone Max. I don't understand the problem?"

"Look Markus, Mike is about to lose his shit. He and Ricky are going on a hunt. That means no one will make it out alive, no one," says Max.

"Max, the Director is out of town, and I am in charge. Unless you have a reason to believe Mike will take things too far, then he has my blessing. Do you have a reason, Max?" asks Markus.

Markus thinks like a company man. He sees no problem with Mike and Ricky ending everything and everyone if need be.

"Sir, Mike will take things too far. I am telling you, he will."

Frankly, in The Trash:

Things in San Diego are going really well. Mike's mom and dad have come to the apartment to help the girls pack. Claire hired a moving crew to transport the boxes, and they are just about done with their last round from the apartment as Rebecca arrives with lunch.

"Mexican perfect!" Claire is completely hooked; she can't believe how much she has come to love Mexican food.

"Good, I'm glad I made the right choice for lunch," Rebecca is pleased with her choice; there are so many excellent eateries in Downtown San Diego that it can be challenging to decide. She puts the food on the kitchen counter with a satisfied smile.

Christina exclaims, "Claire has been eating nothing but Mexican food for the past three days, having it for breakfast, lunch, and dinner."

Max Sr. walks into the room with a box and says, "Well, that's great news because she is just skin and bones! Hey, where would you like me to put this box?"

"Frankly, in the trash, but it's Mike's stuff, so just leave it by the door with the rest," Claire can't help but speak the truth on this subject.

The apartment is almost empty, apart from a few pieces of furniture. All of Mike's belongings are being boxed and sent to Texas. In truth, Claire does not intend to bring most of Mike's things to the new house. His furniture, for example, is truly hideous.

"Do you need me to start taking apart his bed?" asks Max Sr.

"Max, Rebecca, am I being ridiculous if I don't want Mike's furniture in our new home?" Claire has been holding her tongue, and finally, she has to speak up.

Rebecca smiles at Claire and says, "No, I don't think so honey. It's understandable. You don't want to bring his old bachelor life into your new family life together. But I think you should talk to Mike about it, don't you?"

"I will; it's not about his life before me. I know he had a life; it's more that his taste is pretty awful. I mean, this stuff is horrible, isn't it?"

"I don't know. It looks good to me," says Max Sr.

Rebecca laughs, "Of course you would like it Max. You and Mike have the same horrible style. Claire, you should see Max Jr.'s place in Mexico. Believe it or not. It's even worse than this."

Claire turns around, taking in Mike's belongings; she can't help but say, "What could be worse than a Chinese painting of a tiger in black and gold, a Persian rug in red and blue, and a chair that defies description? I'm so glad I'm not the only one who feels this way - thank you Rebecca, for confirming my doubts," Claire is relieved she isn't alone in her harsh judgment of Mike's hideous things.

"How about you call me Mom," says Rebecca

Claire tears up. "Thank you...Mom"

"Oh, come here," Rebecca hugs Claire; and they both begin to cry.

"Well, I feel left out," Christina also starts to tear up.

"Oh, come here dear girl," Rebecca says, pulling Christina into their embrace.

Now all three women are sobbing as Max Sr. walks in with yet another box. "You've got to be kidding me," he says and heads back to where he came from.

I Am on Vacation:

"Mr. Director, I would like to invite you to a party tonight. My dear friend, Emree Özdemir of Özdemir Motors, has invited us to his Château in Cologne." Sheik Zubair Majeed is on the phone with Director Gray.

"I would like that, Zubair. I would like to meet Mr. Özdemir," Gray accepts the invitation.

"Good then, I will pick you up at 7:00 pm. Will that work for you?" asks Zubair.

"That sounds fine, Zubair; I will see you then," says Gray as he hangs up the phone.

"Mr. Director, Markus Delphy is on the phone for you, Sir. He says it's urgent," Director Gray's bodyguard, Bobby Flynn, is holding up his cell phone.

"Bobby, take a message: I am on vacation. I told Markus he was in charge for the next two days. I need that guy to take the initiative for once."

"Yes Sir," Bobby returns to his call with Markus, "Unfortunately, the Director is unavailable. Would you like me to take a message?"

"No message. Tell him to have a nice trip. I just.... Never mind, I will take care of it. Thanks Bobby," Markus hangs up.

"So, what was the message Bobby?" asks Director Gray.

"He said to have a nice trip, Sir."

"The guy just can't get out of my shadow. Oh well, he thinks I am in France anyway," Director Gray tells Bobby.

Ricky passes Elena in the hall on his way back to the hotel room. He is carrying two black duffle bags. They say a quick goodbye to each other and continue their separate ways. Elena is looking for Max; Ricky is headed to Mike.

"Max, I have a plan," says Elena

"Good, because we are all alone here. Markus is supporting Mike," says Max, "What do you got?"

"We go with Ricky's plan, but only me," says Elena.

"I don't think so. Elena, I am not putting you in that place alone. Mike will kill me if anything happens to you, even if he is my brother."

"Max, what will happen when Mike and Ricky show up if we don't get there first? What will happen to the innocent women that are being held captive there? When the blood-lust overcomes the guys, you know what will happen." Elena says, shaking her head in mistrust.

"But I can't help you," says Max, "what if something goes bad?"

"Max, I can take care of myself. You know I can. Now, my delivery will be late if we don't leave. Take me there now, please," says Elena.

The End is Near:

Ricky and Mike begin their ascent up the cliff, a steep climb of over a thousand feet to Emree Özdemir's Château. They have an hour to reach the top and make their way to the house, eliminating any guards in their path. Once they secure the area, the two will enter the house through the front doors, and then it will be a free-for-all until they capture Emree Özdemir and Sheik Zubair Majeed.

"It's a straightforward plan," Mike says, "Everyone dies. That makes it easy." Ricky is the perfect partner for this Mission, as he and Mike share the same philosophy.

As the guys are making their climb to the back of the Château, Max is delivering Cahill's winning 'Acquired' to the front.

"And where is the Mountain Man I paid for?" demands Cahill.

"We had a bit of a problem with him. I promise to deliver him by 10:00 pm," says Max.

Cahill says curtly, "That will not do. Our contract says delivery by 6:00 pm. It is now 6:30. My boss has plans for him. Our contract is void on the male. As for this one, she looks good enough, but we will inspect her. If she does not have all of the attributes presented during the auction or is damaged, the payment will be reduced."

"Yes Sir. I need to give her one more shot, then I'll bring her to you," says Max.

"Good," says Cahill, "hurry up then."

Cahill's eyes are fixed on Max as he inserts a needle into Elena's arm. As the doctor has instructed, Max injects a small dose of heroin, though not as much as Cahill would have administered to his boss's women to keep them docile, but enough to knock her out. In no time at all, Elena's body goes limp.

"Very good," says Cahill, "we can take her inside."

"I got her; I don't need your help," Max picks up Elena, who is very drugged, but before Cahill can get his hands on her, Max shoots Narcan into Elena's nose. This reverses the effects of the heroine, allowing Elena a fighting chance if something were to go wrong.

"Holy shit, that stuff knocked me out, Max," Elena exclaims, her head spinning as she gradually regains sobriety. However, her body is still trembling from the shock.

Max carries Elena over his shoulder into the house. He follows Cahill upstairs into Emree's bedroom.

"Just drop her on the bed!" yells Emree from the bathroom.

"We will check her, Emree. I already told this man that if she is damaged in any way, we will deduct it from the payment," Cahill calls to Emree.

Max looks into Elena's eyes as the two men undress her and lay her on the bed. She is a professional, never letting on that she isn't under sedation from the heroin.

"Ok, she looks fine; you will be paid in full. Go back and bring the man; we will work something out to reduce the payment for him because he is late," says Cahill.

"Yes, I will," Max starts to leave, with Cahill leading him out of the bedroom. But he turns around to look towards Elena.

"Hey, I can't leave you. Emree is naked in there," Max whispers.

Elena harshly whispers back, "Go! I can take care of myself."

Max cannot express what he fears will happen to Elena; all he can say is, "He is coming out now, and I can't do anything to stop him. He is going to...," leaving the sentence unfinished.

Elena is aware of the potential consequences and is prepared to face them; she whispers sternly, "Max, go! I can handle this Mission. You have to leave now."

"What are you still doing here? Cahill will release the funds. Go, she is my property now," says Emree as he walks in from the bathroom.

"Yes Sir, I will go and get the man for you," Max nods to Elena, and she slowly blinks back at him in acknowledgment. He knows this is the right thing to do, but he doesn't want to leave her. He takes a deep breath and reluctantly begins to walk out of the bedroom; his stare remains on Elena until she is out of sight.

"Oh, you are a beautiful one, not exactly my type, but undeniably attractive. I am hosting a party tonight, and I am sure you will be the guest of honor. Yes, with a body like that, you will definitely be the center of attention," Emree begins to admire his new acquisition, running his hands over Elena's naked body, "Yes, you are absolutely stunning and so well-built. It is a shame to have you simply to 'entertain' my guests tonight.

But they are influential men from all over the world, and I need you to ensure they are pleased. How much 'arm candy' have you taken today? Are you able to stand?"

Elena plays the part perfectly, standing but falling as soon as she stands.

"Damn it; you must recover before I can take you to the party and my guests. You just rest here; I need to get dressed," says Emree.

Whew, Elena thinks, *I was sure he would be on me already. And I would have let him, anything for the Mission, but this is a far better outcome.*

Emree returns to the bathroom and shouts to Elena, "I must say that I am not a fan of sharing. I do not usually do it, but tonight is a very special night for me. I am about to enter the U.S. Auto Market, and the Sheik has brought me a powerful American Government official. I need you to keep him company, make him very 'satisfied' for me, and I will reward you with more arm candy for your troubles."

Emree stops dressing and glances at Elena in the reflection of the mirror. She is absolutely stunning, and the urge to *try her out* overcomes him.

"You know what? I have some time, and I hate to be second," he says as he applies oil to his body and makes his way back to Elena.

Seconds later, Emree is on the bed, "I will be quick, just a taste," he mounts Elena to take his taste.

Once Mike and Ricky reach the ridge's top, they unpack their bags and put on their equipment.

"Alright, Ricky, you take left, and I'll take right," Mike instructs, "Call out your hits so we can keep count."

Ricky has been thinking about Mike's Cage the entire climb, and he can't help but think about the women who suffer in places like that. They are not there of their own free will; they are forced to be there. This realization gives Ricky a sense of sadness for the first time in his life as he and Mike are about to do something that he knows will be destructive to these women. He knows Mike's orders, *everyone to be dealt with, with no exceptions.* But Ricky needs to ask, "What about the women Boss?"

Mike has been considering the women himself, and Elena's words echo in his mind, "Let's try to keep the collateral damage to a minimum Rick, but if they are in the way, you take the shot. None of the men inside live to see tomorrow. Do you understand?"

"Got it Boss, good hunting."

"Same to you Rick; let's do this."

The two men begin their hunt, each with their silenced M5 at the ready. Mike takes the first shot killing a guard as they turn the corner in the yard. Ricky is next killing a guard on the second floor looking out over the yard. This continues as the two men make their way to the house.

Silently to herself, Elena screams in anger and pain while tears fall from her eyes. Emree Özdemir bites Elena's right breast, purposefully breaking the skin, causing her to bleed, and hoping to leave a permeant mark.

Emree gazes down at Elena and her now wounded chest, leaving a reminder of his conquest. "I apologize, but I tend to mark my conquests in this manner. But do not worry, I will have Cahill bring you some arm candy to soothe the pain as soon as I depart," Emree resumes dressing, "You are extraordinary, my dear, quite possibly the best I have ever encountered. I believe I may need to keep you for myself, at least for the time being. But I must be going for now; my guests are waiting for my grand entrance. I will return to you as soon as I am able."

Emree finishes getting dressed and steps out the door when Elena goes to work. She utters, *Damn! That was painful - what a fucking Bastard!* She dabs at the blood on her chest, her expression a mixture of pain and disbelief. She needs to dress and leave before Cahill shows up with her arm candy. Elena moves quickly, just not quickly enough; it's too late. Cahill walks in just as she is about to walk out the bedroom door. With no other option, Elena grabs a floor lamp and quickly steps behind the door as it opens.

"Hello, I have your Medicine for you," Cahill enters the room looking for Elena, but she is not on the bed. He turns around to see a metal lamp whorling towards his head.

Elena quickly pulls Cahill's body out of view and rushes down the stairs. Emree is in the living room with a few men. At least a dozen women are meandering and talking with the other guests. They all have the same features - blonde hair, thin frames, and green eyes. *This guy is sick,* Elena thinks to herself. She proceeds to the basement. Inside, she finds a large Cage containing even more women, all with the same blonde hair and green eyes; much to her surprise, they are all pregnant.

"Hey, get up!" Elena exclaims, "I'm here to get you out of this place." The women aren't drugged, but they are kept Caged to keep them under control. Elena works quickly, not knowing where the guards are and expecting to be apprehended at any moment. Fortunately, Ricky and Mike are dealing with the guards, and she won't be disturbed.

Elena opens the Cage and reaches out to help the women unable to stand on their own. She knows she has to get them out of the house before Mike and Ricky arrive, so she quickly opens the door to the basement leading to the backyard. With a sense of urgency, she guides the women out of the house, hoping they can make it out in time.

"What the hell are you doing here?" yells a man in the dark.

"Mike, I need your help; these women must be evacuated out of the house. Please Mike, let's help them," begs Elena.

"You take care of it; I'm staying on 'Target'. The backyard is clear; get them to the shrubs and stay put. Elena, don't come back in here. That's an order!" Mike commands sternly.

Albert is Compromised:

Director Gray arrives at the party and is informed that their "Host" will join them shortly. As he surveys the scene, he can't help but think to himself that the *women here must be prostitutes*, judging by the way they are interacting with the other men in the room. Gray isn't particularly enthusiastic about this type of activity but is willing to give it a try. He sits on one of the large couches and is served food and drinks by some of the most attractive women he has ever seen.

Sitting next to the Director is Sheik Zubair Majeed enjoying and admiring the women.

"Do they all look the same to you, Zubair, or is that my imagination?" asks Gray.

"Emree has a very specific type. In fact, he has a standing purchase order for them," explains Zubair.

"These are your women, Zubair?"

"Yes, they were all ordered from my Network. They belong to Emree now; he is offering them, as his gift, to his guests tonight. He is most generous."

Gray stands, "I am not interested in this, Zubair. Please tell Emree I am grateful for his hospitality, but this is not for me," he wants to leave; this is not what he expected to see. Even though in his mind, he is doing the right thing with the Sheik for his country and himself, he doesn't want to be a part of these women's less-than-desirable lives.

"Nonsense Director, look at this one here. She is lovely. Dear girl, please meet my friend, his name is Albert. Make him feel welcome, will you?"

The young woman walks towards the Director. As she draws closer, Gray can see the numerous track marks and what appear to be cigarette burns covering her arms. Her speech is halting and heavily accented as she says, "You want love? I am very good. I can make you happy. I can make you feel very good and please you nice. I will do anything you like."

Gray is filled with revulsion as the woman gets closer to him. He can see that her body is covered in what appear to be bite marks, indicating that she has been subjected to immense abuse. Gray is overcome with guilt as he realizes *HE* is directly responsible for this woman's abuse and suffering. The Director now understands what Mike has been attempting to explain to him the entire time - Zubair is an evil man who must be dealt with.

"Zubair, this woman needs a doctor. I insist that she gets medical attention right away," demands the Director.

"I believe her time is short Mr. Director. But not to worry, she will soon be out of her misery. Why don't we pick another one for you?" The Sheik glances around, trying to find the perfect mate for the Director. "Ah, that one over there, she has just finished with the Prince. Young lady, could you please come over here? My friend would like your attention."

Emree Özdemir strolls into the room with a dignified air, as if he is a god. His arms are outstretched, and he moves with a graceful gait looking like he is gliding across the surface of a lake. He has chosen to wear a pristine white ensemble, the embodiment of affluence and poise, to make a powerful statement to his guests. His head is held high as he casts his gaze around the room, taking in the sight of his guests in various states of delight due to the 'gifts' he has bestowed upon them. Özdemir proceeds to his old friend seated alongside Director Gray and warmly greets the men. His Desire is to make a favorable impression on his new American acquaintance.

"Hello my old friend," Emree says to the Sheik with a smile that surprises the Director. It is a look of sheer evil, which is hard to describe but undeniably genuine.

"Hello Emree. Thank you for inviting us to your wonderful gathering. This is my friend Albert Gray. He is an American Government official, an important one at that," says Zubair.

"Hello Mr. Gray. I am Emree Özdemir. It is very lovely to make your acquaintance. I do hope that you are enjoying yourself."

Mike and Ricky have most of the guards taken care of; so far, no alarms are going off. Mike says, "So far, so good."

Ricky spots one more that they need to deal with. "Boss, there is one more in the front by the cars," he says, taking aim. Mike is in a much better position to take the shot; the man smokes a cigarette with his back to him. Mike, now focusing his sights on the man's head, gradually applies pressure to the trigger. Suddenly, the man turns his body towards Mike and Ricky, and they see it is Bobby Flynn.

"What the Hell?" Mike calls to him, "Bobby....Bobby."

Bobby hears Mike; his whispered tone carries to him. He looks around to see Mike and Ricky both aiming M5's at him. "Hey, what the hell, guys?" Bobby raises his hands.

"Get over here," says Mike.

Bobby walks over to him, hands still raised, "Mike, what's going on? Why are you here and barring down on me?"

"I will ask the questions. Why are you here? Where is Gray? What is he doing here?" asks Mike.

"He's inside; he is a guest. I have no idea what he is doing. I just do what he tells me," says Bobby.

"Ricky, tie up Bobby! Bobby, you need to keep quiet, or I will have to keep you quiet, understand?" Mike says.

Bobby asks, "Mike, seriously, I don't understand; what are you guys doing here?"

"The less you know, the better Bobby. Please don't make me kill you for doing your job. Just have a good nap." Mike strikes Bobby with the butt of his rifle.

"The boss is here? What the fuck Mike?" asks Ricky.

"Albert is compromised Ricky. He just made the list!"

Elena quickly guides the women from the basement to the outer perimeter of the property, doing her best to hide them. As she turns back to the house, she hears the unmistakable sound of gunshots, glass breaking, and screaming. All hell is breaking loose. "Damn it, Mike!" she shouts. She turns to the women and says, "Stay out of sight. I will come back for you," and runs towards the house.

Justice is Served:

Mike and Ricky begin their assault on the main house. Mike calling out contacts, and Ricky taking the shots. "Target right," yells Mike. Ricky takes the shot, and a man falls from the second floor smashing to the ground with a thud. "Targets left low," Ricky hits Sheik Zubair Majeed's bodyguards, blowing one man off his feet onto the floor and hitting the other before he can pull his firearm in the neck. The man falls to the ground, blood spraying like a sprinkler covering the white marble floor.

As the two Assassins continue their infiltration. Mike's eyes lock on his three 'Targets': Sheik Zubair Majeed, Emree Özdemir, and Director Albert Gray. The trio is clearly taken aback by the sudden and lethal assault on the Château, sitting in shock and disbelief.

In the house, women cry out in terror, and men bellow in outrage. Behind one woman, sitting on a long white couch, is a small man, Gabriel Toussaint. Mike takes aim and fires, hitting Gabriel in the chest. The woman he was hiding behind screams and runs for her life. This encourages more women to flee the house and the horror all around them.

Mike's three 'Targets' have overcome the initial shock and now attempt to escape. He fires a burst of rounds into the ceiling shouting, "Everybody shut the hell up and sit back down where you are!"

Ricky sprints towards their 'Targets' yelling out, "Sit the fuck down!" as he reaches them. He then uses the butt of his rifle to knock the Sheik in the mouth, sending him crashing into the couch, dazed, bleeding, and leaning against Director Gray.

Mike steps towards the men just as Elena bursts through the back doors. "Mike, don't!" she yells, quickly surveying the situation; Ricky has the place locked down. Mike has Gray dead to rights, his hands firmly gripping his rifle as if he is prepared to unleash a much-earned barrage of bullets into him.

Mike, never taking his eyes off Gray, commands, "Elena, take the women out of here." Pointing his rifle directly at Albert Gray's head, "Albert, tell me what the fuck you are doing here!" Mikes says, his eyes full of hate.

Albert Gray can feel the inevitability of his own death; he knows that Mike will be the one to take his life. He can sense it down to his core. He understands that no matter what he says, the result will remain the same. Gray's words are spoken with a sense of finality as if he is aware that these could be his final words. "Mike, it's not what you think. You were right, son. These men are pure evil. I should have listened to you."

"And yet you're sitting next to them, like old friends," says Mike.

"What do you want? Who are these men?" shouts Emree.

Ricky quickly brains the man with the butt of his rifle. "Shut the fuck up!" he yells. Emree is knocked on his side, but he quickly regains his composure.

Elena is urgently gathering the women together; one was severely injured during the attack. A man used her as a human shield, and as a result, she was shot in the stomach. "Mike, she needs help! We have to do something!" Elena shouts desperately.

Mike is focused on Gray, and although he does not want any more harm to come to the women, his main focus is the Mission at hand. "Elena," he says firmly, "get them out. There is a van in the driveway. Take them now. That is an order."

"Albert, who is this man?" Zubair asks. "I thought we had a deal?"

"Zubair, all deals are off. Mike, his Golden Ticket is void," Gray declares.

Seconds later, a shot rings out coming from the staircase. Cahill tumbles down the stairs coming to a rest at the landing. Max stands at the top of the stairs looking at Mike and Ricky. He gives them a nod.

"Max, help Elena. Get these women to safety," Mike orders.

"Yes Bro," Max hurries to help. "Here, let me help you," Elena and Max carry three women out and are followed by the rest. This left the area empty except for the dead bodies, three men on the couch, and of course, Ricky and Mike.

Mike flips his rifle's safety on and slings it behind him; he pulls his knife from the sheath. Then he turns towards Zubair, pointing with the shiny blade. "You, will be last Zubair," he says. Mike then shifts his attention to Emree.

"Hello, Mr. Özdemir, my name is Mike, and you DO NOT want to meet me, but here I am," He pulls a photo from his pocket and then shows it to Emree. "You know this woman, don't you?" He states.

"Why do you have that? Yes, she is...was my niece," Emree admits.

"Emree she is my future wife; she trusted you. She maybe even loved you. You were supposed to be like family to her. What was your plan Emree? What were you going to do with her, you bastard?"

"Nothing, I loved her. I would never do anything to her. You have to believe me," Emree is now pleading with Mike.

Mike hears a voice from behind, "Mike," says Elena.

"Who is this woman?" demands the Sheik, "Emree, who is she?"

Emree answers, "I do not know."

Ricky is holding his rifle just inches from Emree's head, the blood from Emree's forehead streaming down into his eyes. His expression is utter terror as he feels the cold steel of the gun pressing against his temple. He can feel his heart racing and his breath quickening.

Elena stares into Emrees eyes with immense anger, "I am your property, don't you remember Emree? You just bought me today."

Mike stares at Elena, noticing that her blouse is stained with blood originating from her chest. He gently moves the fabric aside and growls in shock, "My God," after seeing the deep, bleeding bite mark on Elena's breast. Mike hands her his knife, knowing she needs this much more than he does.

Elena nods to Mike and slowly makes her way toward Emree.

"You thought I was your property, Emree; now I will take back what you took from Claire and all these others," Elena stabs Emree in the groin severing his penis from his body; he screams in pain, blood pouring onto the couch. Elena then stabs him in the right leg and twists the knife. This action severs his femoral artery. She grips the knife tightly, her gaze never leaving the man's eyes as the life bleeds out of him. She feels no remorse, no regret for what she has done. Saying, "No regrets," loud enough and with conviction for all to hear, as Emree's eyes go lifeless.

Elena removes the knife and wipes away the crimson-colored blood on Emree's now-stained suit. She returns it to Mike with a silent nod. No words are necessary; the look in her eyes says it all as she walks out of the house.

"Mike, this needs to end. Just do what you're going to do," says Director Gray.

Gray has no fear; he simply desires closure. He is aware that Mike has made up his mind and has a list of 'Targets', a list Gray himself has taught him to create. All the names on that list have to be eliminated without exception. Gray knows he is now on Mike's list and has accepted it.

Mike asks, "Albert, do you want to make my introduction to the Sheik? Or shall I."

"Mike, just do what you came here to do," Gray says.

"Albert, we had a deal. You gave me your word!" says the Sheik.

"His word doesn't mean shit Zubair. It's too bad because I loved him like a father," says Mike.

Mike has envisioned the Sheik's death in his mind, and now it is time to make it a reality. He has planned out the excruciating pain he will inflict, slowly peeling away layers of skin and ensuring to keep the agony going for as long as possible. Mike wants the Sheik to feel all the suffering he has caused to so many people, like Marisa, Claire, Christina, Terri, and Sammy. He must pay for all his sins.

Just as Mike is about to begin his carefully crafted torture, he looks up. He notices what is hanging over the fireplace. *That sick fuck bastard,* Mike thinks. There is a portrait of Mike's beloved Claire hanging above the fireplace. Mike can not help but feel an intense longing for her as he stares at the painting. He is certain that she needs him, a feeling that is embedded deep within his soul, and he misses her dearly. Claire and Christina await his return home, and Mike knows he has to go to them. He urgently needs to be with them and be with them now.

This is the first time anything like this has ever happened to Mike. He has changed; his notorious blood lust is fading and fading quickly. Something is calling him home, something he has never felt before....Love, true love. He wants to go home and see his new family..... "Ricky," he says, "I need to go home now." With that, he gives his brother and best friend a nod.

Ricky acknowledges Mike's statement by slowly squeezing the trigger on his rifle, the round blasting a hole through Sheik Zubair Majeed's head, lodging in the wall behind him. The Sheik is crossed off the list.

Albert Gray jumps as the Sheik is disposed of. He knows he is next on the list and wants to unburden himself of his guilt. *I must make Mike understand,* he thinks. Gray has to reconcile with his friend before his death.

"Mike, before you kill me, I want to admit, to you, that I was wrong. I should never have allowed the Sheik to continue his Reign of Terror. I should have listened to you, son. I apologize; I truly do." Gray waits for death, which he knows is coming.

"Albert, I want you to know I mean this with all the honor and respect you have earned and deserve from me...Go fuck yourself!" Mike turns away from Gray, "Ricky, let's go."

The Grand Gesture:

It's a warm Summer evening in San Diego, and Mike and Claire are walking along the shoreline. They have just enjoyed their final meal in California, and tomorrow they will set off for Texas. But tonight, they want to spend some quality time together, undisturbed. The stars twinkle in the sky and the waves softly crash against the sand.

Claire has a huge smile, expressing her sincere appreciation for the fantastic night he has provided. "That was absolutely amazing, Mike. Thank you so much!"

"I had no idea you would love Mexican food so much," Mike laughs, "I had planned to take you to a fancy restaurant, not Roberto's!"

"Mike, this night has been absolutely perfect. I'm really looking forward to trying out the Mexican food in Texas!"

Mike guides Claire towards a cozy blanket spread out on the beach. While they were eating, Christina organized all the items Mike had requested on a blanket; a bottle of sparkling apple cider and a selection of chocolate desserts, all neatly packed in a picnic basket.

Mike coaxes Claire, "Look over here, honey," he gestures to the arrangement on the beach, "Come and join me," they settle down on the blanket, side by side.

"Wow Mike. This is great," Claire exclaims, her eyes widening with delight as she sees the all-chocolate dessert collections. "My favorite! Chocolate Cake. It looks absolutely delicious!"

He makes sure to position Claire to face the water. "That's not all, Honey," turning her gaze towards the water just as the spectacular fireworks display begins. Claire is mesmerized by the beautiful colors and shapes illuminating the night sky. Mike can tell she is both surprised and enamored.

Claire looks on with a smile and softly whispers to herself, *He got it!*

As Claire watches the show with amazement, Mike is ready to unveil his final surprise. The fireworks display comes to an end when the night sky is illuminated with a beautiful heart-shaped explosion, creating a magical atmosphere. Mike withdraws a tiny, infamous Tiffany & Co. blue box from his pocket and gets down on one knee, "Claire Barnes, you are the most amazing woman I have ever known. I can't imagine my life without you in it. You are my dream come true. Will you please do me the honor of becoming my wife?"

Claire soaks up every word Mike says, committing every second of this moment to memory. With a huge smile and happiness that washes over both of them, Claire answers, "Yes! Of course I will. Mike, you can pick any date you want. I love you."

-The End-

Mike McHaskell and his family return for the next chapter of their life in:

Dr. Zim Minister of Death

For more information on our books, character bios, and free content, visit www.marshallblack.com From behind-the-scenes looks to exclusive bonus materials, our site offers a wealth of additional content for fans of our novels. Discover the stories behind your favorite characters and explore the worlds they inhabit in greater detail. Best of all, much of this content is available for free. So why wait? Head over to our website now and take your reading experience to the next level! "

Thank you from our family to yours,

Marshall Black

v:4-29

Made in the USA
Columbia, SC
10 March 2024

fdc247c5-a237-4dc5-aa83-e93717f89257R01